JACKIE

Julie Hamill

Life and Soul Series 2

Published by Saron Publishing in 2019
Copyright © 2019 Julie Hamill

Jackie is a work of fiction. Names, characters,
places, events and incidents are either the products
of the author's imagination or used in a fictitious
manner. Any resemblance to actual persons, living
or dead, or actual events is purely coincidental.
Some Airdrie locations have been used for settings.
All locations stem from the author's fond memories
of living in Airdrie as a girl aged 9-17

Cover photo: 'Young Jackie' (Rose Ann Hamill)
'June' (Pat Hamill)

ISBN-13: 978-1-913297-02-2

Saron Publishing
Pwllmeyrick House
Mamhilad
Mon
NP4 8RG

saronpublishers.co.uk

Follow us on Facebook or Twitter

Also by Julie Hamill

15 Minutes With You

Frank

For Gillian, forever

'One's Better Looking Than the Next'

CONTENTS

THE SHOWS

Viv's eyes were squeezed shut. She took a deep breath in to squeal again, harder and louder this time, as she kept her damp palms clamped around the cold metal bar. Jackie laughed and laughed. She couldn't stop. Her mind was full of this, and only this moment, as she spun in a fizzy feeling, like she was inside a bottle of lemonade. Daniel and Johnny had wanted to leave the bar out, but Viv insisted it be pulled in. She said she had heard that someone fell off once.

'Hands up!' shouted Daniel, and two of his friends obliged. This was their third go on the Waltzer, a favourite for all four friends.

Jackie loved the music and the lights, and she watched as the row of square bulbs above them flashed yellow, red, blue, green, then all white, in time with the beat. Another row of multi-coloured lightbulbs on the side panel flashed one by one like a Mexican wave, then all together, in and out.

The Waltzer boy's gold-plated rings smacked their car, keeping it rolling in a fast twist. As Black Box's *Ride On Time* played loudly through the speakers, Jackie knew the ride would last for one full song - maybe one and a half - her dad told her years ago that's how they timed the rides. He had also told her that, during the winter, the shows were packed up and stored inside the gas work towers in Glasgow, and that's why sometimes the tank was high, because the giant roller coaster and the Big Wheel and the Waltzers were all inside it. As a little girl, this filled her head with wonder, and every time they passed the gas works, they checked to see if the tank was high or low. *'That's the shows packed up!'* her dad would announce, when the roof was high. *'That's them away out on tour!'* he'd shout, when it was low. She never found out that he had made it all up until years later when, on a drive into Glasgow, Jackie mentioned it in passing and Viv nearly crashed the car laughing.

'You just walk right in! Walk walk walk right in!' Viv tried to sing in the direction of Daniel, but her head was locked against the back of the seat and she couldn't turn it.

'I'm gonnie puke!' said Johnny, then laughed. They all erupted in laughter.

'Don't!' they cried. 'No!'

As the song ended, the Waltzer slowed down and the Waltzer boy moved to the booth to chat to his boss. Viv shook her hair out and twenty thin silver bangles rolled and rattled from her elbow to her wrist.

'Oh, my God. That was even better than the last time!' She looked over to the Waltzer operator but he was leaning into the booth. 'Anybody want to go again? I think that guy has his eye on me. He kept spinning us.'

'I've not got much money left,' Jackie replied, feeling in her bag for her purse.

The boys scrambled off each end of the car and held it stationary for the two girls to exit. They quickly checked the seat for coins that may have fallen from their pockets but didn't find any. Viv checked that her rings were still secure on her fingers and quickly counted her bangles in twos.

'Thank you, gentlemen!' Jackie mock-curtseyed.

'Much obliged, gents!' nodded Viv, circling her right arm.

'I'm quite hungry now. Is anybody else hungry?' Johnny asked.

'You're always hungry,' they echoed, and laughed. 'You were going to be sick a minute ago!' Jackie shook her head.

'Let's get candyfloss!' Viv announced.

'I'm getting in on that! My dad and June can share a bar of nougat.'

They took the colourful shallow steps down one by one off the platform as the song faded out and a new one faded in.

'Oh, my God, I love this song! Jackie! *Pump Up The Jam!* They played it in aerobics, remember?' screamed Viv.

'You should do the exercises, Viv!'

Jackie and Viv linked arms and began walking to the beat and singing. '*Pump up the jam! Pump it up! While your feet are stompin!*' Viv stamped her feet and clicked her fingers, looking back to see if the Waltzer spinner was looking. Jackie sang with her. '*Pump it up! A little more, get the party goin' on the dancefloor.*'

Daniel and Johnny hung back, as if they were not with Jackie and Viv.

'*Ow-a! A place to stay!*' Jackie and Viv continued to sing the lyrics together and dance around the circumference of the ride until the song reached the instrumental section, then they posed, pretending to be pop stars in the video.

'*Make ma day!*' Jackie gasped. 'You could teach that aerobics class, Viv!'

'You know it, Jacks!' They stopped dancing to catch their breath and Daniel and Johnny joined them.

'State of youse two! You're a red neck,' Daniel remarked. Johnny slid a long thin line of Wrigley's Spearmint gum from the packet and offered it around. Jackie waved it away.

'I can never blow bubbles with these,' said Daniel, removing the silver foil and bending the gum into his mouth.

'Bubble gum is better for that.' Viv winked and removed a packet of Hubba Bubba from her pocket. She linked arms with Jackie, and Daniel and Johnny followed behind.

Viv chewed her gum to the beat and turned her head to look at Jackie. She blew a huge pink bubble from her mouth and Jackie popped it. They strutted past a gang of young men who were taking cigarettes from a packet.

'Hey, darlin!' they wolf whistled. 'Come over here, sweetheart!' one of them shouted.

'We wouldn't be seen dead with the likes of you,' Viv shouted back, but a smile crept across her face as she turned the other way. The gang whistled louder.

'You want to actually take one of these guys up on their offer of a date one day!' Jackie smiled.

'A date! Ha ha! As if that's what they want. No thanks. I'm saving myself for Tom Cruise,' Viv laughed.

'And I'll take John Travolta when he was Danny. I'm sure he'd go out with me, wouldn't he, Viv?'

'Defo. You really *must* return his call,' teased Viv.

'I really *must* return his call!' echoed Jackie.

Johnny shook his head.

'Fast walk race!' demanded Jackie, laughing. 'I do this with Junie, she loves it!'

She strode ahead, dragging Viv with her. Viv struggled to keep up in her white high heels as her bleached blonde ponytail bounced from side to side. Jackie was in jeans and had told Viv not to overdress for the shows, but knew that she would, just in case she saw somebody she liked.

Daniel and Johnny caught up, and Jackie glanced at Daniel, who, over the past three years, had become a good friend, and one of little June's favourite uncles. She realised that, as a single mother in her twenties, her chances for a boyfriend were getting fewer and fewer, but she and Daniel had no chemistry beyond friendship. Since he'd been hanging around with Johnny, she saw less and less of him, and he was never with any other girls.

Viv took her gum from her mouth and stuck it to the inside of a wrapper.

'Lost its flavour already,' she shrugged. She wrapped it closed and tossed it into a nearby litter bin disguised as an open-mouthed bear.

'We've still got some Merrydown left.' Viv flashed a peek of the plastic bottle she had in her bag. They scrambled in behind the rollercoaster attendant and shared what was left in the two-litre bottle, taking it in turns to gulp the cider, making jokes about what they'd catch from each other, wiping the rim and giggling. Viv back-kicked the empty bottle under a caravan and walked towards the snack van. Daniel scuffed his feet on the spot, kicking up tiny clouds of red ash.

'Quit that! You're ruining my trainers! I just whitened them!' Johnny took a few steps back from Daniel.

'Sorry but I can't resist!' Daniel laughed. 'What is this ground anyway? Is Airdrie built on a volcano or what?'

'Don't know but if you don't stop it, I'll...' Johnny smiled wickedly.

Jackie spotted Viv returning from the van with a huge pink flossy cloud. 'That is massive!'

'That guy's are the biggest. Like, honestly! Look at the size of it, compared to the others.'

'You might not finish it!'

'Oh, I'll finish it. You watch me.'

'I might get a burger,' said Johnny.

'Oh, no, yuck, Johnny, don't eat them! They're out of a tin!' said Jackie.

'When somebody vomits at the shows, there's always bits of burger in it,' Viv remarked. They all groaned and Viv laughed, tearing off a long piece of pink floss.

'You are disgusting!' smiled Johnny, 'And anyway, everybody knows it's bits of carrot.'

Johnny and Daniel walked over to the burger van and stood in the queue, looking at the menu.

'Hamburger, Cheeseburger, Hot Dog with fried onions, Coke, Lemonade, Fanta, Slush,' read Daniel.

'I'm getting a hamburger with onions,' announced Johnny. 'I'm starving.' He stared at the rows of tinned Westlers displayed in the van window.

'Next!' said the man in the white hat behind the counter.

'Uh, hamburger n' onions please,' said Johnny.

Jackie walked over to the stand next to the burger van where Viv had been. She looked down into the pit of sticky pink floss, spinning like a tornado. It reminded her of her mum's old top loader washing machine. She ordered a bar of pink and white nougat and a large candy floss. The man spun the stick in circles around the machine, quickly gathering the floss. It was as big as a beehive. The other three approached.

'He went and did it,' said Daniel. 'Johnny got a burger.'

'Smells all right, actually,' Viv said, her candyfloss almost down to the stick. They stood on the spot, eating. Jackie felt the pink fluff crystallise on her tongue.

'I need to move it for the ten past bus,' said Johnny, checking his watch.

'C'mon then, we'd better get going,' replied Daniel.

They walked to showground exit, turning around every now and then to point at the Big Wheel or the Twister. On the way out, Jackie looked up at the back of the Chapel Street flats and saw a light from a second-floor window. A little girl with sandy-coloured hair and big eyes looked out into the dark night. She had a big Minnie Mouse face on her pyjamas.

'Look at that wee girl up there. I bet she looks out at the shows every night.'

'Aww. Bet she wishes she could go on the high swings.' Viv waved up to the little girl and she waved back.

Her mother entered the room and looked out of the window. Smiling, she wrapped her arms around the little girl and pulled her close. The fairground lights glittered and sparkled on their faces.

Jackie smiled as she thought of how she used to cuddle up to her mum at bedtime. All fresh from a bath, her mum would talcum her feet, comb the tugs out of her wet hair and dress her in a fresh warm Pippa Dee nightie. She longed to feel the soft embrace of her mum again, rub her face against that smooth, shiny, padded dressing gown she wore with the diamond-shaped stitching and the big covered buttons. Just once more. For a second, she thought she could smell her mum's sweet scent, but it was gone.

'Imagine living up there. What a brilliant view,' said Johnny.

'I would absolutely love to live up there,' said Viv. 'Just imagine the shows arriving on a Sunday. You'd wake up and be like, "What's that clink clank noise?" Open your curtains and there they are! Setting up. I'd be pure bouncing if I was that wee girl.'

'She's got the best view in Airdrie,' agreed Daniel.

'Best view in the world, that!' said Johnny.

The girl's mother gently pulled the curtains closed. Viv could see Jackie drifting into deep thought, as she often did when she saw mums with little girls.

'Your dad will be getting June ready for her bed about now,' said Viv, in an attempt to bring Jackie back from her thoughts.

'Oh, my God, look at the time!' Jackie looked at her watch. 'I told my dad I'd be back by eight o'clock!'

'I could have eaten two more burgers off that van. The onions were great,' said Johnny, looking back.

'If we hurry up, I might get home in time for her bedtime story,' Jackie said.

Viv placed her hand on Jackie's shoulders. 'We'll walk fast, don't worry, you'll make it.'

'I really need to bomb it!' Johnny started to run, and Daniel joined in. The girls laughed as they sped ahead.

'You going to bring Junie to the shows while they're here?'

'I'd like to but I'm working. My dad said he'd bring her up tomorrow during the day. Do you want to come in for tea and a *Ripple* when we get down to mine?' Jackie asked Viv.

'I think I'm going to go home. My head's spinning a wee bit,' said Viv. 'Maybe too much cider.'

'And too much staring at that Waltzer guy!' They laughed.

'I'm going to get the bus with Johnny,' Daniel shouted back and waved.

'You on early shift?' Jackie asked.

'Yeah! See you!'

'See you tomorrow!'

Jackie and Viv walked along Chapel Street towards the Top Cross. Viv was talking about how fun fair onions are cut in full circles before they are fried. She noticed that Jackie wasn't really paying attention.

'Are you okay?'

'I'm fine. Just... that wee girl in the window made me think about my mum a bit, you know?'

'Are you still having dreams about her?'

'Yeah,' smiled Jackie.'

'That's really nice. What did she do in the last one?'

'Nothing really, sometimes we're somewhere weird and other times, she's just sitting up in bed, smiling at me.'

'Does she talk to you?'

'Sometimes.'

'What does she say?'

'I can't always remember.'

'Must be a such a comfort to see her.'

'It is. I fall asleep every night and hope she comes to visit me.'

They looked through the windows of Zambonini's café as they walked past.

'I love the pineapple fritters in there,' commented Viv.

'Our June loves the banana ones.'

'Oh, I like them as well.'

'Do you want to come and see her for a bit on Friday? Then we can watch a film or something?

My dad's going to the Working Men's Club - I think Bobby has a job for him, collecting glasses.'

'Oh, that's brilliant! That will keep Frank occupied.'

'And I'm off work on Saturday so we can stay up a bit later.'

'Let me check my diary.' Viv flicked through imaginary pages of a book. 'Well, would you look at that? I happen to be totally free this Friday! Unless of course, Tom Cruise comes over.'

Jackie smiled. 'That could still happen,' she said. 'You really *must* return his call!'

'I really *must* return his call! Viv replied, laughing.

In a church in Birmingham, Tommy Fletcher laid a hand on the lid of his mother's coffin. He thought of her dying wish as he looked down at her name embossed on a gold nameplate. He removed a handkerchief from his pocket and buffed any fingerprints off the gold lettering.

'Filthy pigs leaving smudges like that,' he said. 'People have no manners.'

He put the handkerchief back in his pocket and looked around the empty church. Everyone, including the priest, had gone to the pub to eat the free sandwiches he had laid on after the rosary. He looked up at the crucifix, then back to the coffin and stroked the part of the wood where her head was.

'Don't worry, Mum. I know where she is. They never moved, you see, she's still at her dad's house. Don't worry. I'll get her back, and the baby.' He lifted the framed picture of his smiling mother off the top of the shining oak wood and placed it under his arm. 'If it's happy families you want, it's happy families you'll get.'

He removed a cigarette from the packet in his inside pocket and put it to his lips. 'I know, I'll stop soon.' He sparked a match and lit the cigarette, then inhaled. He tapped the coffin twice. 'I'll be back tomorrow for your big day,' he said, 'then I'll make the trip north.'

He turned and walked briskly down the aisle, towards the foyer. The lit cigarette dangled between his lips as he dipped his fingers in holy water. The blue smoke trailed up towards the stained-glass windows.

'See you later, Jesus,' he said, making the sign of the Cross. He pushed the bar of the heavy church door and walked into the dark night. The door slammed behind him.

Jackie felt cosy and warm. Her mum sat down on the side of her single bed, patting the cover down flat. She was immaculately dressed in a lemon cotton blouse and straight blue skirt. Her hair was set in curls and her face seemed younger. There were less lines around her eyes and cheeks, but she wasn't a different age, she was just - radiant and healthy. Glowing, in fact. Both of them were laughing.

'You look so well, Mum,' said Jackie, faintly.

'Thank you, sweetheart!' Her mum tilted her head to one side and smiled lightly. She looked like a pretty porcelain figurine. Jackie knew they were having a conversation but she struggled to communicate her side of it. Her voice was frail and scratched and drowsy, and she couldn't make it any louder, despite her effort.

'Mum?' croaked Jackie. 'I miss you. Can you hear me?' Her mum smiled and nodded. 'Where are you, Mum?' She tried to reach out for her hand, but her arm didn't move. There was a weight on her chest, as if she was trapped under a sleeping St Bernard.

Her mum stood up and walked towards the door. Jackie felt a tear slide from her right eye.

'Mum?' she forced, as loud as she could, 'stay a bit longer?'

June smiled and drifted away. Jackie's eyes flickered.

FISH AND MAKE-UP

Frank sat at the table with his chin resting on one hand. He stared through the still water in the glass bowl and marvelled at three and a half year old June's red curls dancing around her head as she talked. She was holding a green crayon and scribbling onto a drawing pad. Eighteen other coloured crayons were strewn across the dinner table. There was an empty Crayola packet on the floor, with a half a blue crayon inside it. Frank had a feeling that Mrs Morrisson may have hoovered up the other half.

A goldfish swam around inside the bowl between their faces, its nose darting left and right, cutting through the water, making squares. He couldn't believe it when the woman at the shows said he had won, and that the third golf ball he threw didn't actually bounce out of the empty plant pot.

'Winner,' she had said, casually, without smiling. She lifted a long skinny pole and hooked a bulging bag of water and thrusted it into Frank's hands. He grinned as June danced with delight. They held hands and June pulled Frank's arm to get him to walk quicker.

'That miserable old bint won't ruin my day! I got one of her fish! Your Granda's a winner!' he announced as they walked towards the exit. 'Now, listen, Junie, we're on a roll here! Keep your eyes peeled for pound notes. There's always hundreds of folk that drop their money at the shows. Fivers and tenners and everything! Cash everywhere.' Just at that moment, he spotted a two-pence piece on the ground. 'Ya beauty! See? I told you! Two pence! A few more of these and we'll be rich! You stick with your Granda, hen.'

Frank chuckled to himself as he sat at the table, remembering how she scanned the pavements the whole way home.

'Nearly finished, Granda,' announced June. He looked from the fish back to her and then down to the writing pad in front of him.

'Right, so, come on now. This fish needs a name. We've had it since Monday. Do you want to know what names I've got?' he asked.

'Uh huh...' She finished a scribble by adding dots.

'Okay. Here we go. Do you like Paddie?'

'No.' She shook her head.

'Goldie?'

'No.'

'How about Jaws?'

'No.'

'Jaws 2?'

'Nope.'

'Archie?'

'No.'

'Ah, come on, wee Archie fish!'

'Uh-uh.' She shook her head again, more vigorously.

'Rocky?'

'No!'

'Bob?'

'No.'

'Well, that's all I've got. What's on your list?' She looked down at the scribbles all over the paper, then she looked out the window towards the street.

'I got...Fred, I got Flash, Fishie, Digs, I got Weetabix, Rusty, Jaffa Cake, I got, um, Johnny, Harry, Billy, Emma, Kat...'

'Are those not names off the nursery register?'

'And George...'

'I said Jaws already!'

'No, Granda, George!'

'Zod?'

'No, Granda! GEORGE!'

'Oh! George, right.'

'Granda, you need to wash your ears out!'

Frank rubbed his finger into his ear, pretending to clear it.

'That's got it! I can hear you now!' he smiled.

'Granda, how do you know if the fishie is a boy or a girl?'

'Ah! Good question!' Frank thought before he answered, trying to think of a convincing reply he might have read in an encyclopedia. Coming to his conclusion, he nodded. 'Do you know what? I've heard that, what it is, is, that the goldfish lets you decide that for yourself!'

'Oh!' She looked into the bowl to the fish, her eyes lit with ideas.

'If it's a he, he could be Kermit, or ET, or Pickle...'

'Pickle is a boy's name, is it?'

'Yes.'

'Oh, I see. Now you come to mention it, I don't remember if ET was a boy,' he pondered. 'I know!' he continued, pointing a finger, 'How about Starsky? Or Hutch? We could get another one to go in beside it. A bigger one - Hercules! Or something exotic like Wolfgang, or a punk fish! Call it Sid Vicious.' Frank sneered to try to look like a punk.

'No, Granda, I don't like them names.'

'You could have *A Fish called Wanda*? No, we haven't seen that film. Or you could go for something plain and classic, like, say 'Eric'.

'My favourite is... ET and... Kermit and... Miss Piggy!'

'If you call it ET, we'll have to get him a wee phone. *ET! Phone home!*' said Frank, pointing his finger. Little June slapped her knees and giggled, a habit he recognised from her mother.

'Look! Granda! It's got hair, look! See? It's got yellow hair!'

'Oh, so it has!' he said, looking intently but seeing nothing but general goldfish.

'Just like Miss Piggy! She's just like Miss Piggy!'

'Oh, that's true! That must be her name then. Is that it? Miss Piggy? So it's a she?'

'Yes! Miss Piggy is her name. Miss Piggy! Miss Piggy!' she shouted. 'You're a girl and I'm your mummy, Miss Piggy, and I love you!' she said to the fish.

Frank smiled. 'Shall we give Miss Piggy some food?' He removed a tub of fish flakes from a brown paper bag.

'Yes! I feed her! Are you hungry, my baby Miss Piggy?' Frank popped off the lid with his thumb.

'Just a tiny wee bit now. Only a wee tiny bit,' he said, gently. 'That's it.' June took a small pinch between her thumb and forefinger and dropped it into the bowl.

'Tiny bit,' she repeated in a whisper, fully concentrating. 'There you go!' She raised her eyebrows, as if talking to a baby.

The flakes separated and floated out across the water like leaves on a lake. Miss Piggy paused, rose up and nibbled an edge.

'Look at that! It must have been starving!'

'It's a she, Granda! She! You said "it"'.

'So I did, right, aye. She. You're quite right.'

They watched the fish eat for a second before June resumed her drawing.

'I'll draw a picture for Mummy of Miss Piggy.' She drew circles round and round. Frank smiled at the mention of Jackie, the three of them had a close bond.

'Your mummy always wanted to get a dog when she was your age, but your Granny wouldn't let her.'

'Oh! Can we get a dog?'

'Oh, no. I think a goldfish is enough for now.'

'Would Granny let Mummy have a goldfish?'

'Oh, yes. But I've never been lucky enough to win one until now!'

'Can she see Miss Piggy from heaven?' Frank smiled at how her little thoughts of a Granny that she never met had the ability to take him unawares.

'I can one hundred percent guarantee you that your Granny can see everything, including Miss Piggy, the goldfish.'

'Can she?' She put down her green crayon and selected an orange colour.

'Yes. When people die and they go to heaven - and if they've been good - God gives them special TVs that they can watch their families on.'

'Was Granny good? Is she in heaven?'

'Oh, yes, Granny June was very good. That's why your mummy named you after her! That means you will be good, too, see? A good girl just like your Granny June, God rest her soul.'

'She really has a TV in heaven?'

'She does.'

'Can she see other channels?'

'Oh, I'm sure she still watches *Coronation Street*.'

'And she can see all around the house? All around the streets and in the shops and...' June paused with the crayon to her lip, then continued. 'Pretend that someone took Mummy's make-up out of her drawer... just to look at it... and Granny saw them do it on the heaven TV... but she shouted down, "That's fine now, you can use it for now!" '

'Did this person that took the make-up make a mess?'

'No.' June shook her head.

'Well... I suppose if somebody put the make-up all neatly back into the drawer without Mummy noticing... lids on and all that... and *Granny* said they could use it... then I'm sure it is fine.'

'Just going for a wee wee.' June tumbled down off the chair. A few crayons rolled off the table. He heard her feet thump on the stairs and then over his head, into the bedroom she shared with her mother.

'Miss Piggy,' he laughed as he picked up the fallen crayons. He caught sight of the picture on the mantelpiece. He stood up, walked over and lifted it up. 'Well, I suppose a fish is better than an old dog, eh?' He touched his wife's face under the glass in the frame. 'Where does the time go? Thank God we have that wee bag of mischief you sent us. She's up there now, rifling through Jackie's lipsticks.'

He smiled to stop himself feeling sad. He had not seen June for a few years now, not since she visited him before the christening. Whilst he yearned for her to come back and talk to him, he also wondered if he had ever seen her at all. 'You must be busy up there with your heaven telly and your heaven cream cake and all that. I hope the tea's good. Keep me a cup!'

He put the frame back down on the mantelpiece and walked over to the sideboard. He opened the right hand door and reached in for a shoebox. He opened the box and a picture of June smiled up at him. He lifted out the black and white picture of them together eating ice creams. He looked at it for a few seconds, then selected another, more recent picture of June, on the couch with a drink in her hand, smiling and holding it up as if to say 'cheers'. Digging deeper through photographs and newspaper clippings, he found an advert that had been cut out by her, from when she was a club singer many years before, known as *Miss December*. It was in the *Airdrie and Coatbridge Advertiser*, on the front page with the headline *AIRDRIE'S MISS DECEMBER DAZZLES IN WHITE*. She was walking out of the door of the Working Men's Club, where she had a regular night, when a photographer snapped and captured an iconic picture of her in a white dress, fresh off the stage, looking young, her skin shining, her smile Hollywood, her hair in tight blonde curls. People used to say that she belonged on 42nd Street, not Broomeknoll Street. Behind her to the left of the picture stood another man, Eddie O'Donnell. He was a tall, broad-shouldered man in a sharp three button suit. Nobody messed with him in Airdrie, or any other town. He was an ex-boxer turned manager/bouncer, who had served time in prison for GBH. He was managing June's career at the time. Frank didn't look at him for too long and refocused his attention on June's pretty smile. Looking back at how stunning she was, he couldn't believe that she married him, Frank McNeill, off the railways.

In the silence, a key was pushed into the front door.

'Mummy!' little June shouted as she bumped down the stairs one by one, feet first, followed by her tiny bottom. Frank put everything back into the box and put the lid on. He put the box back into the sideboard and clicked the door shut.

'Careful on the stairs now!' said Jackie, as she put the bag of shopping down in the hall. 'Come give Mummy a big cuddle!' June leapt into the arms of her mother and wrapped her legs around her waist. They rubbed noses and kissed on the lips. 'Oh, I missed you today, my wee baby! Are you wearing... is that blusher?' She took a tissue from her pocket and wiped it off her daughter's cheeks, laughing.

'I did a picture!' she said, as her mother enveloped her.

'Hiya, hen! Tell your mummy what the fishie's name is!' Frank called, peeking his head around the living room door into the hall.

'Miss Piggy!'

'Oh! Miss Piggy! That sounds like the bestest name in the world! Mummy will go and get out of her uniform and then you can tell me more, okay? Dad, can you put this stuff in the fridge?'

'Aye, I'll do that,' said Frank. He picked up the string bag and took it to the kitchen. He carefully lifted out a flat packet in white paper and unwrapped it to have a look. Three haddock fillets in bright orange breadcrumbs. He glanced towards the fishbowl and back at the haddock, then back to the fishbowl again. He gave the goldfish a thumbs up, rewrapped the fish and put it in the fridge to fry later. He rubbed his hands at the thought of fish and boiled potatoes.

Jackie came into the living room in jogging bottoms and t-shirt. June took her by the hand and they leaned in to look at the fish.

'Hello, Miss Piggy! Welcome to the mad house!' Jackie saluted the fish. She smiled at June and flopped down onto the couch and began unpinning her hair from a bun. June retrieved her picture of the fish and climbed onto her mother's knee.

'Oh! You're very artistic. Look at Miss Piggy there! And is that you? You're very talented, aren't you, sweetheart?' She kissed her.

'Was it a long day at work, hen?' asked Frank.

'It was knackering! What a week! Four new patients and three bed baths today!' She placed her kirby grips on the side table.

'Oh, bed baths! Oh, no! You'll not catch me doing that. You'll get a sore back doing all that leaning over and washing bums and whatever else.'

'Oh, Dad! Wait til I tell you! The new nurse had to empty a catheter drainage bag and it spilled *all* over the floor. And DANIEL had to clean it up!'

'Oh! He wouldn't have liked that!' Frank giggled. 'Oh ho ho! A pishy old day for Daniel!'

'A pishy old day for Daniel!' June sang over and over again. She began marching around the living room, singing like one of the seven dwarves on their way to work. The more her mum and granddad laughed, the more she raised her knees higher and moved her arms like levers. Jackie knew she shouldn't laugh but couldn't help herself. She managed to utter, 'That's enough now' between sniggers. Frank laughed freely, he knew no one funnier or more original that his granddaughter.

'What if she says "it's a pishy old day" at nursery? This is your fault, Dad! You're not to say this at nursery, Junie!'

'Pish is not bad language!' he said. 'She hears a lot worse at the swings at the West End Park!'

'Come and sit with Mummy and we'll read this book now.' She cut through her dad's naughtiness with a look to make him stop and he shook his head like Charlie Chaplin and zipped his mouth. June ran to her mother's lap and opened the brightly-coloured pages of a counting book.

'Anyway,' said Jackie, talking to her dad, 'The Sister at work has us all keeping everything immaculate. She's still convinced somebody is going to come in with the *thing*, you know.'

Frank knew immediately that Jackie was talking about AIDS, the Sister's obsession for the past two years. 'Rock Hudson died of that, you know. It's bloody deadly.'

'Well, of course it is!' Jackie rolled her eyes. 'But the Sister thinks you can catch it off toilet seats. She's got us cleaning everything in sight. She's cuckoo!' Jackie twirled her fingers at the side of her head.

'I've heard you can get it off toilet seats, you know. Some pubs have put in paper covers now.' Frank folded his arms. He hadn't seen anything since the Government leaflets and the tombstone adverts with the scary voice a few years before. He hadn't heard of anybody in The Black Dog or the Working Men's catching AIDS, but nobody dared to sit on the toilet in The Black Dog anyway.

'No. You can't get it off toilet seats, Dad. You can't catch it off kissing, or at swimming pools or any of that rubbish. She's ignoring all that, she thinks she knows better! She's absolutely terrified of needles now, won't take blood, always gets somebody else to do it.'

'I suppose you have to be careful with needles and all that. You be careful now!' Frank didn't like thinking about needles. They reminded him of his beloved wife, when she was in hospital, full of drips. He remembered the back of her soft wrinkled hand, deep purple veins sticking up through black and yellow bruises on pale yellow skin. That thick suffocating hospital air. She also had a catheter. He shuddered, ashamed, at his catheter remark, and wished he hadn't laughed.

'What are people going to bring in to the hospital, Mummy? Why is Sister frightened of the toilet seats?'

'She's afraid somebody is going to bring in lots of lollipops and hide them in the toilets because she'll eat them all and get big and big and big and pop!' said Jackie, tickling June, who laughed loudly.

'What time is that up there? Must be time to get the dinner on,' said Frank, moving the subject away from illness and hospitals.

'Two more minutes,' said Jackie. 'I'll help.'

'I'll get peeling.' Frank went into the kitchen and noticed the usual little robin in the garden. He smiled as it looked directly at him, bounced around the grass, then flew away.

He bent down to look under the sink to find the bag of potatoes. Seeing them just behind some Mr

Sheen and the rubber gloves, he reached in blindly and knocked over a rusty can of oven cleaner. It made a clinking sound. He moved the potatoes to the right and forward and there was the clinking sound again, lots of clinking. The sound reminded him of empty milk bottles being collected by the milkman with his fingers. Frank wondered if there were milk bottles in there, or a vase, or something glass. He reached behind the potatoes and around the Dreft and pushed aside a few other cleaning bits and bobs and brushes that he had never used and didn't know what were for. He pulled a few old hardened and frayed towels and torn bits of cloth out from the back of the cupboard to try to see where the sound came from. There was a gap between the base of the cupboard and the back of the wall. A bottle had fallen onto its side and was leaning against the drainpipe. Beside it, just out of sight, he could see another two bottles with red screw tops. Not milk. He leaned in, and gently moved the sickeningly familiar-looking bottle away from the pipe to stand it upright, feeling slightly hypnotized by the sight.

After doing so, he staggered, lost his balance, and fell backwards a few inches onto the kitchen floor. He sat there and stared directly at the red lids, thinking of her fingers twisting until she heard the *crack* she so desired. He thought of the aroma rising up to meet her nostrils. In his mind's eye, he could see her chatting and tearing up old bits of bed sheet to use for cleaning. She kept the rags in the back of this cupboard, under the sink. Nobody used them, they were too hard, all crisp and rough from being left to dry in the dark for years.

This was one of her hiding places. She used her old torn sheets to cover her vodka bottles.

His bottom lip began to shake and he rubbed his hand back and forth over his face. He thought he'd pushed these memories away to a deeper place, boxed them and buried them when he had buried her. A brutal reminder of what killed his wife stood in front of him: not one, not two, but three soldiers of death, reversing his thoughts from loving wife and mother... to staggering, unravelling alcoholic.

Stopping her from falling over, searching for her glasses, picking her up, carrying her to bed, preventing Jackie from seeing her mother. A brilliant mother! A caring mother! A loving mother! A mother that could not live without her poison. A morning drink, an evening drink, an afternoon tipple, a hair of the dog, a wee voddie here, a wee voddie there, everywhere. in the bar, in the house, and now under the sink. *No, no, no...* he thought, *no*. His head felt like it was on fire.

Jackie stood behind him, looking down at her father.

'What's wrong, Dad?'

'I'm afraid there's nothing more we can do for her.' Frank could hear the doctor's voice clearly; his professional tone defeated. *'Nothing else we can do.'*

'Dad!' said Jackie, 'Dad?'

He looked up and saw Jackie, bending down to him.

'What are you doing, sitting on the floor? she asked. 'Did you fall?'

Frank snapped back to reality and fumbled to move the cloths, the Dreft and orange sponges and bucket and anything else he could see, in front of the bottles. He would get rid of them later. *No need for Jackie to know* he thought, *she's only going to start asking questions again.*

'I was just getting the potatoes. You know what it's like under here. Bloody every damn thing gets chucked in. It needs a good sorting out. I'll do it later.'

She put her hand under his arm at the shoulder and helped him rise up with the potatoes in his hand and shut the cupboard doors.

'Do you think you took a funny turn?'

'Maybe, I don't know... I don't think so. I'm fine.'

'I'll peel, Dad, you sit down, you look a bit pale.'

'Will you go back in and sit with June? You haven't seen her all day, I'll peel.'

'Are you sure-'

'I want to peel,' he replied, curtly.

Jackie nodded quietly. She looked at the cupboard doors, then back at her dad, then left the room to put the TV on.

UNDER THE SINK

Frank removed a potato from the brown bag and began peeling it into the sink. He stared down at the blade as he tried to keep the peel to one long piece of skin, without breaking it. The soil muddied his hands and the white flesh of the vegetable was staining with the dirt. He knew he was peeling too thick, and too hard. He turned on the tap and moved his hand underneath the water. The potato gleamed again.

He put the clean peeled potato down onto the sink and picked up another one.

'What's for dinner?' asked little June, standing with a dolly in one hand, the other hand swinging her arm on the door handle.

'Tatties,' said Frank.

'What else?' June enquired. She knew they wouldn't just be having potatoes because there were always three different colours on her plate. He took a deep breath in to reply.

'Delishy Fishies!' replied Jackie, doing jazz hands to make her daughter smile. Instead, June ran to the goldfish.

'No!' she cried. 'No! Miss Piggy is not dinner!'

Jackie followed her to the table. 'Oh, sweetheart no! We'd never ever eat Miss Piggy, she's special! No, no. This is *other* fishies, from the *fishmonger*, big, big fishies!'

'Did the big fishies in the fish shop asked to be eaten?' she enquired.

'Well, kind of.'

'Fish can talk?'

'Maybe. I think so. Sometimes? You have to listen very hard. The fishmongers know, don't they, Dad?' Jackie looked over to Frank, who had his back to her. 'Don't they, Dad?'

'The fishmonger decides,' called Frank's voice, quieter than usual.

'Oh!' said June, 'I didn't know fish could talk sometimes.' She climbed up to the table and pressed her ear on the glass bowl. Jackie moved into the kitchen to see Frank standing by the counter, staring out the window, gripping the knife and a half-peeled potato.

'What's up, Dad? What happened there?' Jackie knew the tiniest thing could set her dad off and turn his happy to sad. He'd be fine for days and weeks, then suddenly something would happen that would trigger him to go quiet or get upset. His grief had a wild element of surprise, creeping into the happiest moments, higher and higher, until he was at a loss, sinking in the repeat of disbelief. 'Talk to me, Dad. Are you thinking about... my mum?' she asked. He breathed heavy and hard. Jackie put her hand on his back. 'I miss her too. I wish she could see June... and the goldfish.'

'Aye, the goldfish.'

Jackie searched his face. It was straight and serious. That face he made when he didn't, or wouldn't, talk. Now was not the right time to question him. *Never was the right time to question him.* Despite their closeness as father and daughter, he never revealed much about her mother. Jackie always had a feeling that he carried secrets, locked up to his heart and only her mum had the key.

'You go and sit down. I'll finish the dinner,' she said. Frank put down the knife and turned and walked towards his chair like a robot toy about to run out of batteries. He sat down and closed his eyes to the low moan of the television.

Jackie washed the potatoes and put them into the saucepan to boil with plenty of salt and hot water from the kettle. She separated the fish out into its three parts, two large and one small. She lit a match for the gas burner and put the heavy frying pan on top. She tapped her nails as she waited for it to heat up. The pot of potatoes began to bubble wildly on the back ring, occasionally splashing big droplets of water into the fish pan and making it hiss. She rubbed some of the block of lard onto the pan as her mother had taught her, and placed the fish gently in the frying pan, in a direction away from her. She turned the gas down to a three for the potatoes to simmer and looked out of the window into the garden and wondered about what had triggered her dad into silence. He seemed fine when he came in to peel the potatoes, then suddenly he was sitting on the floor. She took a fish slice from the drawer and flipped the fish over.

'Four minutes each side, then turn the gas down,' her mother used to say. 'Your daddy loves his fish!'

She opened a tin of peas and carrots on the side and poured it into another smaller pot. She lit the third gas ring. She threw the tin into the flip top bin and it missed. She bent down to pick it up and turned, her eyes level with the cupboard doors under the sink. She dropped the empty tin into the bin, then reached over and tentatively opened the cupboard doors and looked in.

Dreft, bleach, a few onions, rubber gloves, spray polish, the big sponges... the usual stuff. My mum's old cloths. She caught a peek of something sticking out behind a cloth and moved it. Then she saw the thing that he had seen, moving the cloth to the left, one, two, three, bottles revealed. She swallowed, even though there was nothing to swallow, just a bitter taste on her tongue. She put the cloths back over the bottles and stood up. The fish was burning. She threw it into the sink and prepared the pan again and placed in the second slice. She left it for a second to peek around the door. June was sitting in front of the television and her dad had his eyes closed. She watched his stomach rise and fall like waves. Sometimes June climbed on to his knee and cuddled in, just as Jackie did at her age.

They're my mum's bottles, she thought. She raised her eyebrows at the sight of him sleeping and a protective warmth crept over her.

She went back to fry the other fish. She drained the potatoes and halved her fish with June and served up the vegetables and put the three plates onto the table.

'Dad? Your dinner.' She shook his shoulder gently.

'Oh! What time is it, hen?' he asked. 'How long have I been sleeping?'

'It's only six o'clock. Just a wee while. Come and get your dinner.'

'Give us a hand up, will you, hen?'

Jackie offered him a hand under his shoulder. She leaned backwards and pulled him up to standing. She wanted to tell him that she had seen the bottles, but he was dozy from the sleep, so she decided to wait until after dinner.

'Thanks, hen. This looks lovely.' He went to his place at the table, sat down and patted the chair beside him for his granddaughter. 'C'mon, June, your mummy's made us a nice dinner.' June climbed up onto the chair between her granddad and her mother and they ate their fish while another swam around in front of their faces.

'Well, that tasted just like your mum used to make,' he announced, putting his knife and fork down onto the empty plate and pushing it away. 'Fantastic.'

'Hello-o!' called a familiar voice as the back door opened. 'Anybody in?' Viv peeked her head around the kitchen door.

'Oh, Viv, I forgot you were coming! Come in, come in! We just finished our dinner.'

'Auntie Viv!' shouted June and skipped over to give Viv a kiss.

'I've come to hear all about the new addition to the family! Hello, my favourite girl! Is this your new baby on the table?' They leaned in for a look.

'How did you hear?'

'My mum was working yesterday and Mrs Morrisson popped into the shop and she told her. Said Frank had won it at the shows.'

'She's getting like the town crier!' said Frank, quietly.

'She is not!'

'I was only saying, she likes to talk. I bet it was all round Fine Fare before she left.'

'What's up with him?' joked Viv to Jackie as she continued, 'Oh! Speaking of Fine Fare...' Viv reached into her bag and pulled out a packet of Opal Fruits for June and a bottle of wine.

'The old Blue Nun brings her blessings, Jacks!' She waved the bottle from side to side.

'Oh, that's nice of you!' Jackie replied.

'You don't seem that pleased!' Viv said, puzzled.

Jackie glanced at her dad, then held her hands together in prayer. 'Her Holiness is welcome!' she nodded.

'Don't do that!' nudged Frank. 'And anyway, that stuff could strip the wallpaper!'

'Well, lucky you're not drinking it then!' Viv smiled. Jackie stood up and cleared the plates from the table. Viv followed her into the kitchen.

'Don't be going mad with that wine, Jackie,' Frank called as he moved over to his chair. Jackie shook her head. 'How's your dad's leg, Viv?' he shouted.

'Aye, not bad, Frank, he struggles on. He can manage to get to the pub so he must be all right!'

Jackie leaned into Viv's ear and whispered, 'Look.' She opened the cupboard doors and moved the cloths to the side.

'Whose is all that?' asked Viv, her eyes rolling.

'Shh! Not mine and definitely not *his*!' She paused. 'You going up to the Working Men's Club, Dad?' Jackie called.

'Och, I don't know. Maybe.'

'I thought Bobby wanted you to start that job tonight?'

'Oh, aye! It's Friday! So he did!'

'You should go, Frank! It's good to get out,' shouted Viv.

'Bit of money in your pocket, Dad!'

'Aye, okay, you two, I get the hint. I'll go and get a wash in a minute, after I've seen the news.'

'Whose are the bottles?' whispered Viv.

'I think they're my mum's. Remember we found that other stash under the stairs? Same thing!' Jackie pointed to the cupboard. 'It's more of her stash, hidden round the house.'

'Oh, my God. Does your dad know they're there?'

'I found him sitting on the floor staring. I think he had just found them as well.'

'What did you say? Did he see that you'd seen them?'

'No, I- oh, there's our Junie!'

'Mummy, can I get a juice?'

'Yes, darling. I'll just get it for you. Me and your Auntie Viv are going to wash the dishes, then we can cuddle up to watch the telly together.' June took the juice and skipped back into the living room.

'She's quite a plump wee fish, isn't she, Miss Piggy?' said Viv to Jackie very loudly, as she dried a plate, 'She's got a good one, there!'

'Oh, definitely!' said Jackie. 'She's a beauty!' Jackie finished washing the last bit of cutlery and drained the water. She opened the Blue Nun and poured two large glasses, then picked up a clean tea towel and helped Viv dry the rest of the dishes.

'Let's not talk about it anymore,' whispered Jackie. 'We'll wait til he goes out and she's in bed. He seems okay now, since you came round.'

Viv nodded and switched on the kitchen radio, to the sound of *My Prerogative* by Bobby Brown. She turned it up loud and encouraged a reluctant Jackie to bang hips with her to the beat.

'*It's her prerogative!*' sang Viv, pointing to the cupboard.

'Quit that!' Jackie replied.

Hearing the music, June put the couch cushions on the floor and rolled around backwards and forwards with her dolly. Frank watched the news, competing with the volume from the kitchen radio, which was now competing with the sound of Viv.

He went upstairs to get changed, while they did the dishes. He could hear them singing from the kitchen. He loved noise in the house. He decided to shave while he thought through how to get rid of the bottles before Jackie found them and started asking questions about her mum's drinking again.

Jackie turned the TV channel onto *Coronation Street* and sat on the couch with Viv, with June sitting between them. Gail Tilsley was seeing a man much younger than she was, and the shock of the story had made the papers. June cuddled into Jackie with her thumb in her mouth.

As she held her daughter, Jackie thought of how to broach the subject with her dad, without him shutting down. She twisted her cardigan around her finger and gulped her wine, unsure of the right approach.

Frank re-entered the room. 'I won't be long, hen. Don't be having any wild parties now.' He kissed Jackie and June on the head and waved to Viv. He put on his bunnet and closed the back door.

'You'd never think he'd found a thing,' said Viv.

'He's an Oscar winner, is our Frank. That's how he copes. God knows the secrets he carries about.'

'You're as bad as each other.' Viv sipped her wine.

THE COLLECTOR

Frank strode down past the empty market. He rubbed his hands with the cold. He hoped he had hidden the vodka well enough, but it was all done in such a rush he didn't remember. He planned to pour it down the sink in the morning, then bin bag the empty bottles and throw them into the bottom of Mrs Morrisson's bin. *There's no need for her to go under the sink again. The dishes are done.* He turned left into the Working Men's Club.

'Hi, Frank,' said the man in the booth.

'Hi, Alec,' he replied, and pushed the inside door open. Straightaway, he could see Bobby near the bar.

'Hiya, Frank, how's it going?'

'Hiya, Bobby, not bad, thanks.' Frank noticed Bobby's girlfriend Maureen behind the bar and greeted her. 'How are you doing, Maureen?'

'Not bad, thanks, Frank, working away, you know.' She wiped down the countertop in large circles. 'How's Jackie and wee June?'

'All going great guns, thanks, Maureen.'

Frank looked around as some of the familiar members of the club entered in their couples of twos and fours and sat at their usual tables. The wives took off their jackets and the men queued at the bar for the drinks before the bingo started.

'Right, Bobby, what do you need me to do?' he asked, removing his jacket and bunnet.

'I need you to keep bringing glasses back to the bar, especially half pints and tumblers. You know how mobbed it gets in here when Misty get going and the dancing starts. The lassies can't get drinks poured quick enough.'

'No bother.' Frank rolled up his sleeves.

'Then we'll get you a few pound in your pocket at the end of the night and a couple of pints on the way. How does that sound?'

'Aye, sounds good to me!' He smiled.

'Maureen, get Frank a pint, please.'

'Coming up!' Maureen pulled the tap and beer flowed into the glass. Frank felt happy he had somewhere to be and was needed by a friend like Bobby. He sat down on his stool and waited for the Club to fill up. Bobby passed Frank his drink over the bar, then stood beside Maureen.

'Are you going to tell him?' she whispered.

'I'll let him have his pint first,' he answered.

In Glasgow, a once-white coach, now filthy from years of motorway dust, drove speedily through the town. Heaving with passengers, the coach pulled into Buchanan Street Bus Station and the driver swung the big steering wheel all the way around to the left, and then quickly back to the right, expertly aiming to park between the long white lines of the usual designated arrival bay. The bus came to a halt and the air brakes released a loud sigh like an old horse after a big race. The driver pushed a button and the thin electric double doors banged open against each side. He checked the time on the station clock and made a note on his clipboard.

Crumpled up tinfoil balls, empty Kwenchy Cups and chocolate wrappers were scrunched under foot and beer cans kicked down the aisle as passengers shuffled forward to move off the coach. A baby rubbed his eyes and opened them wide to the darkness, one eyelash lost. Elbows bashed into cheeks as people yanked down duffel bags. Two young women helped each other lift their rucksacks down off the overhead racks and swing the straps across each other's shoulders.

Terry stood outside waiting. He watched as passenger after passenger streamed out of the coach, carrying bags, cases, big coats and babies. He searched the shapes for the person he was collecting. He had thought about getting a tea and an iced bun from Greggs but felt he'd better be in the exact place at the exact time he said he would be. Stomach acid rose inside him as he wondered what kind of mood his friend would be in. *At least we parted on good terms after his shop shut. I pity those that didn't.*

A tall, slender shadow began to emerge from the back of the coach, moving slowly forward. Making out the familiar figure, Terry puffed up his cheeks involuntarily and blew air from his mouth. Tommy appeared at the bus steps, immaculate in a black suit and tie. His full head of jet-black hair was neatly in place. Terry thought he didn't look as if he had travelled that far, if at all, as everybody else looked bedraggled and crumpled. Reaching the third step of the bus, Tommy Fletcher threw his duffel bag to the ground and removed a packet of cigarettes from his inside pocket. The people coming out of the bus behind him had to try to squeeze past or wait, tapping their feet, as he lit a cigarette behind a cupped hand in the shelter of the bus doorway and threw away the match. He took the final step down and looked up to see Terry.

'Tommy!' he called, nervously. 'Tommy! Over here!' Terry waved, then pointed to his own head, then put up a thumb. He walked forward to greet his friend, arms outstretched for a pat on the back. It had been three years, but the lit cigarette dangled from Tommy's lips, so Terry dropped his hands down by his sides, then reached for a handshake, which Tommy didn't see.

'Long time no see! How was your journey? Was it good?' asked Terry. Tommy kicked his bag and walked forward a few steps.

'How do you think?' he replied, raising an eyebrow at the crowd and then the bus. 'It was like coming up the motorway in a pram.'

'I thought you would have flown up with your, er, your mum's... what she left you... God rest her...'

'Don't like planes,' he replied, blowing smoke out of the side of his mouth.

'You need a hand carrying anything?'

'Nope.' He drew long and deep on his cigarette. 'Where you parked?' Smoke escaped his mouth as he talked.

'The car's not far.'

'Where is it?'

'Just off Killermont Street.'

'God sake, is that the nearest you could get?'

'Glasgow's all changed since you left, Tommy. Dead busy now, folk can't get parked. I've been here since five o'clock.' He paused to check Tommy's reaction then added, 'But it's no problem! You want a cup of tea or anything or the toilet before we leave the station?'

'No. Let's get going. I've a guy waiting for me to collect keys. In Coatbridge.' Tommy flicked his cigarette towards the vents of a drain and stared as the red ash butt dangled, then dropped down.

He began striding on, leaving Terry scrambling to keep up.

'Coatbridge?' Terry said, almost shouting, 'Are you staying long, then? I thought you were just here for a few months... to settle things... after, you know, your mum... to put something in the *Advertiser*... sorry to hear about that, by the way.'

'Too late for your sorries now, mate, I didn't see you at the funeral.'

'Aye, you're right. I meant to say to you about that. I couldn't get the bus fare together. Birmingham is a long way and it was a bad month, bit strapped,' Terry babbled. 'I did try, but the market can be up and down for customers. Sorry again for your loss.' Terry tripped over an uneven paving stone. Tommy did not look back.

'Pack that job in on Monday. You're coming back to work for me.'

Frank had enjoyed two free pints and Viv's dad had uncharacteristically bought him a half of whisky that he had left behind the bar with Maureen as he made his rounds with a tray.

'This dead?' he asked, holding up any empty glass at each table, making sure he never touched anything with a drop of drink still in it. If he was quiet enough, people carried on their conversations and it was quite easy to hear a snippet.

'She told me he came into £5,000,' one woman said to another, to which the other replied, 'No, it was £10,000, I heard it was a good £10,000.' Frank moved from table to table, picking up news that somebody had won money.

'After he fell out with her, he went down south to stay with the mother, and now he's coming back apparently. I don't know if the mother died, but I think she did.'

Frank wondered who was coming back, who died, how much money the other person had actually won, as it seemed to be going up as he moved around the club.

'It was a pools win, she had, £20,000, and she never spent a penny of it. Kept it for him,' the man said to the other man, who whistled with glee. 'Imagine what you could do with that, eh?' The other man shook his head despondently.

'Imagine the begging letters though,' he said. 'That would be rough. I couldn't stick that.'

'Will you shoosh!' said his wife, trying to listen to the bingo numbers. With a full tray of glasses,

Frank returned to the bar and leaned into Bobby. He set the tray down on the bar and pointed his finger in the air.

'Well,' he announced, 'seemingly somebody has come into money. And somebody else, that has been away, is coming back!' Frank reported to Bobby, who raised his eyebrows. Bobby put money in the till and moved the glasses to the sink.

'Is that right?' he asked, humouring Frank.

'It's like Miss Marple, this job. I'd better get back out there and find out who the millionaire is!' Frank took a quick sip of his whisky, then weaved his way back out between the tables of the main hall.

'Why didn't you say to him?' Maureen asked, nudging Bobby.

'If it carries on like this, I won't have to,' he replied. He turned back to gaze at Maureen's face. 'Anyway, I'm more worried about how you'll be, if I'm honest,' he said to her, and moved a bit of her fringe away from her heavily blushed cheekbone.

'Nothing can come between me and my man,' she replied proudly, and linked her arm into his.

'As long as he doesn't come in here, causing any trouble like he did the last time,' added Bobby.

'I can't see that happening.' Maureen unhooked her arm from his and rubbed both of Bobby's arms. 'He made too many enemies, hurt a lot of people.'

She smiled a little sorry smile and then turned to pull a pint for a customer. Bobby watched her fondly from the side of the bar.

'It was £50,000!' announced Viv's dad, Tam, to his wife, Bessie, and another couple. He slammed his hand on the table. 'Fifty grand he pocketed from her. I heard it in Pender's. He's getting a flat kitted out in Coatbridge with the money.'

'It was never as much as that!' Bessie waved the idea away. 'More like £10,000 or something.'

'No, I heard it was a lot more than that,' replied the other man, 'He's in the money all right and no mistaking. Absolutely loaded.' His wife, wide-eyed, sipped her drink and circled bingo numbers, an expert at listening to two things at once. Frank got close and heard the end of their conversation. *Finally*, he thought, *somebody I can ask.*

'Oh, hello again, Frank!' Bessie kicked Tam under the table.

'I heard you all chatting about this money! Who is it that has won it?' asked Frank. 'I've been hearing about it all night! Was it the snowball? Somebody tell me before I burst here!'

Tam looked at his wife, and the other couple looked down at their bingo sheets. Bessie looked up at Frank.

'You'd better sit down a minute,' she said.

UGLY GREETIN' FACES

At the very end of *Coronation Street* and not a second before, Jackie took June upstairs to prepare her bath. She turned the taps on and June dropped her ducks into the Matey bubbles one by one. Viv joined them and they sang *Three Little Ducks* before she went back down the stairs.

As Jackie bathed June, she thought of her mum bathing her when she was a little girl.

'Mummy's very tired,' she'd say to Jackie, as she attached the cream rubber hose to each tap. Her mum was always tired. Always too tired to take her swimming, or to the school disco. She had learned, however, quite quickly, that asking her mum to sing enlivened her. She seemed to know a lot of songs, but her favourite was by Nancy Sinatra, *These Boots Are Made For Walking*.

'Sing to me, Mummy!'

'Okay, darling. You want the boots song?'

'Yes.'

> *You keep saying you got something for me*
> *Something you call love but confess*
> *You've been a'messin where you shouldn't've*
> *been a'messin'*

And now someone else is getting all your best!

Jackie found herself humming it, while she moved a duck through the water. She thought of her mum's voice, so strong and soulful, loud, powerful and steady. Her mum said she always had to dig deep for her 'recording voice'. Jackie remembered the time she scrubbed her back too hard as the chorus took its grip.

These boots are made for walkin!
And that's just what they'll do!
One of these days these boots are gonna walk all over you!

She'd begun crying with the roughness of her mum's touch.

'Oww, Mummy! Stop!'

Gasping, her mum had pulled little Jackie out of the bath and wrapped her in a warm towel, hugging her and crying and saying she was sorry. She'd put cream on her back and slept in her room with her that night, stroking her hair until she fell asleep. It was the one and only time her mum had hurt her, but she always wondered what made her so cross that day, and why sometimes she got so upset.

Jackie lifted June out of the bath and wrapped her in a towel. She popped her into a fresh nightie and dried her hair. Once tucked up warmly in bed, they read her favourite chapter of *The Lion, The Witch and The Wardrobe*, where Edmond meets the white witch and she gives him hot chocolate and Turkish Delight.

'Go to sleep now, Junie bear. Saturday tomorrow, a fun day! Mummy's off work!' She kissed her forehead and June rolled onto her side, slid her thumb in her mouth and closed her eyes. Jackie lifted the blankets over her shoulders and padded them around her body. She stroked her hair. 'My little china dolly,' she said quietly. She watched her drift off, then put the door ajar and went to join Viv.

As she entered the living room, Viv pulled a second bottle of wine from her bag and a six-pack of Monster Munch.

'Rob Lowe is on in *About Last Night*. Do you want to watch it?'

'Aye, okay, stick it on.'

'What do you think you're going to say to your dad?'

'I've got absolutely no idea.'

Viv opened a bag of Monster Munch and passed it to Jackie. She opened a second bag, then hooked five Monster Munches on each finger and scooped each one off into her mouth, one by one.

'You know, reminders of her... my mum, I mean, are everywhere. And not good ones. Three bottles this time. *Three* bottles... and *full* bottles, Viv. I mean, how much was my mum actually putting away?'

'I don't know, Jackie. I don't know. Maybe she had it stored up for parties and that.'

'No, because then, why would she hide it? Where else is it in this house? In the loft? I mean, she drank a lot, but why? I wish I knew why.'

'Some people don't need a reason to take to drink like that,' said Viv, as she took a long sip of wine.

'I mean, she had everything! She had this house, my dad, a nice life, a daughter. How do you get to the stage where you drink yourself to death?'

'I don't know, Jackie, but it's not fair that you have to think about this again. You should get your dad to try and open up about it.'

'He won't talk about it, I told you before. He doesn't tell me anything. Only that she had a problem, it got bad... he says she "had her demons" but he never says what they were.' Jackie turned to face Viv. 'I want to know about my mum. The young woman she was. I want to know if I'm like her. I mean, look at us, we're sitting here drinking a second bottle of wine. The other night, we had a bottle of cider at the shows. Are we alkies?'

'No, don't be daft. You *have* to have cider at the shows. Everybody has cider at the shows! It's on the notice on the gate at the entrance!' Viv smiled and gave Jackie a friendly punch. 'Anyway. It's Friday night. There's a big difference between a drink on a Friday night and putting vodka on your cornflakes. You've finished a week at work, you're allowed a drink... or fourteen,' said Viv, nodding.

'Is that what you think she did? Put vodka on her cornflakes?'

'No, I don't think that, of course not. That's not what I'm saying. And anyway, you would have noticed if she was doing that.'

'No, I wouldn't have, Viv. I never knew my mum had a problem because I was either too young or too centred on myself. I was always out partying with you before I got pregnant with June, or working. I never knew until near the end. My dad kept it all from me. Some days, she'd be in bed all day when I came home from work, and my dad would say she had a migraine. When I was small, it was my dad that always took me to school. He dropped me off, early, with a piece and jam. Sometimes she waved from the back door in her nightie. Sometimes she was still in her bed. My dad used to say "Shh! You'll wake your mummy!" if I was noisy coming down the stairs.'

'But she picked you up from primary every day! I remember! Her and my mum at the school gate, my mum with a fag, yours all glamorous-looking. At least she never smoked, my mum's got an iron lung, I think, thank God she stopped.'

'She didn't look like that – all glamorous - in the morning. She probably spent all day on her make-up and ironing her clothes and picking out shoes and doing her hair.'

'Jackie, you're being really hard on her... she was a good mum, she just had a problem that she couldn't control. It's a disease, is alcoholism. You wake up, you need a drink.'

'I know that... I know. You know what it is? I just miss her!' Jackie began sobbing in little, slow, hard breaths and Viv pulled her in close. 'I just miss her so much, Viv. And I never knew the half of her.' Viv held Jackie close and rubbed her back.

'It's okay,' she said, 'let it all out.'

'And now these weird dreams... I can't explain...'

After a minute, they separated and Jackie dried her eyes and blew her nose.

'Sorry. Everybody expects me to be over this because enough time has passed. But I feel more sad now than I did five years ago. I can't get past the fact that there was a side of her I barely knew. I mean, my dad didn't even tell me about the vodka under the sink – I had to find that out for myself!'

'He's probably trying to protect you, Jackie.'

'Well, I wish he wouldn't. I'm twenty-five years old, for God's sake. He has just shut her away now, like she only belonged to him. Keeps his memories in a box. Nobody else is allowed to talk about her, bring up what happened to her...' Jackie fell silent. They stared at the television with the sound on low. Viv reached over for the bottle of wine.

'You're going through a lot right now. I'm so sorry.' Viv poured wine into Jackie's glass.

'I'm okay. Sorry about that... meltdown. It just creeps up on me sometimes, I'm fine, and then... I'm not. Anyway. Sorry. Thanks for listening.'

'Don't be daft. You're entitled to cry anytime you like. Especially to me. It's good for you.' Viv held up her glass. 'To ugly greetin' faces.'

'Ugly greetin' faces,' Jackie smiled. They sat in a comfortable silence watching the film and sipping their wine. Rob Lowe offered Demi Moore a drawer, and Viv started fidgeting on her side of the couch. Leaning to her left, switching to the right, adjusting her cushion. She put her glass on the carpet, picked up again, then put down again.

'What's up with you? Ants in your pants?'

'Och, it's these new knickers I got, the elastic is digging in.'

'For God's sake! You and your bargain knickers! You shouldn't buy off the market!' Jackie laughed.

Viv stood up and flopped down onto the couch again, then released a huge exasperated sigh, ending in a noise of bubbling of her lips.

'Just take them off and throw them in the bin. You can put your tights back on!'

'It's not the knickers.'

'Oh, God, what is it?'

'I don't know how I'm going to tell you this,' said Viv. 'I haven't been able to tell you yet, because we were talking about your mum and that.'

'Tell me!'

'Argh!' Viv exclaimed, annoyed. Jackie quickly put her drink down on the side table.

'What is it? You seeing somebody?' she gasped, folding her knees under themselves. 'Have you had a one night stand? Oh, my God, tell me! Are you pregnant?' Jackie gasped again, louder, her eyes wide with realisation. 'Oh, my God – is it AIDS? Have you got AIDS?'

'No! I've not got AIDS, for God's sake. It's none of that.'

'Well, what is it?'

'I'm really sorry, Jackie...'

'Sorry for what?' She stopped still and leaned a hand on Viv's arm. 'You're worrying me, now!'

'There's a rumour going round...'

'What rumour? What?'

'There's a rumour going about that Tommy is coming back.'

'Tommy?' Jackie pointed to her chest. 'My Tommy? Tommy Fletcher? How do you know?'

'My dad said he heard it in Pender's. He says that guy that used to work in the bookies with Tommy is collecting him from the station.'

'What guy?'

'That big Terry guy. The one on the fruit stall. You know him! He used to drink with Tommy in the Working Men's Club. Big tall guy with ginger hair.'

'Oh, I know who you mean! Aye, they are pals, definitely! Oh, no! Oh, Viv! This isn't good.' Jackie shook her head. 'When's he coming?'

'Well, my dad says it's soon, apparently.'

'And he's definitely coming to Airdrie? Do you know how long for?'

'I don't know how long, but my dad said he's got money. He's rich. Thousands. Rolling in it, now.'

'Oh, no, Viv, what am I going to tell June? What if he wants to see us?'

'Well, you should get some of his money for a start. Compensation for the way he treated you.'

'I don't want his dirty money. He probably got it off a drug dealer or somebody. This is so bad! I thought we had seen the last of him.'

'No, the money's off his mum. She died.'

'Oh... well, that's a shame. But I never knew her so...'

'We can only hope that he doesn't coming knocking back for you. Not just for your sake. For June's, for Maureen's, for your dad's, for poor Daniel's... for all the people he hurt.'

'I forgot about that night he bust Daniel's nose!'

'I wish I had panned his melt in! Finished him off!'

Jackie sighed and poured the last of the wine into their glasses.

'I wish I'd let you,' she said. 'But not the face.' They both laughed. 'He was some looker, though, wasn't he? I wonder if he's kept his looks?'

'Aye, he was. Pure evil underneath but a good-looking devil.'

'Why do all the bad ones have to be good looking?'

'I think it's in the rules somewhere...'

BLADES

Jackie waved Viv down the street from the front door. Viv didn't have far to walk and always rang Jackie's house phone three times to let her know she was home safely. The wind whistled outside and a streetlamp flickered. Jackie felt warm from the wine and wanted more. She closed the gate and walked into the kitchen, then leaned against the back door for a few minutes, thinking about Tommy, then remembered the vodka. She decided to have another look in the cupboard. She reached in behind the pipe and took out a bottle and stopped to examine it for a few seconds. The glass felt sticky. She knew she should put it back, before her dad saw, but she kept hold of it, hugging it to her body. Her drunkenness compelled her to *try it, taste it; taste what your mother craved*. She walked into the living room and sat in her dad's chair. Her mum smiled out at her from the picture on the mantelpiece. *Was she sober or drunk when that was taken?* Jackie wondered. *What happened that night? What happened any of those nights?*

She unscrewed the bottle and took a sip of the vodka. It burned her throat.

'Jees-o, Mum. This is rough without lemonade!' She took another sip and talked to the picture. 'Did you hear that Tommy's coming back?' she slurred. 'If he's come back for me or my baby, he can hop it.' She took a few gulps, forced the drink into her body, in front of her mother's smiling face. She held the bottle down the side of the chair until she recovered from the sting in her gullet. 'I wonder what you would have made of him?'

She got up and staggered to the sideboard and pulled out her dad's box of old photos. She knelt down, holding the neck of the bottle in her fist. She tossed the lid off the box and tipped the photos and clippings onto the floor, spreading them out around her knees. She found some newspaper cuttings.

MISS   DECEMBER   OPENS   AIRDRIE SUPERMARKET read the headline on a cutting from 1951. There were more cuttings, one of them an advert.

MISS DECEMBER!
LIVE - EVERY THURSDAY AT AIRDRIE
WORKING MEN'S CLUB

She knew that her mother had been a club singer before Jackie was born but didn't realise she was such a local celebrity. Jackie swigged the vodka and admired her mum's beauty. Platinum blonde hair in perfect curls, *she was a big star!*

She singled out a picture of her mum and dad and her in front of them in a pushchair. The three of them smiling. Jackie wore a knitted dress that she remembered being itchy at the collar. Her mum looked tired, but happy. *Was she drinking then? When did it start? Was she always drunk?* She took out another picture. Jackie was cradled in her mother's right arm, held high. Her mum had a little monkey in her other arm. Although she had only been a toddler when this was taken, Jackie was sure she remembered how it had felt to be held by her mother's soft, strong forearm. She had a very vague memory of that day, in Arbroath, the man with the monkey, stopping people and asking if he could take pictures of them in the street, holding his tiny pet. The monkey wore a striped knitted jumper and had a long tail. He took their address and payment and posted the picture later.

Jackie searched her mother's face for similarities to hers but couldn't find any. People always said Jackie looked more like her dad and that she had his round eyes. She stared at her toddler self, wondering why she had no smile, next to her radiant smiling mother who had a look of gentleness. Even in her forties, she looked so young.

She leaned back onto the sideboard and took another swig of vodka. She felt herself begin to sway. She gathered up the pictures and clippings and put them back into the box and into the sideboard. She leaned back and put the lid on the bottle and rolled it across the carpet, to see how far it would go.

'Why... you... drink... Mum?' she asked, staring at the bottle.

She watched the bottle gently touch the wall, then crawled across the carpet to pick it up. On her knees, she rolled the bottle back across the carpet to see how far it would go the other way, and it rolled along and stopped at the other wall. She crawled over and picked it up again, opened it, and forced down some more of the cruel drink, then screwed the lid back on. She stood up and staggered towards the kitchen. Her thoughts buzzed like a thousand bees. *Is this what it felt like, Mum? Like this? You looked after me like this? Drunk? If you're raised by a drunk, you become a drunk! Like mother like daughter! What am I going to do if he wants to take June? Why can't he leave us alone? Am I a drunk like you?*

She found herself outside in the garden, bottle in hand. The wind blew her off her feet slightly but she was able to grab a washing pole to steady her legs and continue. She searched the sky for a few seconds, then closed her eyes. The wind pushed her backwards towards the door and she grabbed the washing line just before the back step. Her breathing began to get heavier and heavier and her head lulled forward. She let out a low, primal moan full of angst.

'MUUUUUUUM!' she cried.

The bottle flew out of her hand and smashed against the back fence.

'I WANT MY MUM!' she cried, then noticed what she had done. 'YOU STUPID, STUPID, STUPID!' she slurred, and stumbled over the grass to collect the pieces of glass. The bottle neck was intact so she started scrambling to find broken glass and drop it inside the neck so that she could take it all to the bin. The wind blasted her hair back off her face. Leaves danced around her head and a small tree branch landed on the grass beside her.

'Need to get it all,' she swore through gritted teeth. She picked up the tree branch and used it to poke around the grass. Unable to find any glass, she felt around with her hand until a sharp pain pinched her finger. 'Ow!' she cried. It was instantly wet and sticky.

Suddenly she felt a warm, firm grip on her shoulders. She noticed her dad's trousers flapping around the edge of his ankles, and she could see his Pac Man socks. She laughed through her tears and looked up at his face.

'Hiya, Dad. I've made a mess. Big mess,' she cried.

In the silvery twilight, Frank caught sight of her hand, covered in blood, and the red label of the vodka bottle.

'Did you drink that?' He held her by the shoulders, steadying her in a sitting position. She nodded. Frank was calm, not angry, not shouting. 'Let's get you in. Your hand's bleeding.'

'I need to find... glass! I smashed it, Dad... all over...' she stumbled.

'I'll get it.'

'... before June plays...'

'I'll find it.'

Instinctively, Frank put her arm around his neck and helped her up. He led her into the kitchen, washed her hand under the tap and watched diluted blood drain down the plughole. He checked there was no glass in the cut, then opened the cupboard where they kept bandages, plasters and pills. A bandage unravelled. He stopped the bleeding with a tea towel, then wrapped her hand tightly in a bandage, attaching a safety pin.

'That's not how you put a bandage on...' she slurred. 'I'm a nurse!'

He poured her a glass of water from the cold tap and forced her to drink it, then he took her up and put her into the bed beside little June's. He put a blanket over her and she mumbled a few words about December, then fell straight to sleep.

She looks just like her, he thought, and he felt unease nudge a corner of his mind. Frank was used to putting a person to bed. He had done it for years.

He checked on little June who had slept through it all. Closing the door, he went to his room and got changed into his pyjamas and slippers. He put on his dressing gown, then went back downstairs to get his torch and a dustpan and brush. Once in the garden, he was relieved to see that the bottle had remained fairly intact in large chunks of glass and he was able to find it all, as it gleamed from the grass against the torchlight. He collected it all, then brushed it out of the dustpan into some newspaper. After wrapping it up, he put it in the outside bin. He went back inside, reached under the sink and grabbed the other two bottles, checking there were no more. He poured all the vodka down the sink, watching it glug quickly down the drain. He wrapped the two bottles in newspaper and put them with the smashed one in the outside bin.

He put the torch back into the kitchen drawer, washed his hands and went back into the living room to his chair. He took a deep breath, his hands starting to shake. He looked at June's picture, then reached for it, before pausing for a second. He pushed it face down.

Tommy had arrived at the West End Flats and collected his keys and sent Terry home straight-away. He was in his newly-acquired fourth floor abode and was pleased with what he saw - a freshly decorated and refurbished two-bedroom flat, fully furnished with a blue crushed-velvet Chesterfield three-piece suite in the living room, a television, and a video recorder. A fringed standard lamp stood in the corner next to a matching footstool, and as he clicked on the main lights, he found that the dimmer switch worked perfectly. A full-length ornate mirror leaned in the hall, next to the phone table, as instructed.

In the immaculate white brick-tiled kitchen, there were lots of brand new stainless steel electric gadgets on display, including a fancy kettle, coffee percolator, a huge microwave with digital screen and an electric tin opener. He smiled as he saw the electric knife.

The bedroom housed a large queen-sized bed with soft white quilt and soft beige bedside lamps and tables. The wardrobe had been custom-built to his instructions with sliding mirrored doors and double hanging space. He slid a door open to find a selection of shirts, suits and shoes, some still with labels on and two suits zipped under suit bags marked Burton's. He slid the wardrobe door open at the other side which had plenty of empty hanging space and specialist square shelves made to hold ladies' shoes.

The second bedroom contained a single bed decorated with fairy pictures and fairy lights. There was a princess chair with vanity table that had little Hollywood lights around the outside of the mirror and a pink wardrobe that had a sign that read 'Fairies Live Here!' A huge doll's house with miniature furniture adorned the other wall, sitting neatly under the window.

The bathroom contained a large shower and a bath with jacuzzi pumps. The two sinks sat side by side with fresh towels either side. A stack of toilet rolls stood beside the heated towel rail. He took a pee and decided that the designer's taste was spot on, it was the nicest bathroom he'd ever seen.

He washed his hands and returned to the living room.

He took a cigarette from his inside pocket, held it between his lips and unzipped the duffel bag. He removed several items and placed them on the coffee table - a large brown envelope filled with £50 notes tied together neatly in flat bundles, a toothbrush and toothpaste, a three inch flick knife, and the framed picture of his mother, which he took over to the window ledge and placed down gently.

'She'll never be able to resist this place,' he said to himself, looking out to the empty swings blowing back and forth in the West End Park playground, in the dark and dusky night.

GLASGOW'S MILES BETTER

The phone rang in Daniel's house. Nobody budged.

'It will be for you, anyway,' remarked his dad, from behind a newspaper.

Daniel dropped his spoon into his bowl of Frosties and rushed to the hall to answer it. It was Johnny.

'Coming into Glasgow tonight?' he asked buoyantly.

'I don't know, I'm a bit skint after the shows, I was going to stay in.'

'What for? *Blind Date*? Don't be daft. Come out, I want to go to that pub I told you about.'

'Oh, I don't know, Johnny, I don't know if they'd let me in.'

'Why wouldn't they let you in? You'll get in if you're with me. It's great! Come and see it. Just go inside and look. And if you don't like it, we can leave.'

'Do you promise me because, once you get somewhere, you know what you're like... you'd stay all night!'

'I promise. And we'll take the next train home straight back to Airdrie.'

'Okay. What time?'

'Meet me at six o'clock at the train station. That gives you six and a half hours to do your make-up!'

'Ha ha, very funny. I'm still in my pyjamas here. It's not midday yet! Do I need to wear shoes or trainers?'

'It's not that kind of place. Wear what you like, they let anything in!' Johnny laughed, but Daniel wasn't sure what he meant. 'Just to say, you might see a few folk wearing some... different fashions, and some dress up, but don't worry, it's a good laugh.'

'What about Jackie and Viv, should we ask them?'

'No, it's not their kind of place. Just a night out for us. Lads on the town.'

'Okay. What's the pub called again?'

'It hasn't really got a name. Some people call it Pauline's, after the owner, but it doesn't matter, I know where it is.'

'Okay, I'll see you at six at the train station, then.'

'Great! See you after. Cheerio!'

Daniel hung up, nervous, excited and curious about what he'd agreed to. He returned to the dining room. His dad sat at a table in the centre, calling out different horse names and odds, to no one in particular. His mum walked swiftly into the room in her apron. She placed two doorstep white bread cheese sandwiches in front of Daniel, and his father leaned back in the chair with the paper under his arm and a pen behind his ear. She returned with a stainless steel hot pot of tea and a plate of Caramel Wafers and tea cakes. Putting these down she moved back into the kitchen and came back with three empty mugs and a small stainless steel jug of milk. She poured the tea and added the milk, still standing up.

'Frosties is not enough, Daniel. You're in that bed too long. You need to eat.'

'Where's yours?' asked Daniel's dad. He took a bite of his sandwich and squeezed the bread.

'I'll get mine in a minute. Who was that on the phone? Was it Jackie? You going out, son?' She sipped her tea, still standing, watching Daniel eat his sandwich. He took three bites and examined his teeth marks in the bread.

'No, it was Johnny. He wants to go into the town tonight.'

'Into the town?' echoed his mum.

'The town? Glasgow town?' asked his dad, taking another bite. 'What are you wanting to go all the way in there for?'

'It's not that far on the train,' said Daniel, taking a last bite of his first half.

'You're taking the train? That'll not be cheap. How much is a ticket now? How will you get home?'

'For God's sake, Barbara, give him a chance to answer.'

'Johnny says we don't need to pay if we get off at High Street. I'll get the train home again.'

'Of course you need to pay! You'll get arrested doing that. Check the times with the man at the station. I'll give you the money for the fare. Oh, I don't know about this, Brian, I don't know about him going into Glasgow! There's a lot of weirdos hang about. There's your druggies, your drunks, your down and outs...' She counted out the list on her fingers.

'Mum, I'll be fine. I won't be on my own.'

'Are Jackie and Viv going as well?'

'No, just me and Johnny.'

'Whereabouts are you going, anyway?' asked his dad.

'Pauline's. A bar in town.'

'Pauline's... is that in the West End?' His dad pondered the familiar name. 'I'm sure there's one of they new poncy wine bars in the West End called Pauline's.'

'I don't know. Johnny does. It's near the Barras.'

'Oh, my God, Brian, don't let him go to the Barras at that time.'

'You stay away from the Barras, you hear your mum.'

'I'm not going to the Barras it's just *near* the Barras.'

'He says it's not at The Barras, it's only *near* The Barras. Anyway. He'll be home right after closing time. Won't you, son?'

'Aye.'

'Have you got enough money for a drink, Daniel? The beer's not cheap in that Glasgow.'

'Will you stop fussing over him, now, Barbara?'

'I'm not fussing, I'm just *asking*.'

'I've got some money...'

Barbara put down her tea, reached for her handbag and removed a large purse. She unclasped the metal spring and removed £5.

'Take this,' she said, squeezing it into the palm of his hand and clasping his fist shut again. 'Be careful. You might be twenty-three but you're still my baby.'

'Big man-baby,' smiled his dad, opening his paper.

'Promise me you'll be careful, Daniel.'

'I'll be careful, Mum.'

'Okay then, son.' She kissed his head, then went into the kitchen with her tea. Daniel heard the usual kitchen sounds, hot tap running, washing up liquid squirting, cupboard doors opening and closing, rattling crockery. His dad peeked over the top of his newspaper.

'How much did she give you?' he asked.

'A fiver.'

'A fiver! Well, you're getting no more out of me.'

'I didn't ask for any more!'

'A fiver will do you fine. Your mum could get a full family shop with that-'

'And still have change... I know.'

'And still have change...' his dad mumbled. Daniel smiled.

He left the crusts on the plate and went upstairs into his room. He gathered up t-shirts and socks and other bits of laundry he'd left on the floor and took them down to his mother in the kitchen.

'There's my good boy,' she said.

'Right, that's me away, Barbara.' Brian stood up from the table with the folded paper back under his arm, a familiar sight that Daniel recognised. He knew he was going to Airdrie to place his bets. His dad was still annoyed that his 'lucky bookies' - as he called it – had closed down. It was boarded up but the bold sign still hung there with the word *SOLD* emblazoned over it - *Fletcher's Bookmakers*. Daniel hoped it would never open again. One punch from Fletcher was enough. Luckily, he had managed to keep the story of that night safely hidden from his parents.

'Mum, will you iron my green t-shirt, please?'

'Bring it down, then, son. Two bets and no more, Brian!' she shouted after her husband.

'Aye, two bets, two pints!' he replied, and the door slammed.

Daniel grabbed two Caramel Wafers off the table, unwrapped one and took a bite. He rushed back up to his room, taking the stairs two at a time, munching and swallowing the chewy chocolate.

'COOEE!'

Jackie walked down a narrow corridor. Her mother led her into a living room with four armchairs. Her head teacher from years ago was sitting in one chair, and the lady she remembered from the first Holy Communion class was in another. A fire crackled behind a guard. The TV was on, flashing colour pictures, but turned down low. It might have been Des O'Connor. Her mum wore a bright yellow cardigan, one button open at the top, one button open at the bottom, with a grey skirt. Her hair was in tight curls, close in against her scalp.

'I remember you!' said one of the women from her chair. 'Lovely girl!' The other lady agreed. 'How you've grown!' she exclaimed.

Jackie sat in the chair beside her mum's.

'It's good to see you!' she said, patting Jackie's hand. 'I've been watching a lot of horror films, you know! Loads of them! I really like them. You know, the Stephen King ones. They're very funny!'

Jackie said nothing, she smiled. She didn't know where she was but she didn't care. Horror films? They were laughing. The two ladies told stories to each other as her mum continued talking to Jackie.

'There's one with a clown. Oh, my God, that clown is hysterical! And there's a priest one – not Stephen King, I don't think - the one with the girl with the head that goes woo woo! and twists. The head goes all the way around, you know! My God, I was laughing! Oh, Jackie! You should come around more often!'

The other two ladies agreed.

'You should, Jackie! You really should!'

'Come around more often, Jackie!'

Jackie's old headmistress poured vodka to the top of her glass, leaving no space at the rim.

'There!' she said, 'Perfect! Say cheers now!' The three ladies clinked glasses.

'Drink your drink, Jackie,' said the communion woman. Jackie took the full glass from the table beside her and took a sip and winced.

'You really should come round more often, Jackie!' said the headteacher.

'Come back again, Jackie,' added the other lady, drinking the vodka like it was water.

Jackie nodded. She stared at the fire and watched it crackle. She felt the welcoming warmth in the room, as if these ladies had been sitting chatting for days. She wanted to stay in this strange place for longer, but knew she had to leave. They encouraged her to swallow all of her drink, ending in a loud cheer, then her mum stood up, as if to say goodbye. Jackie stood up and felt her mum's soft cardigan rub against her face in a cuddle. Jackie breathed in lavender and smoky embers. Their brief embrace ended too quickly as June patted Jackie on the back gently, indicating that the hug was over. Jackie turned and walked towards the front door with rounded shoulders.

'Straighten up now, Jackie, that's the girl.'

Jackie tried three different doors to exit, all leading to different rooms. All of them contained a dried-up mop in a bucket.

Why don't I go around to see her more often? I haven't seen her for ages. I should see her more often!

She found the front door and opened it to lots of steps, like an Escher painting.

Why don't I see my mum more often?

She took a step outside and the cold air brushed her cheeks. A familiar feeling began to rise upon her in the most sudden way.

The room window was open.

No... don't open your eyes...

The breeze from the street caressed her face. She rolled onto her side and squeezing her eyelids tight, tried to eliminate the light from the gap in the room blinds. She wanted to get back to that house.

'Mummy...' left her lips, barely audible, and she fell back into sleep. For a while, her sleep was deep, but she woke again in a light, hot sweat with daylight on her skin. Her daughter's voice nudged her thoughts from one world into another.

'GRANDA! When will Mummy wake up?'

'Now, Junie, I've said before, she'll wake up when she wakes up. She's very tired. Finish off your beans, now, that's a good girl.'

'But when will it be, Granda?'

'Very soon. You eat your dinner now. Good girl.'

'I think she will be up in ten minutes. Will she be up in ten minutes?'

'Yes, maybe in ten minutes, or maybe more, you never know.'

Jackie heard her dad's kindly voice talking to her daughter and it made her feel like *she* was a little girl again. Her heart panged when she realised she'd had another, very realistic dream about seeing and talking to her mother. She tried to make sense of the headteacher and the other lady and the steps, but none of it would figure out, except the excessive glass of vodka. Jackie instantly felt sickness rise upon her as she remembered rolling her mother's vodka bottle around the living room carpet the night before and the wind in the garden. She couldn't fathom how she got to bed.

She felt a deep disappointment, like she could cry a million tears. Her head pounded and her body shook. She turned her face towards the window but it made her feel worse. She turned back again and started to worry about Tommy taking her baby.

'Cooee!' said a voice, with a double knock to the back door, then the same voice adding, cutely, 'Cooee, Junie!'

'Hello, Mrs Morrisson!' shouted little June, turning from the table.

'Shh now, Junie,' said Frank, a finger to his lips.

Jackie leaned up on her elbows, she could picture her dad's half-annoyed, half-delighted expression.

'Jackie still sleeping?' asked Mrs Morrisson.

'Aye, she's still in her bed,' replied Frank, 'Exhausted.'

'She works too hard. Too many shifts!'

'That she does. Day off today though.'

'Did you hear that wind last night?'

'Not really, no.'

Jackie slowly moved her long slender legs out of bed and placed her feet lightly on the carpet. She noticed her bandaged hand and remembered being at the kitchen sink with her dad, seeing the bandage unravel and fall down from the cupboard. She rushed her other hand to her temple, squeezing her eyes shut. She noticed she was still in yesterday's clothes. She fumbled to remove them and pull on her dressing gown. She went to the toilet and hung her head over her knees. She brushed her teeth, then managed a one-handed shower. She scrubbed her face hard with the sponge with her wet hand, like she deserved to be punished.

She towelled down her wet body as best she could and changed into a soft cotton fitted t-shirt and denim skirt. Wearing nice, clean clothes helped her feel better. She struggled to button the fly with one hand, it felt stiff and too big for the hole. Every small movement was an effort. Giving up for the moment, she sat down on the unmade bed trying to muster up the energy to brush her wet hair. She reached for her Pond's Day Cream and applied it to her thirsty skin. She combed down her fringe and hair and blasted it with the hairdryer, using the curling brush to turn it under at the ends. She added a little bit of light foundation to calm the red patches on her cheeks, rosy from scrubbing with the sponge, she thought, or perhaps from the alcohol.

'Do it again!' June was laughing at Frank, who was performing a trick with his thumb by bending it, but making it appear to be cut in half.

'Some wind last night!' Mrs Morrisson noted. 'My God, was that some wind! I could hear things crashing... and bashing... and smashing! There were a lot of weird noises! Did you hear it, Frank?'

'Not really, no. I'll make us a cuppa.' He got up, patted June's red curls and went to boil the kettle.

'Well, when I got up this morning and looked out my window, the street was in a right state! My bin was knocked over, them next door's bin was over, Sadie Ward's garden chair was stuck up on the dyke, there was bits of tree and rubbish and all kinds of garbage lying about. There was even a shoe! There was a shoe lying in the street! Somebody's shoe must have been blown clean off!'

'The wind is very naughty!' nodded June, and shouted to the kitchen, 'Granda! Granda! GRANDA! A shoe fell off... but the sock stayed on!'

'That's right!' Mrs Morrisson gasped. 'You're quite right, June. Now you come to mention it, I saw no sock.' Mrs Morrisson nodded to the little girl with an air of mystery. She pointed one finger in the air. 'Not one single sock!' she said. June looked at her own socks and swung her feet back and forth.

Frank took a quick look outside to check his bin was still standing, and it was in the exact spot he left it. He closed the door over again.

'And, you know, it didn't look like an old shoe,' continued Mrs Morrisson, leaning into June, 'It had a good heel. T'was a man's shoe, I think.' She leaned back in her conclusion. 'A smallish man!' she nodded. 'It could have been Mr Gupta's, when I think about it. He's not too tall. I mean he's not small, but, what is he? Five foot six? Is he five foot six, Frank?'

'No!' called Frank, 'He's at least half a head smaller than me! I'm five foot seven and a half. Five eight. Five nine, maybe. He must be five... four or something.'

'Do you think I should give his door a knock?' she shouted, then paused. 'The poor man without a shoe. I might give his door a knock.' Mrs Morrisson continued to talk in a quieter tone. 'They'll all be up and about now, it's lunchtime. Mrs Gupta will be frying her samosas. Lovely smell. Mind you, I've never tasted one.'

Frank came into the living room with a cup of tea for Mrs Morrisson and one for himself.

'Beware a man with one sandal!' he said, and carefully gave her the hot mug. She held it around the rim with the tips of her fingers, then took the handle.

'What are you on about, now, Frank!'

'The shoe! Beware a man with one sandal - it's from the Bible. Or it might be from a film? I think it's from a film, *Jason and The Argonauts,* I think?

Or *was* it out the Bible? I think it was the Bible it was in. What was it again?' They sat in silence, sipping.

'Oh, but the wind! You must have heard it now, Frank? Did you not hear it?'

'Never noticed it! Was probably fast asleep.'

'An earthquake couldn't waken him!' said Jackie, smiling cautiously at her father as she entered the room.

'Mummy!' exclaimed June, 'Mummy's awake!' She lifted both arms up for a cuddle. They hugged and kissed at the table. Jackie stole a glance at Frank who looked over his reading glasses and briefly and quickly shook his head. Jackie took this to mean he had not said anything to Mrs Morrisson about the night before, and that she wasn't to mention it.

'Ah there she is! Nurse Jackie! Late shift last night?'

'No. Just tired, Mrs Morrisson.'

'You do look a little bit tired, hen. Maybe an early night tonight.'

'Jackie has been doing a lot of night shifts,' interrupted Frank. 'There's a build up with that, you know, that lack of sleep...' Jackie smiled at him.

'There's beans in the pot, Jackie.' Frank shifted in his chair.

'Ta, Dad. I'll just make a tea for now.' Jackie went into the kitchen and flicked the kettle on. She looked out the window onto the back garden grass to see if she could see any traces of the bottle. Frank followed her in to get biscuits from the cupboard.

'Dad,' Jackie whispered, 'I'm sorry. I didn't mean to - it was in my hand and then-'

'Let's not talk about it now. It's all cleared away and binned. Just act normal. I don't want "anybody" to know anything.' He opened a packet of Garibaldi and arranged them on a plate.

'I'm so sorry, Dad!' she whispered, louder. 'I feel terrible about it. I don't know what came over me!'

'Shh.' He patted her shoulder. 'We can talk about it after.' He took the biscuits into the living room.

Mrs Morrisson beckoned June over to sit on her knee and June walked over expectantly and pulled herself up using the layers of the old lady's skirt. With her arms around her, Mrs Morrisson gave an exaggerated wink and nodded her head towards her handbag. June reached around behind her into the bag and removed a small white paper packet.

'SWEETIES!' she bounced.

'Shh! You'll get me into trouble with your Granda!'

June giggled, and peeked into the bag. 'Can I have one now?'

Mrs Morrisson looked left and right. She grabbed a tea towel that was lying on the side of the couch and threw it over Frank's face.

'What's that? I can't see!' cried Frank.

'Okay! The coast is clear! Make it quick. Go!'

June gobbled the first sweet she picked from the bag without looking at what it was. Mrs Morrisson shook her head. Frank left the tea towel on his head as if he hadn't noticed it was there.

'What's that you've got?' he asked. 'I can smell something nice and tasty!' He yanked the tea towel off his face and looked at the white packet.

June squealed and Mrs Morrisson hugged her tightly.

'Oh, you lucky... and I've just got a rubbish old Garibaldi here! Give your Granda one!'

'No!' June protested, holding the bag close.

'Ah, go on, give your old Granda one! Look at all I've got. An old stinking dry Garibaldi. Look! It's got a beard on it. Probably been in that cupboard for ten years. Give your favourite one and only Granda a sweetie, hen.'

June opened the top of the paper bag wide and put her fingers inside. She rummaged around and selected a white mouse. She bit the chocolate head off and laughed in his face.

'Oh, she's brutal!' Frank smiled behind his mug.

June popped the remaining severed chocolate body into her mouth, then carried the bag over to her granddad and tore off a whopper that was stuck to another three whoppers. She handed it to him and he popped it into his mouth.

'Delicious!' He chewed, then sipped his tea.

'Look at that, eh? Such manners, at her age! I've never seen the likes of it!' Mrs Morrisson shook her head and smiled.

Jackie came back into the room, blowing on her tea and smiling at June.

'You lucky girl!' she said.

'What happened to your hand, Jackie?' asked Mrs Morrisson.

'Clumsy with the carrots...' she answered.

'You're needing more sleep, hen. Your mum needed a lot of sleep, as I remember, she used to get very tired, God rest her-'

'June, where is your dolly? I want to see her new hairstyle,' interrupted Frank.

June ran from the room to find her Sindy.

They sat in silence for a few seconds, waiting for June to return. Mrs Morrisson glanced from Frank to Jackie and back again. She sensed a subject change was needed, sometimes the way when the late June McNeill was brought up.

'Oh! I can't believe I haven't told you yet!' she exclaimed. 'And there's you mentioning the Bible and all! There's a new priest up at mass!' She sat up in her chair, being careful not to spill the tea. 'You want to see this! Everybody but everybody is talking about him!' Frank sat up. He was keen to obtain information he didn't already have on a new priest he'd already heard might be coming to the parish.

'Now, I heard about this!' he said. 'Some nephew of Father Cleary's – is he actually a priest?'

'I believe he is *not* a priest, at least, that's what Sadie Ward told me. But some say he is a young priest in training, a Seminary or maybe a Deacon.'

'So you don't know if he is a priest?'

'Well, Father Cleary told Sadie and she told me that it's his nephew from Paris – the Father's sister lives there – and he's over helping out because he's *thinking* of being a priest.'

'Oh, he's *thinking* of being a priest, I see!' Frank leaned back and pondered. 'I wonder how long you're allowed to do that for?'

'As long as you like, I suppose, if he's only thinking about it. I mean, you don't see many young priests these days. Maybe he wants to live it up a bit first.' Mrs Morrisson laughed. 'Live it up!' she repeated. 'Imagine that! Live it up at old Father Cleary's!' Frank and Jackie smiled along with her.

June returned with her Sindy doll. She showed Frank the dolly's long blonde hair and then took it to her mother and they plaited it together. Mrs Morrisson cleared away June's beans plate and cup, despite Jackie's protests and Frank's half protest.

'Oh, my God,' said Mrs Morrisson, blessing herself, returning to the room. She removed her marigolds, rolled them together and put them back into her handbag. 'God forgive me, but you should see him, Jackie – the young father - Father Cleary's nephew, I mean.'

'Is he nice? I haven't seen him yet,' said Jackie.

'He's only just got here, you wouldn't have seen him, nobody has seen him,' Frank said. 'I haven't met him, but we'll probably get a personal introduction tomorrow after mass. I know Father Cleary very, very well.' He nodded to himself. 'Close personal friend. He'll want me to meet the boy.'

'Oh, he's no boy, Frank. He's a *man*.'

'Get a hold of yourself, Mrs Morrisson!'

'I'm telling you, I've seen him up close, and he is *very* handsome, Jackie. Oh, he's tall and he's got dark hair like Elvis. And he's dark-looking, you know, that olive skin the colour of maple syrup. And the eyes of him! Eyes like planets!'

'Oh, for God's sake! What are you talking about? How close were you to the poor laddie?' Frank scowled into his tea, annoyed at Mrs Morrisson that she had all this information before he did.

'Browns and greens and blues, I don't know what colour they are. It's kind of a mixture. Like the planet earth colours. My son has a shower curtain in his bathroom in Linlithgow, you know. It's got Jupiter and Pluto and Earth and Mercury and the rest of them on it... what's it called... The Sailer System.'

'Solar System! "Sailer System"!' Frank corrected her and Jackie laughed.

'Anyway, you should have seen him pulling up the big weeds around the nasturtiums, Jackie, the muscles of him –'

'AWAY FOR GODSAKE, MRS MORRISSON!' said Frank loudly, 'Enough is enough now... There's a child in this house!' June and Jackie giggled at their antics.

'I'm only saying that I passed by the church during the week, you know, I had to go that way to go down to meet Esther for the coffee club, and he was working in the garden.' She looked directly at Jackie and raised her eyebrows.

'I never knew you drank coffee, Mrs Morrison!' Jackie said, sitting up.

'Oh, I don't touch the stuff. No, no.' She paused. 'Anyway, Jackie, between us, and God rest our

John, but if I was a younger woman, twenty years younger or so...'

'More like forty years!' said Frank. Mrs Morrisson patted her hair.

'I think you look really good for your age, Mrs Morrisson!' said Jackie. 'Doesn't she, Dad? She looks good for her age, doesn't she?'

'How would I know?' said Frank, reaching for another Garibaldi. 'I know nothing about what women are supposed to look like.'

'Thank you, Jackie,' said Mrs Morrisson. 'Don't be ridiculous, Frank! I'm not after the young priest. You know that my heart still belongs to our John!'

'Aye, just as well. It's getting like the bloody *Thorn Birds* in here.'

'Stop it, Dad!' Jackie laughed. 'What's his name, Mrs Morrisson?'

Mrs Morrisson put her index fingers up in the air, as if setting the name on a sign, and paused after each word. 'Jean. Paul. Julien! Have you ever heard a name like that? Jean. Paul. Julien. I have *never* heard a name like that. It's got the double barrel. Of course, my John was called John but it's not the same 'Jean' if you know what I mean. This one is *French*. It's spelt differently.'

'That's a lovely name.' Jackie looked behind the net curtain. The sun was peeking through the clouds after a spell of rain. She looked at the clock. It was five past two.

'Jackie, why don't you have some beans on toast, then you can take the wean up the street? I've the grass to cut,' said Frank.

'Oh! Go to Christie's! Oh! A cream ring from Christie's, now, Jackie!' breathed Mrs Morrisson. 'The ones with the coconut are absolutely beautiful! Bring me one back, will you, Jackie, please.' Mrs Morrisson fished her purse from her bag and removed 50p. 'You want one, Frank?' she asked, to which he nodded, and she fished out another 50p.

'Give that to your mummy, Junie. That's enough for four.'

'Can we go to John Menzies?' June shouted. 'For felt tips?'

'Oh, okay!' said Jackie, thinking it would be a good idea to get out and give her dad some space. 'Mummy will eat something and then we'll get ready to go.'

'Poor Jackie! Ah! You must be exhausted.'

'The fresh air will do her good,' said Frank.

Frank watched Jackie sitting down to eat. He told himself that everything would be fine, they didn't need to talk about it and it would pass by in time. *No need for any more upset. She's not like her mother. Her mother would have had another drink by now. It's just a hangover. That bloody wine. She's not like her... she hasn't got it. And there's more important things to think about such as Tommy Fletcher...*

'Want me to make you a wee sandwich, Jackie, instead of beans?'

'No, that's okay, Mrs Morrisson.'

'What kind of sandwich?' asked Frank.

'You just ate beans on toast, Frank O'Neill!' she smiled playfully. 'And five Garibaldis! If you don't need me for anything else now, I'll be off.' She kissed June on the forehead as put on her coat. 'Don't forget to eat all the sweeties! And give him none!' she whispered to June with a wink and kissed her again on the cheek. She turned to look at Frank before leaving and noticed something strange on the mantelpiece.

'You've knocked your picture over, Frank.'

Frank nodded. 'Oh, must have been while I was dusting,' he said, and set the framed picture of June upright.

'Oh! Is that pigs I see flying, Jackie?' Mrs Morrisson laughed. 'Dusting, my behind...' She closed the back door behind her and walked outside into the brightness of the day. The shoe that the wind had blown over was still in the same spot, so she picked it up and headed off to Mr Gupta's.

Jackie drifted into the kitchen to put her plate in the sink.

'Sun's out. I'm away to sit on the back step, then I'll get the mower out,' said Frank, walking past.

'Dad, I've got some news to tell you.'

'We'll talk once June is in bed tonight.' He continued walking.

Jackie sighed. *He's brushing it under the carpet, again.*

Frank sat down, his bum cold on the icy step. The clouds broke further apart. He raised his face towards the blazing sun and closed his eyes.

CHOP, CHOP

It was an unusually warm Saturday afternoon in Airdrie when Jackie and June arrived in town, and Graham Street was buzzing with people at the shops. Outside Woolworths, a group of teenagers showed each other their new tapes and singles and albums they had bought, unfolding tape sleeves to check lyrics, discussing chart positions and removing inner pockets to see pictures of the band. One had bought a poster of Elvis Costello and was trying to roll it back up. Another one had *Smash Hits!* and was examining the cover which had a picture of a band Jackie hadn't heard of, The New Kids On The Block.

Jackie remembered doing the same thing not too long ago with her best friend, when Viv bought *Guilty* by Barbra Streisand. She wouldn't let Jackie touch the white cover or open the LP to see the bigger photos inside the gatefold.

A vinegary aroma wafted from Antonia's chippie across the street as someone crossed the road with an open bag of chips. It was a warm, salty, paper smell that automatically made a person feel hungry, even if they had just had a full meal.

'Mmm, smell that, June, vinegary chips! The best smell in the whole wide world!' June threw her head back and sniffed in deeply.

'I love chips!' she announced loudly.

'Me too! Maybe we'll queue up and take some home for dinner, later, eh?'

'Yes! And cream rings, Mummy. But first! Felt tips!'

'Yes, of course, felt tips, we can't forget the felt tips.'

Continuing her walk up past Woolworths, Jackie pondered that perhaps Viv would not let her touch the Streisand album that day because she had a big bag of Antonia's hot mushy chips in her hand.

June skipped along lightly beside her mother, happily holding her hand but singing a made-up song in a world of her own. Jackie was feeling back to herself again. She was glad that she added more mascara, blusher and a light lipstick. On earlier inspection, her hand only had a little cut, thankfully, which was now covered with a plaster. She vowed to herself that she would never drink vodka again. She thought about what a terrible mistake it was, she had got into a mess and felt ashamed in front of her dad. She thought briefly of the dream of her mother and tried to make sense of it. As they walked around Airdrie, she kept one eye out for Tommy Fletcher or any of his friends. She wanted to keep things normal for June, keep her carefree, and so she held her hand tightly and made everything fun for her, as best she could.

Passing the butcher shop, they jokingly held their noses to avoid the 'meat' smell and headed into John Menzies. June knew the aisle she wanted and rushed on ahead to the back of the shop. Jackie waited patiently while June took her time looking at different pens and colouring pads and discussing them with her mother. Finally, they agreed on a packet of ten coloured felt tips, under the strict agreement that the pens were only to be used for drawing on paper, and never on the bumpy wallpaper or on the table, no matter how tempting that may be.

They walked back down into Woolworths to admire the large selection of colourful Pick N Mix, some in shiny wrappers, some boiled, or 'bald', as June called them, due to their shape and lack of wrapper. They decided not to buy any as they were very expensive and June already had the sweets that Mrs Morrisson gave her. They made their way down to the back of the shop and June pushed lots of different-shaped buttons on as many noise-making toys as she could, while Jackie looked at some of the clothes next to the toy section.

Outside they crossed the road to Antonia's to join the queue that was always out the door on a Saturday. Jackie stood patiently with June in her arms near the entrance. The guy that was almost always in Antonia's was near the front. He looked like the singer Bobby Gillespie, with the dark, lank hair and skinny build. People always said it *was* Bobby and that he used to travel from Glasgow to buy his chips *only* at Antonia's. Jackie wondered why, if this was true, he wasn't surrounded by fans every week. He brushed past them with an open bag and the queue shunted forward. Jackie ordered two battered sausage and chips and the server soaked them with vinegar and salt, double wrapped them tightly in white paper and put them in a bag. Jackie handed over a £5 note, took her change and they walked back down the street and crossed the road to Christie's. They stood outside and admired the Domino cakes and strawberry tarts in the window before they joined the queue, which was also long but moving quickly. When it was Jackie's turn, the baker placed four coconut-topped cream rings in a white box and closed it firmly and put the box flat inside a bag. Once they got out of the shop, they began the walk back down Graham Street. June talked about the cream rings and felt tips the whole way down as they reached The Spud Spot.

'Jackie!' called a booming voice. Two men walked towards her, one of them waving animatedly. The sun shone in her face so she held up her hand to make out the larger shadow.

'Jackie! How are you keeping?' he said. It was Father Cleary, the priest from their local church, with a younger man, and Jackie figured this must be his nephew. Coming into focus, the sun seemed to beam around the young man, almost as if he were solar-powered. Jackie thought his dark tanned features so unusual and exotic for this neighbourhood. They came to stand in front of her, side by side, their skin colours contrasting like two flavours of ice cream in the same bowl. Father Cleary reviewed Jackie's shopping bags.

'Chips tonight, is it? Lovely!'

'Hello, Father, hello...' Jackie waved her hand close to her body.

'You been into Christie's as well? Well, it's a big feast at your house, tonight, Junie!' The priest laughed. 'Let me introduce you to my nephew, Jean Paul, who is over from Paris at the moment. This is Jackie and this little lady here is June. This is the McNeill family I was telling you about.'

'Fronc and Jackie? Oui?'

'Yes, that's right, Frank and Jackie. And June, of course. Frank is Jackie's father. Does the odd bit of work around the parish, paints the statues and so on, but he isn't here today. Or, wait, sorry, is he with you today, Jackie?'

'No, he's at home, cutting the grass, Father. Although he's probably sitting on the back step, enjoying the sunshine.' Father Cleary laughed and his peaky jowls wobbled.

Jean Paul stared intently at Jackie. He had never seen a woman with such porcelain skin. She was pretty, eyes bright and green, if a little tired at the edges. He admired the small dots of freckles on her cheeks and nose. Aware of his staring, Jackie straightened her skirt.

'Quite right too! I'd be the same if I didn't have to get up to Fine Fare before it closed. Mrs Clark offers to do it for me on the weekends, you know, but I like to do it myself, Jackie. We'd better hurry up now, look at the time!'

'It is a pleasure to meet you, Jackie.' Jean Paul leaned in to kiss her on both cheeks. He felt warm against her breezy skin. Father Cleary made a remark that a handshake would have been fine. Jackie blushed.

'You can probably tell that Jean Paul is, as I said, French, and they do things differently over there, Jackie. I'm teaching him, you know, the ways of how Scottish people greet each other.'

'Nice to meet you,' she said, fumbling for words. It had been a long time since she felt such a fond kiss on her cheek, and she caught a brief scent of musky aftershave. Jean Paul smiled and bent down to shake June's hand.

'Pleased to meet you, Mademoiselle June,' he said. June curtseyed and bowed her head forward. Jackie laughed at her antics.

'He's not a prince, Junie!' smiled Jackie, 'you don't have to curtsey.'

'Mais, non, but she looks like a princess! I should bow!' Jackie laughed as he bowed.

'Believe me, she doesn't need rescuing!' Jackie felt the clumsy sentence leave her and wanted to swallow it back in again.

'Well, we had better get on, now,' said Father Cleary. 'Don't let those chips go cold! We'll see you all tomorrow at twelve o'clock mass. Jean Paul is helping out for now as he considers his... future.' He glanced at Jean Paul who was smiling broadly at Jackie. 'Right then! I expect to hear you singing nice and loud tomorrow, Junie! As always!' He winked at Jackie. Jean Paul smiled at June.

'Be seeing you, petite fleur,' he said. 'Au revoir, Jackie.' He reached for Jackie's hand to shake it, but only brushed his warm fingers against her cold hand as she moved it away so he didn't touch the plaster on her palm. For a second, she caught the strange colours of his eyes that Mrs Morrisson had tried to describe.

'Goodbye, Fathers!' said June.

'I am not a priest, little June,' said Jean Paul.

'Not *yet*,' said Father Cleary, marching on.

Jackie and June continued walking down the street. After a few steps, Jackie decided to turn her head and look back. Jean Paul was looking straight back at her, a row of shiny white teeth beaming from his face. Jackie looked away quickly and continued walking. She felt a rush. As she turned the corner out of sight, her cold fingers reached up to her cheek and touched the place where he kissed.

Frank finished putting away the lawn mower and stood back to admire his cut grass. It had taken him forty-five minutes to get around all the corners and he was pleased that there was no sign of broken bottle anywhere. The little robin that frequented his garden landed lightly on the freshly cut lawn and bounced around looking for worms. He felt his scalp tighten and knew it was time for him to go inside out of the sun. He went in the back door and washed his hands at the sink. He took a tea towel and ran it under the cold tap, screwed it out, then put it on his head, before running the hot tap. The water thundered against the plastic bowl. He squirted in washing up liquid. He removed his socks and shoes and placed them in the hall, then took another tea towel from the kitchen drawer and placed it on the floor in front of his chair. He turned off the tap and tested the water with his elbow.

'Perfect!' he said. He carried the basin of high bubbly wobbling water into the living room and put it on top of the tea towel. He sat down in the chair and rolled up each trouser leg. He placed his right foot into the basin first, gently down through the bubbles into the soothing heat, just hot enough not to burn but too hot for a full bath. He placed his left foot in beside it and relaxed back into his chair. The basin was just wide enough for him to be able to stretch out his toes, and he luxuriated in the soapy suds, the bubble sounds popping against his ankles. He pondered how he was going to tell Jackie about Tommy. Viv would also know by now. He knew he would have to tell Jackie tonight, before somebody else did.

The Coatbridge car dealer hovered around Tommy Fletcher, fussing over his every whim as he circled cars and opened doors and boots, then slammed them shut again.

'We have a beautiful Ford Capri if you'd like to look at that. New in - flashy red colour, very good price. Marie, get Mister Fletcher a coffee. How do you take it, Tommy?'

'Two sugars.'

'Two sugars. Any milk at all?'

'No milk.'

'No milk, Marie, come on now, hurry along, get the kettle on, now, two sugars, chop chop!' The receptionist scuttled off into the building. His eyes followed her as he continued talking. 'She makes a good coffee but she's a bit dim. You know what women are like. She's easy on the eye, though. You need a good-looking bird at the desk, don't you?'

Tommy ignored him and continued browsing cars. The dealer began to turn the single sleeper earring in his right earlobe.

'See anything you like at all? I've got a lovely purple BMW convertible that would suit you - keeping it stashed round the back for special customers only. Highly polished in wax. Two door, cracking stereo. Zero to sixty in-'

'I want a four door,' interrupted Tommy, 'with decent boot space.'

'Four door, family car, eh? The sophisticated man, of course! Right, let's see...' The dealer rubbed his hands.

'In black.'

'Right,' the dealer nodded. 'I hear you there, black is very popular these days. Good choice. Any budget in mind, or...' He had heard in the pub that Tommy Fletcher had a new influx of cash. Nobody knew how much, but he was determined not to let him leave without buying something. He tapped his finger and looked around, surveying the car lot.

The receptionist returned with the coffee. She handed it to Tommy who took it from her without taking his eyes off a fur-covered sports steering wheel. She turned to go back into the building and the dealer slapped her behind and made a whip cracking sound.

'Get back to the desk and get that phone answered,' he joked, but nobody laughed. She marched off, red with rage.

Tommy moved over to the SOLD section. His eye caught a Ford Sierra Sapphire RS Cosworth. He opened the driver side door and looked inside. He left it open, walked around the other side and opened the passenger door and leaned in. He walked around the back and opened the boot.

'Ah! She's a beauty, but she's sold. Buyer is collecting tomorrow.'

'Is that right?' Tommy lit a cigarette, inhaled and took a step backwards. He stepped forward again, bent down and looked underneath the car for rust. He stood up and kicked each tyre, then sipped his coffee. 'Shame.'

'Yeah, shame, it's a top, top motor, that. I'll see what else I've got in similar.'

'Shame that the sale fell through.' He climbed into the driver's seat. 'Get the keys, Alan. *Greasy* Alan.' The dealer swept a hand over his hair. 'And rip this sticker off the windscreen...'

'But it's Mr Dalziel that's bought that... It's for his wife... the paperwork is done... I can't...'

Tommy reached into his top pocket and removed his flick knife. He clicked and the shiny blade appeared.

'Mr Dalziel *thought* he bought it. There was a mistake with the paperwork, wasn't there, Alan? You did say your receptionist wasn't so clever. Now get the keys, go on, hurry along...' He slashed the knife through the air left and right as he laughed. 'Chop chop! And I want it cheaper than what Dalziel was paying.' Alan walked to the front desk as quickly as he could, biting his cheek and squeezing his hands in and out of fists.

PAULINE'S

Johnny passed a can of lager to Daniel and he pulled back the ring curl in one swift motion. The old train carriage swayed from side to side and Daniel had to take a few quick gulps so that the liquid didn't froth over. He looked out of the window at the passing terraced houses and trees while Johnny talked about how not to worry about train tickets because there was no guard at this time of the evening and anyone could walk straight through High Street Station. Johnny hurried Daniel to finish the can – he had another one waiting for him in the bag.

'A wee drink before you drink saves you money!' said Johnny. Daniel looked at the side of his can. There was a picture of a blonde woman smiling back at him. 'Who did you get?'

'Pauline.'

'Ha ha, no way! Pauline's is where we're going!'

'That's mad.'

'Our Pauline doesn't look like that, though. You might see her but she doesn't always come out to the bar unless she's dressed in her best.'

'Typical barmaid, eh?' said Daniel.

'She's not a barmaid, she's the owner. She likes to mix with the punters.' Daniel thought that Johnny made a smirk as he looked out of the window. The train drew into High Street and they gulped down the remainder of the cans, crushed them with their shoes and left them on the floor. They strolled through the station without a ticket, just as Johnny had said, and turned left to walk down towards The Barras.

'This way,' said Johnny. They ducked around a few corners and Daniel started to hear some music. *High energy! Your love is liftin' me!* 'Oh, my God, it's rammed!' said Johnny. Daniel couldn't see inside the pub as the windows were blacked out. Lots of men stood outside in a queue waiting to get in. Daniel felt aware that his longer hair was not the correct style as most of the men going in had short skinheads or neat crew cuts. His jeans were also baggy and most of the other guys in jeans were cut offs or drainpipes. One bigger guy had very small shorts on. *Well, it is July,* he thought. They joined the queue.

Johnny was smiling widely. 'I've been dying to bring you here for ages! You're going to love it!'

'The music isn't really my kind of thing, you know? I like more of an indie sound.'

'It's a disc jockey! We can ask for something you like when we get in. They play a real mix. Last time I was here, they played *Shoplifters* and *Xanadu,* back to back!'

'I don't really like Olivia Newt–'

'Three pound,' announced the bouncer, holding out his hand. The other bouncer stamped the backs of their hands with the initial 'P'. As they entered, they passed a throbbing speaker. Daniel felt his chest bounce with the sound. The place was in darkness with disco lights flashing, despite the daylight outside. The only natural light came in when the door opened and closed.

'It's a bit loud!' Daniel leaned in towards Johnny, nervously.

'What?' said Johnny, pointing into his ear.

'I said, it's a bit loud!'

'It is not! Let's get a drink.' Jonny motioned for Daniel to follow him. They passed a man with a comb over hairstyle. He was in full make-up with large ruby lips and a star on his cheekbone. His eyes travelled from Daniel's face down to his High Top trainers and back up again. He raised one perfectly shaped eyebrow.

'Well, hello, baggy jeans!' he nodded, approvingly. Daniel smiled nervously and politely nudged his way through a sea of shoulders to stay

behind Johnny. He felt like everyone was looking at
him like a new boy at school who had turned up
wearing the wrong uniform. More and more men
entered the bar and started dancing or chatting
animatedly. The atmosphere was jubilant, in a way
that Daniel had never seen before.

The DJ changed the record to Madonna's *Into
The Groove* and a loud cheer erupted. Two men
with overcoats and briefcases came out of the
toilets, rubbing their noses. They pushed past
Daniel to get to the dance floor. One of them stuffed
his coat through his briefcase handle. A few other
nearby men pulled at his tie and flicked it around.
He laughed, clearly enjoying that he'd kept his tie
on. The man noticed Daniel staring while Johnny
was getting served at the bar.

'Was at a conference yesterday!' he shouted. 'Not
been home yet!' Daniel smiled nervously and gave
the man a thumbs up, keeping one hand in his
jeans pocket. The other man grabbed his tie and
pulled him closer, and both of them danced face to
face with the briefcases at their feet. It was not
possible to get any nearer the dance floor as the
entire pub heaved and shook with bodies, some of
them now topless.

'Take it!' shouted Johnny, one arm poking
through two tattooed necks. 'Take it!' Daniel's

plastic pint of lager sloshed over the sides. He grabbed it from Johnny's hands and took a few gulps to lower the liquid so it wouldn't spill if he was bumped. Johnny tried to get out from the front of the bar towards Daniel but several customers were trying to squeeze into the tiny gap he left.

'I've never seen it so busy!' he shouted as he made his way to stand in the space Daniel had kept for him. Daniel recognised the opening tin guitar of Abba's *Gimme Gimme Gimme*. As the keyboard joined in, the crowd began to part. They cheered and whistled. The man in the make-up that had referred to Daniel as 'Baggy Jeans' passed through the gap in the crowd, slowly, pausing to touch faces with a red satin glove, or smile and pose. His comb-over was no longer present. Now his locks were lush and shiny in a perfect neat brunette wig, and a red, off-shoulder vintage sparkly dress was fitted so that his body had curves. His elegant gloves stretched all the way over his elbows. Daniel was bamboozled by what he could see, and immediately wondered what his dad would think, and how he would comprehend it. Maybe he would laugh? It was hard not to. This he, now a she, clearly had grace, so confident in her heels, she sauntered and shimmied and pouted to cheers of encouragement. She could have been Raquel Welch, entertaining troops in

Vietnam, a vintage beauty, enrapturing all those around. Bodies pushed in on Daniel, and nobody seemed to have a problem with the lack of personal space.

'*That*'s Pauline!' shouted Johnny in Daniel's ear, so loudly it made it buzz. 'But she's only Pauline when she's in here. During the day, it's Paul. I've seen him in the Post Office. Not everybody knows about it, if you know what I mean. That would be a no-no.' Daniel continued to watch her move and Johnny shouted again. 'If you're lucky, she might stop to speak to you!'

'I've already met her!' he shouted back. 'I mean him. I mean, I mean *her*.'

'Have you? Oh, my God! Get you!' Johnny laughed. 'Straight in at the deep end! What did she say to you?'

'She liked my trousers, I think, my jeans, called me 'Baggy Trousers' or 'Baggy Jeans' or something like that.'

'Oh, God! Pauline christened you! That's amazing! On your first time here! You're Baggy now! This is perfect!'

'Is it?' Daniel drifted, as Johnny laughed. He felt suspended in time as he paused with his mouth open, watching Pauline being lifted by two chunky men up onto the podium where she began to dance and mouth the words to the Abba classic. *'There's not a soul out there! No one to hear my prayer...'* she sang, moving her arm around in a semi circle.

'Gimme! Gimme! Gimme!' sang the crowd. She pointed towards Daniel at the third 'Gimme'. He looked around and people smiled at him. Johnny clutched his stomach and laughed loudly. Men roared for Pauline's every move and clapped hands, joining in with the song. Some others hugged and waved along. The two businessmen kissed. Daniel's eyes darted to Pauline, then back to the men kissing and hugging. It was a lot to take in. Hundreds of men, squashed together in this tiny pub, in their own private blacked-out euphoria. People jostled and danced and bounced and waved and he swayed when they pushed past him.

The pink lights flashed against the glitterball, throwing tiny patterned squares of light all over the room. Daniel felt pushing, touching, glancing, sweating, laughing..., everybody having a good time, dancing to the music, singing and hugging, and he began to withdraw into his own private thoughts.

I'm not like this... like them. They're all out 'there' and I'm in 'here'.

Johnny noticed the change in Daniel. He had hoped it wouldn't go this way. Daniel's pint thudded to the floor and the beer splashed upwards, soaking surrounding shoes, socks, jeans and some hairy calves, although nobody seemed to notice. He was caught in a sway. Somebody opened the bar door and he saw the bright evening sunlight pour through. Squinting, he followed the yellow triangle shape on the black floor until he was outside. He cleared the crowd and took a deep breath beside a small grass verge.

Johnny placed his pint on a ledge and pushed through after Daniel. Out on the street, he called after him but Daniel had already begun to walk away. He ran to catch up and pulled him around by the shoulder.

'Hey! Where you going?'

'I'm going home.'

'Why? What happened? Did somebody say something to you?'

'No, it's okay. I told my mum I wouldn't be late.'

'You're not late! We've only been in there half an hour!'

'I just want to go, Johnny. Sorry.' Daniel looked down at his feet. 'Sorry to let you down, I just... I don't know if I'm ready...'

'No, *I'm* sorry. You've no need to apologise. I shouldn't have taken you to there... probably too soon.'

'I don't think it's my kind of place, Johnny.'

'Didn't you like it?'

'Kind of a... I could see everybody was having a great time, I mean, I just felt a bit dizzy, you know, it's hot in there.'

'Dizzy, like you're going to be physically sick?'

'Yeah.'

'Are you all right now?'

'Yeah. Probably something I ate.'

'Oh, okay.'

'Yeah. I'll head off. You go back in. No point in me ruining your night as well as my own!' Daniel made a face, pretending he might throw up. Johnny smiled reluctantly. He knew that Daniel wasn't telling the truth but thought better to let him have space. He waved him goodbye and went back into the pub.

Daniel walked quickly through the side streets. He did not want to get into a discussion with Johnny until he had a chance to organise his thoughts. It was best just to get away. If Johnny asked questions now, it might be too difficult to change the answers later, and he hadn't really asked himself any questions, although he could feel them rise within him.

ENDEMIC

'That's her away to sleep. She was spark out.' Jackie flopped down onto the couch.

'She made a right mess with that cream ring.'

'So did you! There was bits of it in your hair.'

'That was June's fault!' Frank rubbed his head where the remaining hair was. 'What did Mrs Morrisson say when you dropped off her cake?'

'She said thanks.'

'She didn't need to say thanks. It was her that bought them.'

Jackie and Frank sat silently staring at the television as the *Blind Date* candidate shouted 'Number Three!'

'I can't believe you bumped into that new priest.'

'I know! He's not a priest, though. I don't think he wants to be either.'

'What was he like?'

'I told you. He was exactly like Mrs Morrisson said. He's French and dark skinned. Well-tanned.'

'And he knew my name?'

'He called you *Fronc.*'

Frank sat back in his chair with a pleased grin and folded his arms.

'Dad,' Jackie turned to face her father. 'I just want to tell you again how sorry I am about the... bottle. I really don't know why I drank it, or how I ended up in the garden... my head wasn't straight. I was drunk and I suppose I just wanted to know... what it felt like... for her.'

'I told you to forget it now, Jackie.'

'I'm a bit worried, though... if I'm... like her. Am I like her? I've read that you can inherit these things.'

'No, you're not. It was just that Blue Nun. Probably made your head a bit... spinny. Easily done. Viv should know better. You don't think clearly after that bloody wine. Nobody does. Still, at least you're not drinking Buckfast. I saw three young ones last night – must have been fifteen if they're lucky. The bloody brass neck of them, standing at the Airdrie Savings bank, swigging from a bottle of Buckie, passing it about and eating wine gums.'

'They were probably heading to the Staging Post. That place is full of under-agers.'

'Well, it's an endemic, is Buckfast in Airdrie! An endemic!'

'Where did you read that?'

'What?'

'Endemic.'

'I know what endemic means! Away for Godsake.'

Julie Hamill

They sat watching a couple riding a rollercoaster in Blackpool.

'Dad?'

'It's a disease that spreads around a particular area.'

'No, I wasn't asking that.'

'Well, what is it, then? I'm watching this.'

'I think Tommy's coming back,' Jackie blurted out.

'Who told you that?'

'Viv. Her dad heard it from somebody in Pender's. She says he's coming back soon, if he's not back already.'

'Well, see, thing is now, Jackie, I'm glad you brought this up...'

'Did you know?'

'Well, I did. I got told last night. I was going to tell you, in a minute,' he pointed to the TV, 'after they finished their ice creams.'

'Who told you?'

'Viv's mum. Bessie. She told me just as the bingo finished.' They watched as Cilla Black asked the couple if they'd like to see each other again. Jackie shook her head. 'Viv said that his mum died and left him money.'

'I heard. He'll be back to flash that about, all right.'

'I know. Oh, God, Dad, what will we do? What if he wants to see June?'

'We will do nothing. He won't be seeing the wean! We knew this day would come! You need to think about how he left. Wasn't even sure she was his, remember? He even tried to blame his best pal because of the colour of June's hair. He's a dirty, filthy, horrible article. He won't be putting a toe over that door for our Junie. You steer clear of him, Jackie, do you hear? Stay out of trouble.'

'Oh, don't worry, Dad, I won't fall for that again.'

'And, Jackie?'

'Uh-huh?'

'You're not like her. Not like that. In other ways, yes, but not like that. For a start, your mother would have had a drink in her hand right now. And you don't.'

'Right.' Jackie paused. 'Dad, do you remember when you thought... well... we weren't sure if my mum was visiting you?'

'Well, yes, but you know, that was probably my imagination, who knows...' Frank shifted in his chair. He still felt sure it was really June that came, but deep down, he didn't know anymore.

'I don't think it was your imagination. I've been dreaming about her a lot. Really weird dreams that don't make any sense.'

'It just means you're thinking about her. Perfectly natural. Everybody does that when they lose somebody close. Just mixed up; a lot of nonsense, probably.'

Jackie fidgeted with her sleeve, as the *Blind Date* titles rose.

'Having said that, you're very lucky to have those dreams', he said, looking at the television. 'If it is her, tell her I said hello.'

'You just said it was a lot of—'

'Never mind what I said.'

HEAVEN AND HELL

Jackie took the three small stone steps one by one, holding hands with June who climbed up carefully in her red patent shoes so as not to scuff them. Frank followed directly behind them, touched the holy water and blessed himself. The familiar scent of incense filled his nostrils.

Jackie was taken aback to find the church so packed. Their usual pew was occupied so they had to find a seat a few rows back. Frank didn't recognise old Mary at first – even though she had sat two rows in front of him for over thirty years - her white cloud hairstyle had a new big red bow fastened on the back.

'Hark at Baby Jane there. What's the bow about?'

'Shh!' replied Jackie. She was looking around the church and noticed it was mostly women occupying the seats, with a few of the old men scattered around who usually collected hymn books and bulletins at the end of mass.

She noticed Viv across the aisle, sitting with her mum and dad. Jackie recognised Viv's mum's gold-coloured jacket that she had seen her wear to June's christening a few years before. She also noticed that

Viv's hair looked extra bouncy as she kept flicking it back off her face and then letting it slide back in front of her eye. Viv's dad was wearing a crisp white shirt, brown jacket and checked waistcoat and her mum fiddled with his tie. Mrs Morrisson and her coffee club friend Esther sat in the second row from the front on the left, both in floral patterns. Esther's pearl earrings dangled as she talked.

Many of the older ladies were wearing more than their Sunday best, in fact the crowd was so smart and colourful, Jackie thought she could have been at a wedding. She was relieved she'd worn her favourite white summer sundress with the pretty patterned buttons and a pink shawl and sandals, and little June had told her she looked beautiful.

The bell dinged twice and everyone stood up and the priest entered. Shortly after he reached the altar, the reason for the fancy clothes and busy church pews soon entered behind him: Jean Paul Julien. Jackie realised why it was so busy, and probably why, at the last minute, she had decided to go for the sundress.

Viv's mum took a tissue and mopped her brow, old Mary stood up straighter, the front row sang loudly and somebody on the same row as Jackie, a woman in her late forties, held up opera glasses. All eyes were turned slightly left for Jean Paul Julien, who stood to the side of the altar dressed all in white. His black hair gleamed and the bronzed skin on his face looked darker against his starched white serving robes. The beams of bright light that shone through the stained-glass windows landed on his cheekbones and squared his jawline as if it had been sketched. People responded to prayers automatically but paid no attention to Father Cleary. Jackie had a little giggle to herself. *This mass is on autopilot*, she thought, and she looked up towards the gold stars on the blue ceiling above the altar. She found her mum's star (or at least, the star she chose for her mum), looked at it and smiled, and shook her head. She would have loved this scene, and they would have laughed at it afterwards. Looking back at the altar, Jackie caught the eye of Jean Paul and he quickly looked away. The organ struck up the chorus to the offertory hymn *All That I Am*, and Frank turned to Jackie as he passed the plate.

'What's going on?' he asked. Jackie shrugged and took the plate and put the envelope in. She nodded up to Jean Paul's direction.

'I think... you know... it's for *him*,' she said.

Frank rolled his eyes. 'You are kidding me! That's desperate,' he said, to which Jackie replied by mouthing the words, 'Fresh meat.'

She suppressed a laugh. Without admitting it, she knew why she was so airy and giggly today, and a great feeling of excitement danced under her skin. *There is something*, she thought.

He looked at me – but does he look at everybody like that? Jackie looked at June, kneeling on the kneeler, playing with her blue My Little Pony. She combed its tail with the special plastic comb and repeatedly tried to tie a tiny white ribbon around the top of the mane. She started again, with her tongue at the side of her mouth, combing and untying and re-tying the ribbon until she got the bow she wanted. Jackie bent down and kissed her on the cheek, then stood up again.

People shuffled out of the rows for communion. The woman with the opera glasses topped up her lipstick, closed her compact and clicked her bag closed. She sashayed down the communion line, ensuring she was in the correct line for the priest and not the Eucharistic minister, whose communion line was very short. Jackie walked behind her with little June in front, her arms crossed to her shoulders. Father Cleary gave June a blessing, then offered Jackie communion. She took it in her hands as Jean Paul held a gold plate underneath. They both avoided eye contact. She returned to her seat and watched the rest of the congregation file down to the front and back to their seats again. Some of them began to nudge and chatter. Mrs Morrisson fanned herself with her folded bulletin. Father Cleary finished and wiped the chalice, then folded the white napkin and placed it on top in a square. He looked up and the church fell silent.

'Nice to see so many of you here today,' he said, with a hint of sarcasm. 'May I introduce you all to my nephew, Jean Paul, who will be staying with me at the parish for the rest of the summer. By way of a welcome, tea and biscuits will be served in the church gardens today. May the Lord be with you.'

'And also with you,' the crowd murmured their response.

As soon as the final blessing was given and the last hymn verse sung, there was a rush to the back door of the church.

'You'd think it was Tom Jones in here! The state of some of the women! He's a priest, for God's sake.'

'He is not!' replied Jackie, smiling.

Frank put his hymnbook in the pile at the end of the pew and Jackie helped June with her My Little Pony styling tools. They put them all into her backpack and zipped it shut.

After lighting a candle, they made their way slowly outside and a trestle table was surrounded by chatting churchgoers. Old ladies helping out poured large pots of stewed tea into waiting cups. Teacups clinked against saucers and digestive biscuits were dipped and munched in the sunshine.

'There's Bourbons! I'm going in before there's none left!' Frank rushed to the table. Jackie stood with June at the doors and a lady named Ruth brought June a cup of orange squash and a biscuit. Frank had nicknamed her 'Roots' because he could always see two inch-thick lines of grey hair around her parting.

'You enjoy that, hen,' she said, to which June replied, 'Thank you, Roo...' She looked up at her mother, then gulped down the juice.

Jackie smiled politely as Ruth walked away. She could see Jean Paul in the distance, surrounded by women of all ages. Mrs Morrisson stood with her friend Esther, as they cornered Frank with a plate of biscuits. They were waiting their turn to talk to Father Cleary and Jean Paul. Viv stood with her mum, drinking tea, then spotted Jackie and walked over.

'Hiya!' she smiled, as she hugged June. 'Seen the new talent?'

'This is just so hilarious!' replied Jackie.

'I know! The collection plate must be heaving this week. Old Cleary will be able to have a nice holiday on the back of it! Hopefully he leaves his nephew behind, ha ha!'

Viv's mum and dad waved at Jackie and June. Behind them, a familiar figure caught Jackie's eye, in the distance. He was standing among the graves, holding a large bouquet of flowers. Blue cigarette smoke lingered by his lips as he looked directly at her.

'You have got to be *kidding* me,' said Viv. 'The absolute gall of him! Do you want me to tell him to beat it for you, Jackie? I took him down once, I can do it again.'

'No, it's okay, Viv, can I leave June with you for a few minutes while I quickly just see what he wants?'

'Are you sure you want to go over there by yourself? You know what he's like. Jackie, don't fall for any of his crap, okay?'

'I won't. I'll be back in a minute. I'll get rid of him.' Jackie walked off towards the graveyard and Viv sighed and shook her head.

'Let's go get a biscuit, Junie,' she said as she led June towards a tower of Custard Creams being poured out of a packet. Viv looked up and saw Jean Paul looking over to the graveyard. His eyes followed Jackie through the crowds as she walked across the grass through the large gates. Viv nudged her mum.

'Mum, look,' she smiled. 'I think Jean Paul is checking out Jackie.' Viv's mum strained her neck to look at Jean Paul until he turned and caught them. He excused himself from the people he was talking to and went back inside the church.

'It's unholy to lean against a person's grave,' said Jackie, loudly as she marched towards Tommy.

'Hello, Jackie.' He stood up straight and extinguished his cigarette by expertly flicking it onto the path. 'You're looking fantastic.'

'What do you want?'

'I just came to give you these.' Tommy held up the largest bouquet of flowers Jackie had ever seen. It was full of pastel colours and pretty blooms. She had never been given flowers before and felt a great pang in her heart where romance once was.

'No, thank you,' she replied, curtly. 'I'll ask again, what do you want?'

'Nothing. I just came to say hello. I knew you'd be here.'

'Just to say hello? I find that hard to believe.'

'Jackie, I want to tell you... I'm sorry. For leaving like that. I'm not the same person. I've changed. My whole outlook, everything. I've even cut down on the fags.' He raised an eyebrow and a devilish grin spread across his face. Jackie remembered how handsome he could be, then dismissed the thought. 'Now, please, take these flowers, or I'll have to give them to one of these unlucky ladies.' He pointed the flowers towards some of the graves. He took a step towards her and placed the bouquet gently in her hands. 'Take them,' he said quietly, lifting both of her hands to accept. 'Seriously, give them to Mrs Morrisson if you don't want them.'

Jackie looked up into his eyes.

'I didn't know you knew...'

'I know Mrs Morrisson. And I also know how much she has helped you since you lost your mum. Much more than I ever did. See, Jackie, I was selfish. I didn't appreciate what you were going through. But I do, now.' He looked down at the ground. 'I lost my mum, a few weeks ago. Massive stroke. Died right there on the spot. My heart broke. I only had those three years with her after I left Airdrie. But they were three of the best years of my life. She set me straight, Jackie. She sorted me out. Made me see what I had lost with you and the baby. A few weeks before she died, she said she wished I'd come back and find you. That's why I'm here. And I'm all set up. I've got a nice flat, with lots of space. I'm starting a business in Coatbridge. I've got a family car, parked just over there. A really nice one. Leather seats and a tape recorder. I've got a Human League album in there. *Dare*. You used to like them, didn't you?'

Jackie couldn't help herself. She smiled a tiny smile and nodded. Tommy could be so charming, but she knew where it ended, and the smile dropped from her face.

'I know how you must feel about me, Jackie, and I don't blame you. All that business with punching your pal, running out like that... Maureen. I'm ashamed of myself. I'm not that guy anymore. That time with my mother... and her death ... it changes a person. I'm sure you hear me on that, you know where I'm coming from there.'

Jackie looked up the hill to where her mum was buried.

'I'd better get back to-'

'To June?' He smiled. 'I'm sorry about that too. I'd like to know her, if you'd let me. I'd like to know you... again.'

'I don't think so, Tommy. Too much time has passed. I'm genuinely sorry about your mum. I'm sure she was a nice lady. Thanks for the flowers.' Jackie turned to walk away and Tommy grabbed her arm.

'Jackie, wait!' She turned around. 'I'm serious. Come and look at my new flat. In Coatbridge. It's got all the things you like. Electric tin openers and all that. Big microwave with loads of buttons. That buzzy knife you love; brand new,' he smiled, 'and a special room for June, all decorated, with fairies. Her own room. Imagine that! You two share, don't you? I bet she'd love a room of her own.'

Jackie often wondered how she'd ever afford to leave home on a nurse's wages, and for June to have her own room.

'All I'm asking is that you look at the place. Come over. Cup of tea, then go. Just come and see it. I can meet you there or pick you up. Whatever. Just come and see it.' Jackie began walking away, towards the church and he walked quickly after her. 'Just once, just look, that's all I ask. And I want to contribute towards June. Dresses, shoes, school uniform, food, whatever you need. Anything. And I can drop you off anywhere, in the car. Jackie! I can pick you up from work. We could even go to the pictures. Make up for lost time.' He stopped at the cemetery gates and she continued walking.

'The pictures? You have got to be kidding me!'

'Well, anywhere! Anywhere you like! For my mother, Jackie. Her dying wish! I want to give her this, at least. Let me try.'

147

Jackie felt a jolt at the word 'mother' but she continued walking through the gates. June ran towards her. Viv walked quickly behind June.

'Oh, pretty flowers! Who is that man?' Tommy waved at June. She waved back. Jackie thrust the flowers into Viv's hands and scooped June into her arms. 'Who is the man, Mummy? Are you crying?' She walked back towards the church door. Her dad was laughing with Father Cleary. Mrs Morrisson clasped her hands together with delight at his happiness.

'Are you okay, hen?' Viv's mum stood in front of her face, fussing over Jackie, trying to console her. Viv was beside her.

'The nerve of him showing up here! Jackie, I can take care of him – just say the word!' Viv was clearly angry that her friend was upset and Jackie couldn't think clearly.

'Mummy, who is that man?' June asked over and over and Jackie didn't have an answer for her.

'Mummy just needs to go to the toilet, darling, I'll be back in a minute, wait here with Auntie Viv.'

'Auntie Viv, who was the man?' asked June.

'Just somebody that used to live round here. Somebody your mummy knew a long time ago.'

'What does he want? Why did he give Mummy flowers? Does he want to marry her?'

148

'No, darling, no, I think he was just saying sorry for something. Look! There's more cups of juice! Let's get some!'

Jackie pushed open the heavy church door and walked down the aisle. She had intended to go straight to the toilet to get some tissue but she paused to look up at her mother's star and decided to kneel down. Overcome by a rush of Tommy's revelations, she collapsed into tears. She paused and looked up to the gold star on the ceiling.

'What am I supposed to do now, Mum? Tell me what to do...' She sobbed into her hands for a few minutes, then searched her bag for a tissue, finding only a corner. She used what she could to dab the edges of her mascara. 'What if he *has* changed, Mum? Has he? This could be my shot with June's dad. A chance to make things neat and tidy.' She allowed the silence of the church to envelop her, the sleepy scents giving her comfort. Then she heard something dropping on the floor. She looked up to see Jean Paul, now in jeans and a t-shirt.

'Excuse moi, my uncle left his glasses in here, I was just collecting them and they fell, I did not mean to disturb...'

'No problem.' Jackie stuffed the tissue corner back into her bag.

'I hope you don't mind me asking, are you okay?'

'I'm fine, thank you.'

'I saw you talking in the... how do you say, gravestones?'

'Ah, yes. Well... graveyard,' Jackie smiled. 'It's called a graveyard.'

'Ah.' He returned her smile, as she stood up. 'Can I help you with anything? Escort you back outside? A glass of water, perhaps? Or tea?'

'No, I'm okay, honestly. Thank you.'

'As long as you are fine.'

'Yes, I'm fine.' Jackie brushed down her dress.

'Fronc - your father - just invited us to your house for lunch next week, in the evening. I am looking forward to that.'

'Oh, did he? That's nice. The word for that is "dinner".'

'Yes. Dinner. I hope he checked with the boss first, no?' Jackie laughed at his attempt at humour.

'No, but that's okay. You're both very welcome.'

'Do you enjoy to cook?'

'If you like sandwiches,' she said.

'Oui, yes, sandwiches are magic, as you Scottish say.' He walked towards her, putting the glasses case in his back pocket.

'What about you? Do you like cooking?' Jackie asked, trying to powder her face.

'I am not good cook, but as a Frenchman, I like to eat bread, cut the cheese and of course, drink wine. Where can I go wrong?'

He offered his arm.

'That's settled then, cheese sandwiches it is!' Jackie smiled, clicked her compact closed and put it into her bag.

'Let me escort you back to your family.' Jackie slid her arm through his, and it felt natural and warm. 'It is nice to see you smile, Jackie, I know that you are sad. My uncle told me about your mother, and your old boyfriend. So much *tourmente*. I am sorry for that. You seem so hurting.'

He reached for a tissue from behind the candle stand and handed it to her.

'Oh! Look at that,' said Jackie, 'secret stash.'

Jackie dabbed her eyes with the tissue in her left hand. Her right arm was still linked with Jean Paul's. He seemed to radiate such kindness towards her and she wasn't used to it. Her experience of men and relationships had Tommy's sharp-edged sarcasm. She had never had the gentleness of someone like Jean Paul. His strange eyes sparkled under long lashes and one part of his hair had fallen forward, which she had to restrain herself from pushing back into place. This was the second time they had touched, the second time she felt a caring feeling, but there was no question that her guard would remain high.

'Anyway, Jackie, as I said, if you ever need someone to talk to, please call on me. At the moment, I am live in a church house, and I think that makes me qualified with the ears.'

Jackie smiled. 'I might take you up on that.'

'I hope you don't mind me saying but, mon Dieu! Your hands, they are freezing!'

'Ha ha! All Scottish hands are cold, honestly, touch anybody, they'll be freezing.'

'I don't want to touch anybody, Jackie.' He hesitated, then blushed.

'Well,' said Jackie, 'maybe it's not that we are cold, it's that you are hot,' she said. As the words left her mouth, she wished she could suck them back again immediately.

'I am hot?' he asked, then laughed and shook his head. Jackie shook hers and put a hand to her head. They walked towards the side door he held it open for her. Flushed, Jackie glanced up at her mother's star, and it twinkled. Holding on to Jean Paul, she wondered if new joy could erase old heartache.

THE FATHERS ARE COMING

'I've still got it. I went to Mr Gupta's door with it the other day and he wasn't in. I don't know whose it is. I don't know what to do with it, but I'll tell you this; I'm lumbered with it now.' Mrs Morrisson put the shoe in her bag and shook her head.

Jackie smiled politely at her. She was tired from the highs and lows of a very strange Sunday. She had put June to bed at six thirty, much earlier than usual. She had watched her little girl drop right off to sleep after she had read her *The Town Mouse And The Country Mouse*. She managed to distract June from asking who the man in the graveyard was for a while, but it played on her mind as to how to deal with it. *How to tell a little girl that her daddy wasn't a nice man?*

Viv suggested to Jackie to never tell June that Tommy was her father. Jackie thought of her words, *Cut him out! He has no right to see June anymore - it has been three years.*

Jackie didn't want to lie to June, and considered if she and Tommy could be friends, while he visited his daughter. She wanted to do the right thing by her but her stomach churned in sync with her mind.

She allowed her thoughts to drift away from Tommy to Jean Paul. Her eyes glazed over as she bathed in that moment in church when she held his arm. She was only half-listening to Mrs Morrisson, who carried on talking about the missing shoe, when Frank came in from the hall.

'That was the Father Cleary on the phone,' he announced, holding his reading glasses. He kept them both waiting for a few seconds as he took his time to settle into his chair. 'They're still coming on Thursday and he says to tell you that he's a vegetarian now.'

'Aww, what?' Mrs Morrisson sat forward in the other chair.

'That's absolutely fine!' said Jackie.

'Did you hear him, Jackie? He said Father Cleary is a vegetarian? Ah, that's a shame for him, now, isn't it?'

'No, not at all, it's okay. It's just sandwiches and a few cakes, right? We can do him cheese and egg and potato salad and bits like that. It will be all right, Mrs Morrisson.'

'Ah, but poor man. You have to get pills for that. Being a vegetarian.'

'No, you don't,' Jackie giggled. 'They're probably vitamin pills that you're talking about.'

'What does he eat then? Oh, God, I was going to make a beef casserole as well, but he can't eat meat.'

'Beef casserole would be nice,' said Frank, 'they can eat round the meat.'

'I can't do a beef casserole now, can I? Can I, Jackie? Can I do a beef casserole, do you think? Could they eat the vegetables out of that?'

'I don't think so, maybe, I'm sure you could and other people could eat it and he could eat something else. I don't think it's that he can't eat meat, it's that he doesn't want to.'

'Why not? What about fish? Does he eat fish? Oh, my God, now!'

'No, he said no to fish,' said Frank. For once, he was glad he answered the phone, victorious in the knowledge that he had gleaned more information than Mrs Morrisson.

'Well, what does he eat then? Oh, my God, what does he eat?'

'Mrs Morrisson, don't worry about it. I'll do sandwiches and tea. I know he likes Custard Creams, I'll get them as well.'

'No, Jackie... you can't do all that, straight in from your work and there's a priest and a half-way priest coming round. All that food to make. More than sandwiches will be needed to fill them up. A bit of chicken maybe... does he eat chicken?'

'No. He does not eat chicken, beef, pork, or fish, or anything. No. Animals.' Frank sat back in his chair and rolled his eyes bigger.

'Well, I wonder why he's done that? Could it be a religious thing, maybe? Or a diet? Maybe it's a diet! Do you think it's a diet he's doing, Jackie?

'It could be,' said Jackie, raising her eyebrows.

'I think you're right! I think he's on a diet. You're on to something there, Jackie. Maybe he's trying to lose a few pounds. And about time too. Good on the man.' Mrs Morrisson blessed herself, then walked to the kitchen to wash her cup. 'I'm off now. I need to have a good think about what we could make the Fathers. I suppose you're going to sit on your arse, are you, Frank? While we're doing all the work?'

'I am not! I will be putting the biscuits out on a plate. I'm good at that.'

'Don't worry about my dad, Mrs Morrisson, I'll have him busy with the duster before they get here.' Jackie smiled at Frank and he scowled.

'You get to your bed early tonight, hen, you're back at work tomorrow. It's been a busy weekend.'

'I will do, Mrs Morrisson, I promise.' Mrs Morrisson closed the back door. Frank and Jackie sat in comfortable silence watching the television for a few minutes, Frank in his chair, Jackie lying on the couch.

'Her head will be spinning with that. Vegetarian. Spinning!' Frank picked up his paper and laughed.

'Wee Mrs Morrisson is such a worrier, isn't she? She worries too much, poor thing. She's so lovely and caring about everybody.'

'She's a feeder, is what she is.'

'Well, I don't hear your belly complaining.'

Frank put his paper down again. 'I meant to say earlier, but you did the right thing, not telling our June about that Tommy. Let him see he can get nothing from you, then he'll be off as soon as he got here. I guarantee you that.'

'I don't know, Dad. June asked again when I was putting her to bed, who was he and why did he give me flowers. See, that's the thing,' Jackie sat up. 'I don't know if I should tell her Tommy's her dad. I don't know what's the right thing to do. When she asks where her daddy is, I just say he lives abroad. I feel terrible about the whole thing. And now he says he's changed. He does seem a bit... softer... Oh, I don't know.'

'What? Like hell has he changed!' Frank tutted and looked around. 'Where are the flowers he gave you? I never saw them. Was it a big bunch?'

'Massive. I told Viv to give them into the wee woman at the church office.'

'Oh, right,' he paused. 'I bet they cost a bomb. But changed? No way has he changed. Jack the Lad. Now don't you believe him. June doesn't need a dad. She's got a Granda. Everything she needs is right here, in this house.' Frank pondered that Jackie might leave, and he was not ready to live alone again. The first time was hard enough.

'Yes, but she has a right to know, though, doesn't she? And it's a funny old set up, isn't it? You, me and her, don't you think? People must think I'm a right saddo; a single mother that lives with her dad, no boyfriend, shares a room with her daughter. It would be nice for her to have a dad.'

'And what's wrong with the set up? Daniel still lives with his parents, doesn't he? And anyway, nobody out there knows where you sleep or how many rooms are in this house! I don't care and have never given a damn about what people think. We're a family and that's that. Families come in all shapes, most of them are all messed up, bloody fights on Hogmanay and divorces on New Year's Day and the rest of it. We are better than most, whatever the shape of us.'

'A wonky triangle?' Jackie smiled.

'You behave.'

'No, you're right. June is happy here. I am too. I'm just trying to figure out the right thing about

Tommy. June is going to want to know the truth about her dad eventually, maybe want to meet him. She's already asking! Maybe I should just tell her, now, Dad? It's not good to keep secrets, is it?'

'No, but sometimes secrets are for the best. We can make adjustments when the time comes. You have to protect your own. Even if you did tell her, you have to think about what kind of dad he would be, what the family set up is.'

Jackie leaned back and thought about her dad's words as he looked back between his newspaper and the television. She studied the side of her dad's face. One of his wrinkles ran from the corner of his eye all the way down his cheek to meet the indentation of his smile. She loved that line, there for as long as she could remember, his A-road of laughter.

'What? What is it, now?' he asked her, aware of her staring. 'Is it about Fletcher?'

'No. I want to know something. About my mum.' Frank looked away from the screen to Jackie.

'What about her?' he asked.

'I want to know... was there a reason she drank so much?'

'Och, Jackie, we've been through this before, hen. I don't want to talk about it. It's all in the past.'

Jackie stood up and sat on the arm of his chair and placed her arm around his neck.

'Dad, please tell me what I want to know. Don't shut me out and keep secrets. We can't keep finding bottles, and I think it's why I tried it. I know you're trying to protect me but I'm a grown woman. I need to know about the person I came from. I know she had a problem, you've told me and yes, I did see it at the end. I want to know how it started.'

'There's nothing really to tell you, Jackie.'

'I know how hard it must have been for you. Seeing her like that. Especially after, well, she was so beautiful in the "Miss December' stuff".' Frank looked at her, puzzled. 'I've looked, Dad. I read it all. I'm sorry.'

'You've been in my box?'

'Yes. I know she was quite famous round here, wasn't she?'

'You're not to go rummaging in there, Jackie. Those are my things.' Frank was being led into territory he didn't want to be in, and he didn't want to share stories of the past. He pushed himself up and went into the kitchen to put the kettle on.

Jackie knew he wanted to shut her down, so went quietly to the sideboard and removed her dad's box. She took it to the table and sat down, opened it and waited for him to come in.

'I'm making a tea. Do you want one?' he shouted.

'Yes, please,' she replied, lifting out pictures and clippings one by one, and spreading them out.

Frank came back into the room and placed the mugs on the coasters on the dinner table.

'Why is all this... my stuff... out? Put it back, please.'

'No. Sit down, Dad.'

'Put my stuff back, Jackie. This is my box. I don't want it disturbed.'

'It's my stuff too. There are pictures of me here, look.'

'I know but I want to keep it good.'

'I haven't done anything to it. It's all as you left it.' She placed her hand on his hand. 'Dad, please sit down and tell me about my mum.' Frank slowly pulled out his chair and sat in it. 'Wasn't she absolutely beautiful, Dad? I mean, look at her! I never knew what a success she was!'

'Aye. Well, she didn't boast about it. She had a touch of class. Och, it was years before you were born.'

'She had such pretty little features, didn't she?' Frank could see that Jackie was enamoured with this idealistic view of her mother. Pure, perfect, young and beautiful. He surrendered and let her look for a bit longer. He watched her read through

161

the clippings and pictures, like she had discovered a cave of diamonds. He felt conflicted; he had kept the past from her, but always thought it was for the best. Now he felt guilty and stupid. He noticed the picture with the ice-creams.

'You're like her in this one, I think,' he softened, pushing the picture of the three of them towards Jackie. 'You got my eyes but you've got her wee face. You sound like her, as well!'

'Do I?'

'Oh, aye. Sometimes I have to do a double take if you shout down from up the stairs. She was full of cheek and charm when she was your age. Got away with murder, always up to mischief.' They both sat, smiling at the picture. 'I'll tell you who else is like her.' He pointed upstairs. Jackie laughed.

'Do you think? But look at her hair! Wee June's hair is red!'

'The wean gets that from me!' He stroked a few whiskers, proudly. 'My beard comes in red, you know that.'

'My mum's hair was really blonde then. How come my hair-'

'Platinum blonde, aye. Straight out the bottle. Her natural hair colour was the same as yours. Exactly the same colour. She dyed it until she couldn't manage anymore... you know, it was grey

162

right before she left...' They shuffled pictures and articles around, until Jackie came across a picture of her mum at the club door, wearing white.

'Look at her there, wow! She's stunning!' Jackie ran her finger over her mum's dress.

'Aye, she was very glamorous.'

'Who is this man?'

Frank took a long sip of tea. 'Eddie O'Donnell,' he said, quickly.

'Who was he? I've seen him in a few pictures.'

'He was her... manager... kind of.'

'Oh! She had a manager? That's amazing. He looks like he wouldn't take any nonsense off anybody, anyway.'

'He didn't. There was many a black eye when he was about. Ex-boxer.'

'What happened to him?'

'I don't know,' said Frank, finishing his tea. 'You finished?' he asked, pointing to Jackie's mug. She shook her head. She hadn't even taken a sip yet. Just as fast as Frank was opening up, he was closing down again, and Jackie wasn't about to let him shut the door on her questions just yet.

'Leave the cups, I'll wash them,' she said, urgently. Frank was halfway out of his seat and slowly sat down again. 'How come you changed your tone there, when I asked who he was?'

'No, I didn't.'

'Aye, you did.'

'I did not. Let's put all this away now, I think there's something good on-'

'Cooeee!' came a quiet call from the back door.

'Away, for God's sake,' Frank muttered. Mrs Morrisson walked into the kitchen and quietly closed the door.

'Sorry to call so late. I thought you'd want to know that it *was* Mr Gupta's shoe that I found! He was so grateful-' As she entered the living room, she stopped. Frank was trying to gather up everything into the box and Jackie was holding onto the picture they had been talking about. 'Oh,' she said, 'Sorry, I'm interrupting! I'll leave you to it.' Jackie noticed a little fright in her face as Mrs Morrisson saw the picture in her hand.

'No, Mrs Morrisson,' she stood up, 'you stay! Join us. We're just reminiscing about my mum's younger years, aren't we, Dad? I'm sure you've got memories of my mum I'd love to hear as well, Mrs Morrisson. You were neighbours for a long time. I'll make you a cup of tea. Mine has gone cold anyway.' Jackie took her cup to the kitchen. Frank glared at Mrs Morrisson and she shrugged her shoulders and mouthed, 'I didn't know.' She put her bag down and took a seat at the table next to Frank.

'Did you tell her?' she whispered as she pointed to the picture of Eddie O'Donnell. Frank shook his head. 'Are you going to?'

'No. I'm putting it all away. There's no need.'

'You might as well tell her now. What if she finds out from somebody else round here?'

'Finds out what?' Jackie asked. She placed a cup of tea in front of Mrs Morrisson. 'Is this about the man in the picture?'

Frank looked down into his tea. Mrs Morrisson's eyes darted round the room then focused on the goldfish. Neither of them looked at Jackie, or Eddie O'Donnell.

KNITTING

Daniel lay in his bed with his music on low, watching the grooves of the record cradle the needle. The same album had been playing on repeat all day, one he had bought a couple of years ago in Woolworths, *Animal Magic* by the Blow Monkeys.

He had avoided Johnny's phone calls and told his mum he felt too sick to go to work at the hospital that afternoon. When he had arrived home early the previous evening, she was ecstatic to see him safe and sound. She kissed him on his forehead and both cheeks and told him what a good boy he was and what a relief it was that he was home from Glasgow as she had worried all evening.

He couldn't wait to feel his pillow. He felt that sleep would stop him thinking too much, and it did for a while, but he had slept all night and been upstairs in bed all day, and all he had done was think. Think about what he had seen, but what he didn't want to look at. What he heard but didn't want to listen to. About who he was and who he may have always been. He was confused, and quite frightened. All the thoughts wired around each other like Mister Messy's body. He was angry at

166

Johnny, feeling forced into making a decision, because of him, to join his 'club', one from which he denied himself entry.

His favourite track, *Digging Your Scene,* played. *'It'll get you in the end it's God's revenge,'* sang Doctor Robert.

He wondered if HIV would get Johnny in the end, or one of those men in Pauline's. Any of them could have it. It was easily passed on, all it would take is one mistake, but certainly not one that Daniel was prepared to make. The thought of how contagious it was terrified him, and there was still no cure. He had read of people dying, in his dad's newspaper. He was nowhere near that stage, or any stage, come to think of it.

He struggled to order his thoughts into what he feared the most about broaching the entire subject with himself. Frustrated, he scrambled for a pad and pencil from his bedside drawer and wrote a list:

Telling Mum

Telling Dad

Considering that I <u>might</u> be 'G'.

Daniel crossed this out and moved it up to number one.

The shame

Daniel crossed this out and moved it up to number two.

Telling the others - Jackie, Viv, Frank, oh, God, Mrs Morrisson? Does everybody HAVE to know my business?

Catch AIDS + die

Johnny's 'I told you so'

Get head kicked in by Fletcher

It's easier just to hide it

Can't hide it forever

Yes, I can

!!! Die of ignorance etc etc etc etc

He threw the pencil at the wall and the pad into the drawer. He turned to face away from the stereo and shut his eyes tightly. Still, in his head the phrases whirled around.

If I say it, then I am it but I'm not it. I don't think. (Yes, you are).

Over and over, thoughts swirled around his head. Denial, confrontation, failure to progress, again and again. He rolled over to the other side of the bed near the stereo and lifted the needle off the record. He stood up to go into the toilet next door. As he opened his bedroom door, he was met by the low murmur of the television and click-clack of his mother's knitting needles, fast paced and urgent, like the sound of a car indicator. His mother always knitted, whatever the weather. It was a comforting sound he had loved since he was a child. He laid his hands on the upstairs bannister and hung his head low. The click clacking continued. A sound he may never hear again, if he was to tell her.

'Is there something I need to know about him?' asked Jackie, picking up the picture of her mother and Eddie O'Donnell. Frank remained silent, deep in his thoughts, as Mrs Morrisson's fingers fiddled with a tissue. Jackie looked from her dad's face to Mrs Morrisson's. Aware she was being kept in the dark about something, she began to feel slightly heated, and adrenalin nudged the dark edge of discovery. 'Sometimes secrets are for the best, you said. You have to protect your own. Is this one of those times, Dad? What are you keeping from me? Has he got something to do with my mum's drinking?'

Mrs Morrisson blessed herself, the tissue still between her fingers. Frank looked up to Jackie, then back at his mug. 'Jackie you don't need to know these things, hen, don't make a big thing out of it.'

'If it's no big thing, then why can't you tell me?'

'Holy Mary, Mother of God, Frank, will you tell her? It's better coming from you.' Mrs Morrisson restrained herself. Her slight outburst surprised her.

'But it's not about her!'

'It doesn't matter!'

'Oh, for pity's sake, right. Your mother went with somebody else when we were first married. A long time ago. Way before you were born. She went with him. Eddie O'Donnell. 'Big Jock' was his nickname, from the boxing. There. Now you know.'

Jackie put her hand up to her mouth. The tiny hairs on her arms stood on end so she absentmindedly rubbed them. 'No way!' she said, 'I can't believe this!'

Mrs Morrisson motioned to Frank with her finger, then turned to Jackie.

'Twas hearsay now, Jackie. People are such terrible gossips. People don't think that a woman can succeed of her own accord unless she's sleeping with a man!' Mrs Morrisson sat back in her chair.

'We'd been together for a few years, about three, I think, when he came along,' Frank continued. 'We were only young. She was singing in the Working Men's Club and he offered to manage her. He was good at the start. Got her into lots of places in Glasgow. She loved it. We all went to see her. He kept telling her she'd make it big. Filled her with dreams and ideas, blew her head up like a balloon.'

'He doesn't sound like a very nice man.'

'Oh, Big Jock was charming, all right, he took a lot of people in, make no mistake,' Mrs Morrisson interjected, then looked at her nails. 'He walked around like he was Casanova. Reeked of expensive aftershave, so he did. A lot of women liked him.' Frank shot her a look of confusion, then continued.

'She fell under his spell, and I *saw* it happening. All the time she told me, I wasn't supporting her - I didn't believe in her, but I did. We were arguing because of him. I'd go to pick her up from visiting her mum's and she'd be leaving to do a show at a club with him, last minute. He had her working in every place across Scotland and working every week in the Working Men's Club. She was out all the time and when she wasn't out, she was in the paper. I couldn't keep up. I couldn't afford to go to every single place to see her. I had to work, Jackie! I'd have lost my job! He gave her what I couldn't - champagne cocktails, fancy bars... the gold star treatment. By the time I found out about it... well, I was the last to know. The whole town was gossiping about them. And as soon as she started not wanting to leave the parties and loving the lifestyle a bit too much, what *he* started, *he* finished. He just... dumped her.' Frank looked up from the picture. 'And I was there, like a young mug, ready to take her back.'

'You're not a mug!'

'We picked up the pieces and just carried on.'

'Oh, Dad!'

'That's why I never told you. I didn't want you to think less of me.'

Jackie reached out and stroked his shoulder. His shrunken frame slouched, his fleecy cardigan felt like one of June's teddies. 'I think anything but. I think more of you. It's amazing that you forgave her.' Jackie tried to say more, but she couldn't manage the words.

'Your dad loved her, Jackie. And she loved him. It was right that she came back. She would never have had the life she had if it wasn't for your dad.'

'She never got over him, Patricia, you know that and I know it.' Jackie had never heard her dad refer to Mrs Morrisson by her first name, but she didn't interrupt their discussion.

'Nonsense!' she tutted, 'that's not true. You don't know that to be true! You gave her everything she wanted and more. He only gave her a show! You gave her a life, a house, a daughter to be proud of, happy times, all this, a good marriage.' She patted his hand. 'You are what she wanted. Think about it. She never went after him, did she? She could have found him if she wanted to. She came straight back to you and stayed with you until she died.'

'Did you ever talk to her about it, Dad?'

'No. We never talked about it. She just came home one day, said her singing was over, and that was that. We moved on.'

'Oh, Dad!' exclaimed Jackie.

'Don't, now, Jackie. No sympathy. I loved your mum and that was that. We did have happy years, but every now and then, she had that sad stare, you know, big eyes into nowhere, like a deer, and I did wonder if she missed him, or if she was thinking about when she was a singer. It was those days that she started to disappear down into the bottom of a bottle like a genie.' The three of them fell silent until Frank sat back in his seat.

'I'm so very sorry, Dad.'

'Oh, don't be, it's ancient history. And by God, she was a great wife, home-cooked meal for me every day, clean socks, ironed shirts, a smile. We hardly ever argued.'

'Why do you keep this picture of him?' asked Jackie. 'You must hate him.'

'I don't know, I've never thought about it. It was a long time ago. Maybe I want to feel that her drinking wasn't my fault, it was his. But then, it was my fault too. I was proud of her and... I should have told her that more often. Maybe then, she wouldn't have looked elsewhere...' Frank broke off, staring into his mug, and Mrs Morrisson continued for him.

'She worked hard, your mum. She was a true star for a while, and she was a brilliant singer. The songs filled her up to here! Her voice was one in a million. She was always smiling when she sang. Oh, the audience loved her, Jackie! The story goes that O'Donnell pushed her too far, then he dropped her when she was about to hit her peak. But your dad was there, as he said, waiting, and your mum and dad were one of the happiest couples I knew.'

'Now let's put this stuff away.' Frank began to gather up the clippings and pictures and put them into the box. 'I'm sorry, hen,' he said as he reached for the lid. 'Don't let it change how you feel about your mum. She is and was still your mum and she loved you. You were the wee girl neither of us thought we'd have. We just didn't think we could have children. When you came along, it was the best day of her life. And mine. I had the marriage with her. Years and years, we were happy. Remember that, not him. Promise me.'

'I promise...'

'I know it is a lot to take in, but it was a long, long time ago, way before you. Nothing to do with you. As for your question about the drinking, people don't always need a reason. She would have maybe started anyway, of her own accord. She would have found something else.' He walked over and put the box into the sideboard and clicked it closed. 'I'm sorry I didn't tell you sooner. It all happened before you were born. Everything changed after that. For the better.'

'I'd best be off.' Mrs Morrisson reached down and unclicked her handbag, put the squashed-up tissue inside and clicked it closed again.

Frank nodded to Mrs Morrisson. She knew he was thanking her and she returned his nod.

Jackie followed her through the kitchen to the back door. She put her hand on the handle and paused.

'Now, Jackie, listen to your dad. Don't carry this around in your heart. Everybody makes mistakes. Your mum was a good woman. Your dad always defended her honour; he protected her. They loved each other very much, and, very deeply. He's a fine, fine gentleman, your dad, one of the very best.' Mrs Morrisson kissed Jackie on the cheek, then walked over to the side gate. She didn't turn around. 'Don't ever tell him I said that,' she muttered.

Jackie smiled, closed the door and locked it. She looked at the picture of her mum on the mantelpiece and wondered about that faraway look in her eye that her dad had referred to.

ORDERS

Terry stood at the doorway of the new Fletcher's Bookmakers. At six foot two, he filled the doorframe, which Tommy told him not to lean on. He had also been told not to touch anything. The inside was so much better and more high tech than the last shop. Tommy had clearly spent money on it. He looked around and admired the smooth painted woodwork of the booths that he'd be standing in and pictured himself putting on people's bets behind glass screens just like the ones they have in the bank. He'd miss the fun and jokes he had with the regular customers at the job on the market but not the cold weather. Tommy could be, at times, a bit aggressive, but he was one of Terry's oldest friends and Terry knew he could never say no to him anyway.

Tommy carefully supervised the shop fitter affixing the new till into the worktop. Another shop fitter swept the floor. Small pads and pens were laid out neatly around on thin ledges with high stools placed beside them. Five televisions were switched on, all on different stations with racing horses and dogs.

'That's you all set. All plugged in and ready to go. Do you know how to work it?'

'Yes, I do,' replied Tommy, tapping the till.

'State of the art, that,' said the shop fitter, 'good luck with it.'

Tommy turned to Terry. 'We open in twenty minutes. Go next door and talk to Pender. Invite him in for a free bet and a look round. I want him sending punters my way. All his staff, their pals, get them spreading the word.'

Terry nodded and turned to go to the butcher's next door.

'When you come back, you can test out the kettle,' he shouted after him. The shop fitters finished tidying up and waited around for a few minutes. Tommy thought they wanted a tea or coffee, or worse, a few pounds, so told them if they were finished, they could go and he would settle up with their boss later.

Once alone, he reclined into his black leather chair. He spread his arms out, then clasped his hands behind his head and waited.

Jackie sat down in the nurses break room and reached for a chocolate muffin from a basket left by a patient's grateful daughter. She peeled back the paper case, took a bite and chewed slowly.

'Hey! You look exhausted.' Daniel walked in and placed his mop and bucket in the corner. 'You okay?' he asked.

'Standard nurse face.' She nodded and took another bite. 'You're looking pretty knackered yourself.'

'I didn't sleep very well last night,' he whispered. 'I phoned in sick yesterday – had a bit of a day in bed.'

'Were you not well?'

'No, just took a skive,' he smiled. 'Don't grass me up.'

'As if!' she replied. Another nurse came in, took a cake and ate it in two bites, then walked out again.

'Staff Nurse Mary is looking for you, Daniel,' she called back. 'Mrs Williamson spilled a full jug of juice on the floor.' Daniel rolled his eyes.

'Oh, right, thanks, I'll head there in a minute.'

'Did you do anything on Saturday?' Jackie asked.

'Not much. Few drinks with Johnny in town,' he replied.

'How is Johnny? I've not seen him since we all went to the shows. Or you, much, for that matter. You okay?'

'Aye, he's fine. Same old, same old.' Daniel hoped Jackie wouldn't ask for details. 'I've not seen Viv since that day either.'

Jackie yawned. 'I saw her yesterday at mass. She's doing great.' Jackie yawned again. 'She loves that Avon job. Better get a coffee before I go back.'

'You okay? You seem wiped out.'

'Just stuff,' she replied. 'I want to go to visit my mum's grave today. I've not been for a while. I'm a bit worried about my dad, though.'

'Is Frank all right?' Daniel was exceptionally fond of the old man, who had welcomed him into the heart of his and Jackie's family.

'He's fine, absolutely fine. Just a few wee... family things. Run off my feet with June, as well, and I'm sure you know the score with Tommy.'

'No. What score? Tommy Fletcher?'

'Didn't you know? I thought you knew! Oh, my God, sorry! I thought I was the last to know. He's come back. He's living in Coatbridge. He had the cheek to come to church yesterday and wait outside in the graveyard with flowers. Says he's changed. I don't know if I believe him, but I don't think you have to worry. He said he felt bad about punching you that time.'

'Jesus. That's all you need.' Daniel opened the fridge and looked inside. He felt the rosiness in his cheeks rise when he thought about that evening. He pretended to look for something.

'My dad says he'll be gone again soon, Daniel. He's sure of it.' Daniel looked up from the fridge. Jackie could see he was embarrassed. 'Let's not talk about him.' Daniel nodded. 'Speaking of my dad... well, you'll never guess what? This will make you laugh. He went and invited Father Cleary round for dinner. Can you believe it? I need to get sandwiches sorted for him and his nephew this Thursday.'

'Oh! The nephew! I heard about him. My mum says he's the talk of the town. What's he like?'

'He's actually lovely. Really nice guy.' Daniel noticed Jackie's eyes sparkle.

'Oh! I saw that!' He walked closer to her, pulled out a chair and sat down.

'What?' she smiled.

'You fancy him!'

'Don't be daft!' She couldn't stop a smile creep across her face. 'Oh, all right, then! Maybe a wee bit!' She stood up, flicked the kettle on and spooned coffee into a chipped Libra mug. 'Me and everybody else! He is nice, though.' She turned and faced Daniel. 'He's handsome but he's gentle and kind. And funny. He's really quite smart and funny.'

'Ah, Jackie! That's so great! What was it like when you met him?'

'I don't know how to describe it. Awkward? He kissed my cheek but he probably does that with everybody he meets cos he's French. He's so... warm. It's like the sun comes out whenever he's about, anywhere I see him, the weather is... nice. It's so weird,' she added, dreamily. 'I saw him again yesterday after mass and he asked me to take his arm and his skin is so brown and soft and his fingernails are so clean... and, Oh, God! I accidentally told him he was hot but it's not what I meant, Daniel!'

'Oh, Jackie!' Daniel clapped. 'You got it bad! What are you going to do?'

'I don't know. I've only met him twice! I don't know him. It's probably all in my head. Anyway, guess what? He might want to become a priest! Just to complicate matters...'

'And he's coming to your house on Thursday with Father Cleary? Oh, my God, Jackie!'

'Daniel!' called a voice from the corridor, which he recognised as the Staff Nurse. He stood up.

'You'd better go!' Jackie stirred her coffee and added milk.

Before Daniel could respond, he was ushered out of the break room by the Staff Nurse. He followed behind her dutifully towards Mrs Williamson's bedside, his blonde hair flopping forward as he carried his mop and bucket.

Jackie took a few rushed sips of her coffee, checked the time on her fob watch, then rushed back to the ward, leaving the coffee cup three-quarters full.

Frank was finishing drying the dishes in the kitchen with the window open in front of him. He watched the washing on the line as he piled up the plates to put away. Three of his white vests waved back and forth, side by side in unison with the light wind. The vests looked like they belonged to a giant compared with the rest of the clothes on the line, including many of little June's small belongings that pranced lightly around beside them. Her frilly whites and lemons and pale pinks tickled the air as the clouds parted to welcome a stretch of blue sky. He thought of all the people the same age as him, who were sick in hospital, or couldn't walk, and those that were dying, or friends that had died. All the funerals he had been to of people in their seventies and younger. How much they'd love the chance to pinch wooden clothes pegs around wet cloth, standing barefoot on damp green grass.

He took a peach from the fruit bowl and ate it over the kitchen sink. The juice ran down his chin. He felt happy, and lucky, that he had made it this far, and tried to keep going, to focus on the little things, to enjoy this juicy, furry, dripping fruit. He made a mental note to transfer another £20 into the savings account he had set up for Jackie, for when his day came. He wondered if she was okay at work today, after learning about Eddie O'Donnell. *All out in the open now*, he thought, as he took another bite.

'Granda, can I go in the garden with my bubbles?' asked June. 'The sun's out!'

'Aren't you tired after nursery, hen?'

'No, Granda, I'm not tired!' She shook her head from side to side as if to prove it.

'Aye, on you go then, my wee dolly.' Frank opened the door for her and helped her onto the lawn. He felt one of his vests, it was half dry. Jackie had taught him to hang clothes upside down so he didn't leave peg marks in the middle of the chest. June blew bubbles and he sat on the wall and watched her. 'Give me the bubbles. I'll blow and you pop,' he said.

June handed the bubbles over to him and she clapped three quick claps as he blew a gigantic bubble. It floated into the air and he blew out hundreds more as she ran around, clapping her hands against each one, making sure it was burst.

Mrs Morrisson paused her dusting. With polish and cloth in either hand, she stood watching at her upstairs bedroom windowsill. Frank blew the bubbles over and over again. She smiled and opened the window to hear June's laughter, then carried on dusting with a smile.

Viv pulled up into the car park of the small L-shaped shopping centre on Bank Street in Coatbridge. She reached over to the passenger seat floor and picked up a second pair of shoes. She slipped off her driving flats and scooped her feet into black patent heels. She pulled down the sun visor above the wheel to look into the mirror, then unclicked a briefcase which contained eye shadows, mascaras, lipsticks, glosses, blushers, foundations, brushes and compacts in all kinds of shapes and sizes, all marked Avon. She selected a lipstick and topped up the colour she was already wearing. Checking her eyes and cheeks for shadow and blusher, she gave herself a nod of approval. Clicking the briefcase closed, she placed a thick, pink triplicate order pad under her arm, and an Avon pen in her jacket pocket. At four o'clock, there was just enough time to do one more appointment before the little chemist closed.

'Mrs Patel!' she said, closing the door. 'The autumn colours have arrived in advance. I thought of you straightaway when these came in. I said to my boss, I said, Mrs Patel will *love* these.'

Mrs Patel smiled and motioned for her son to take over behind the counter as she came around to be by Viv's side.

'Now I'm only in to show you the eyeshadow palettes. All of the range is new, of course, but I don't want you to worry about that because there's a lot of products. We'll focus on the eyes today and see what you think.' Viv unclicked the briefcase and unfolded separate sections of colours, brushes and foundations. 'Sapphire Blue is the hot colour. It has come in ahead of the party season,' she said, pushing a brush in circles. 'Take a look.' She popped a mirror in Mrs Patel's hands as she sat down in a chair and Viv got to work on her face. She applied eyeshadow right up to the woman's brow, adding lighter and deeper shades to highlight different areas. Her son shook his head and shrugged his shoulders as Mrs Patel oohed and ahhed in the mirror. Bit by bit, she encouraged Viv to show her eyeliner, mascara, blusher and lipstick, just as Viv knew she would. In make-up, nobody liked an unfinished face. After seeing all of the range, Mrs Patel placed an order and Viv helped her fill out the form, ensuring she signed her name and gave the advance payment. She was tearing off Mrs Patel's copy of the receipt when the bell above the door rang and a customer entered.

Terry walked up to the counter. Viv stayed quiet, even though she recognised him as Tommy Fletcher's friend. He ordered a packet of indigestion pills and took two on the spot. As he paid, the young son asked him how it was all going.

'Painfully,' Terry replied. He noticed Viv on the way out of the shop. He admired her black fitted jacket and matching skirt with violet blouse before he recognised her face.

'Hello!' he said, without thinking.

'Hello,' she replied, briskly.

'Okay, then!' he said and pushed the door back open. Viv turned to see where he was going. She put down her pen and walked over to the shop window. Her eyes followed Terry as he entered a new shop.

'Great. Just great,' she said, quietly.

Jackie pressed the button to get off the bus and approached the familiar gates. She was glad it wasn't raining but the wind was on the rise. She pulled her jacket lapels into her neck. She walked up the hill, passing all the headstones, some old, some new, some with flowers, some bare, with absolutely nothing, some overgrown. Quite a few enormous and ornate carvings of angels and saints. She passed by the saddest stones of all; for babies. She read a few baby epitaphs, then had to look away.

She was struck by yet another similarity between her and her mum. She had considered her life with a God-fearing good man versus an exciting, successful, more dangerous one and, objectively, Jackie was able to appreciate a woman's dilemma in the attraction of both. Jackie experimented with feelings of anger towards her mother. She *did* go back to her dad, they really *did* love each other, he certainly loved her deeply.

As she reached the peak of the hill, the white stones of her mum's plot came into view. The small plant that Frank had left was blooming with pink flower heads. She looked around to check that nobody else was at a nearby grave, then she spoke.

'Hiya, Mum. I don't have anything for you today. I was at work, came straight here. See, the thing is, my dad told me, well, you probably know he told me, right? About you and...? My dad says you see everything. So, assuming you do... well, I don't know how I'm supposed to feel about it, really. All I've got are more questions that you can't answer, and he won't...'

Jackie stood quietly, focusing on the words 'beloved wife and mother' which were carved into the stone under her mother's name.

'I suppose you fall for the charms of the wrong man. I've done it myself. My dad says O'Donnell finished with you. Did you love him, Mum? I mean, you went back to my dad, I know that, but then you drank...' She scraped her shoes on the grass. 'It was good of my dad to take you back and look after you... But would you have rather been with Eddie? Was my dad your safe choice?' A bumble bee hovered around above the pink flower and then landed.

'You loved my wee dad, didn't you? Who couldn't love him?' She paused and straightened her dad's flower plant. The bee looked cute and furry up close and she felt compelled to stroke it, but thought it better not to disturb his wings. 'I suppose you also know that Tommy is back? Maybe you saw. He wants to see me and June and I might have to tell her who her dad is, even though she's never really noticed she hasn't got one. He's all set up, money, car, the whole lot. Says he's changed, who knows, it could be true. Then there's this other guy, you'd like him, he's really nice. But then he might be going to be a priest, I don't know yet. He's called Jean Pa-'

Before Jackie had finished saying the name, a high wind swooped up and blew through Jackie's hair, swirling it around in all directions. After a few seconds, the wind dropped back to nothing, leaving a white feather falling in the air, left and right. Jackie's eyes followed it down, as if watching a game of tennis, until the little feather settled atop her mother's stone.

SANDWICHES

Viv never like to tell half a story, and she didn't like to be interrupted when she was in full recount. Jackie sat on the phone seat attached to the table in the hall and listened intently.

'He said to me, "What are *you* doing down here, all dolled up?" and I said, "For your information, I work round here. And this is my *work* uniform, but what it's got to do with you anyway?" I said, and then he was like, "There's no need to get all touchy and whatever." And that Terry was there, he works in the shop as well. I don't know why he hangs around with Tommy, he actually seems like a nice guy. Anyway, I had a look inside the new shop, posh as you like. Great big tellies, tall stools, a fancy electronic till. He must have some money, Jackie.'

'I knew he was setting up in Coatbridge. He told me that. Was it busy?'

'Pender was in getting the grand tour and a few old guys were in putting bets on.'

'Was he nice to you?'

'I wouldn't say nice, no. I'd say, his usual self. Trying to be charming but he has that sly way about him... you know.'

'This shop means he obviously intends to stay, I suppose. I'm going to have to tell June now, aren't I? God, I don't need this right now.'

'Listen, Jackie, has it ever occurred to you that if he does have all this money, and you have his baby, that you might be entitled to half of it?'

'I don't want his money, Viv.'

'I know you don't, and I wouldn't either, but it's worth thinking about. He owes you for how he treated you. And it could be useful to have a bit tucked away for the future. You should think about that.'

'Even if I wanted his money, I couldn't get it, we were never married.'

'So what? Common law wife! You have rights. Anyway, stuff him. I've got to get off the phone, but I can come and help you with the priest sandwiches tomorrow, and we'll find time to talk about it, okay? I just got a big order off Mrs Patel so I can finish early and get round at about five-ish.

'Eyeshadow trick?'

'Yep! What time are you finishing?'

'Five.'

'Right. What time are they coming?'

'Half six.'

'Okay, see you tomorrow.'

Viv hung up and Jackie quickly dialled Mrs Morrisson's number who told her that Mrs Patel was planning on making extra samosas and would drop them over to her house during the day.

Jackie relaxed with June. She fed her dinner, played building bricks, bathed her, then put her to bed. After another long day, she couldn't wait to get to sleep herself, so she got into her pyjamas and climbed under the covers. Despite her tiredness, she tossed and turned in a light sleep, and it took her a few hours to settle. She could sense something nearby, behind the room door. It definitely wasn't her dad, and June was in bed. Jackie didn't feel afraid. She opened her eyes wide and addressed the door.

'If you're there, come in,' she whispered. 'Come in.' She heard and felt nothing but a strong feeling that someone was standing by the door. She waited a few minutes, repeated her whisper, then closed her eyes and fell back to sleep. Then again, she woke and felt it, something near in the dark of the night. Her eyes flew bolt open. She looked to her left into the faint streetlight that came in through the curtains. Floating in the air was a circle, swirling shapes inside it, like water, or the moon, except it was transparent. She reached out to touch it. Her fingers ran through it, all at different times, but they touched nothing. The circle stayed there with her hand inside, fingers still moving. Suddenly aware of what she was doing and seeing, fear gripped her and she clamped her eyes shut.

The next day, Frank collected June from nursery at midday and they discussed her day on the walk home. He peeled a tangerine and gave her segments between her reporting whose name the teacher drew a smiley face next to and who got in trouble.

When they arrived back, Mrs Morrisson was standing at the back door about to enter with a tray of food covered with a square plastic lid. Frank opened the door and, military style, Mrs Morrisson put the tray straight into the kitchen and walked back out again. Frank lifted the cover to have a peek.

'Leave it!' He dropped the lid back down. Mrs Morrisson returned with another tray, and then another. Frank and June sat down and watched her move around their living room. She carefully lifted the goldfish and put it down on the tiled ledge in front of the fire. Then she took a white linen tablecloth from a bag and threw it up into the air with two hands and it unfolded and landed gently onto the dining table like a parachute. She flattened it out with her palms.

'Hope you've not got any beetroot, it'll stain like a big bruise,' said Frank, feeling like he was helping.

'No beetroot, only white pickles,' she replied, rolling her eyes. June smiled at Frank and rubbed her hands. He did the same.

'Are we going to have a party, Granda?'

'A little party, yes. Only a wee one.'

'Will there be crisps?'

'I've got crisps for you, my darling.' June ran into the kitchen and returned with a packet of *Space Raiders*.

'Don't be spoiling her dinner, now,' said Frank, smiling. 'Speaking of, Mrs, what is for the dinner?'

'I've done sandwiches and Mrs Gupta handed over a tray of samosas and there's a bit of potato salad and coleslaw and what not.'

Frank scowled at June and she laughed. 'Sandwiches isn't a dinner,' he whispered.

'And I've done a beef casserole,' Mrs Morrisson called, 'as I knew you'd say that about sandwiches not being a dinner.' June laughed and Frank punched the air.

The back door opened and Jackie and Viv shook umbrellas.

'Hi, Mrs Morrisson! That's the rain on, all of a sudden. I'll just wash my hands. What do you need us to do?'

'Nothing at all now, Jackie, it's all done, hen. You look soaked.'

'What? No way! You've done it all?'

'There's plenty here. We could feed the five thousand.'

'Oh, that's amazing.' Jackie reached over and kissed Mrs Morrisson on the cheek.

'Jackie, why don't you go and get a nice hot bath and you and Viv can go up and get ready. I'll get it all set up for you. This kitchen is just not big enough for the three of us!'

'She's right, Jackie, let's go choose your outfit!' Jackie and Viv giggled. Jackie scooped June up into her arms and stole one of her Space Raiders from the bag.

'The priesties are coming!' she said. 'Let's go put on something nice, Junie.'

'Mummy, he's not a priest, remember?'

'She certainly does!' said Viv, with a broad grin. Jackie put June down and chased her upstairs with Viv following after.

'Granda says sandwiches are not a dinner,' she squeaked.

'Right, Frank,' said Mrs Morrisson, 'Quick Hoover round, please, and don't dunt the table legs.'

'I'm on it, Your Majesty!' he said, strolling to the hall with a salute.

'Have we enough chairs? We've not got enough chairs. I'll go and get more chairs.' Mrs Morrisson darted back outside to her house.

'I had another dream last night,' Jackie said to Viv, as she towel-dried her hair and Viv pulled hangers apart, looking disdainfully at Jackie's clothes. 'Do you believe in signs? I think my mum is sending me signals.'

'You're acting like how your dad was.'

'Well, I'm beginning to wonder... I went to visit her and there was this bee that landed on my dad's plant... and then a white feather blew around in a wild wind and landed right in front of me on her gravestone after I mentioned JP's name.'

'Jackie, we really need to take you shopping,' said Viv. 'Right, you're done, Junie, you can go downstairs to Granda for inspection!'

'You look like a princess, Junie,' said Jackie. June twirled her pink dress, then left the room obediently. 'Go down on your bottom, good girl.' Jackie brushed her hair. 'I think my mum likes Jean Paul!'

'Jackie,' said Viv, with authority as she laid out a navy wrap dress, 'everybody can see that he likes you. It's blatantly obvious by the way he was staring at you outside the church. You need to just go for it, but be cool as well. Don't pin all your hopes on one tail. It's not clear yet what his plans are.'

'I don't know how to be cool! I haven't had a boyfriend since Tommy!'

'Let him do the work! You said yourself he was chatty and nice. Did you think about what I said about Tommy by the way?'

'I haven't had a chance yet. What do you think about the feather and the bee?'

'I think it's lovely. Comforting. Where's the harm in believing, I say. Now try this on, with these.' She pulled out some cream sandals. 'I'll do your make-up. We'll call it a freebie, this time,' she smiled.

'Eh? I've never paid before!'

'I know! And think of the millions I've lost!'

Jackie pulled the dress over her head and Viv looked on at her friend as she slipped the shoes on. She clasped her hands together.

'Beautiful,' she said. 'Now let me at that hair and make-up, please.' Jackie pulled a face and they both laughed.

Mrs Morrisson returned with the chairs as Frank was putting the Hoover away.

'Final checks!' she said, adjusting June's dress and fixing Frank's tie. Jackie and Viv came into the living room. 'Oh, now, Jackie, you look lovely! Doesn't she, Frank?'

'You look smashing, hen. What's that on your eye?'

Jackie put a finger to her eye and looked at Viv, who tutted.

'It's eyeliner, Frank, for God's sake.'

'Och, Frank!' Mrs Morrisson gave him a tiny push and he laughed.

'Well, I don't know, do I? Surrounded by women, here! I like your eyeliner, hen, very... well, it goes round the eye in a very nice... round way.'

The doorbell rang and June began jumping on the spot. Mrs Morrisson tore off her apron and threw it into a cupboard. They all started shoving each other towards the door. Frank accused Viv of shoving first and they all joined in. Nobody knew who should answer the door so they all rushed forward, squashed together like a tin of beans. They opened the door and Father Cleary and Jean Paul stood there, staring in confusion at the laughter.

'Hello! You all seem happy! What's the joke?' Father Cleary looked on joyously. Jean Paul beamed at Jackie.

'Just something Viv did, I mean, said, Father. Do come in! In you come, move out the way, please, everybody, come on now, make space, make space.' Mrs Morrisson, Jackie, June and Viv shuffled up to stand on the bottom few stairs as Father Cleary entered and removed his large overcoat.

'Have you no coat, Jean Paul?' asked Frank.

'He thinks it's the summer out there!' said Father Cleary.

'It *is* summer!' echoed Jackie and Jean Paul together.

'It was raining very heavily an hour ago!' Father Cleary hung his coat.

'That's true. Twenty degrees every day, Jean Paul!' Frank joked. 'Ten in the morning, ten in the afternoon, a splash of rain and a peek of sun, that's your Scottish weather for you!'

'Four seasons in one day!' Mrs Morrisson smiled and stood back until everyone had entered the living room and sat down on the couch and chairs. She made her way through to the kitchen and boiled the kettle. She had one final check of the food and had her bag on her shoulder as Frank entered the kitchen.

'I'll come back and help with the clearing up later, Frank.'

'Where are you going?'

'I'll get out from under your feet now.'

'Don't be daft, you're staying, Mrs!'

'No, Frank this is a family visit.'

'You're practically family. You're staying and that's that. Viv is staying too. Now take that handbag off your shoulder and help me with these drinks.' He smiled, a cheeky little grin, and she gently and slowly placed her handbag on the countertop.

'Thank you, Frank,' she said, quietly.

'AND HOW ARE YOU KEEPING, YOUNG JUNE?' Father Cleary's voice boomed around the room.

'Fine,' replied June, holding onto and twirling her mother's skirt.

'Shall we put a record on, June?' asked Viv. 'Come and help me choose one!' June looked at her mother, then walked over to Viv and knelt down beside her.

'I hope we get a song from little June later! She sings like her Granny used to, you know, Jean Paul, her Granny was a lovely singer.'

Jean Paul exchanged glances with Jackie who was trying not to look at him, but each time she did, he was looking back. Frank came in with a tray of drinks.

'Whisky for the father, small whisky for the other, I mean, Jean Paul, smallish wine for Viv, smaller wine for Jackie, small sherry for Mrs, diluting orange for the wean, small to medium whisky for myself. Right! Cheers, everybody!' Frank held his glass and everybody said, 'Cheers,' and took a sip of their drinks.

'I'll get the food out,' said Mrs Morrisson as Frank sat down. They sat in silence, sipping drinks, until June put a needle on a record and it began crackling at a loud volume. June smiled at everyone around the room.

'This is Junie's favourite, isn't it?' offered Viv.

'To Bombay, a travelling circus came,' began the singer.

'Oh, my God, Viv!' laughed Jackie.

'Jackie! And in front of the Fathers!' tutted Frank.

'What is this?' asked Jean Paul.

'This is *Nellie The Elephant*!' nodded Father Cleary. Viv took June to the centre of the room and clapped as she bounced to the chorus.

'Maybe turn it down a wee bit, Viv,' shouted Frank.

'No way! We're enjoying it, aren't we, Junie?' June bounced her knees along to Viv's clapping. Father Cleary clapped along.

'I'm quite familiar with the Toy Dolls,' he shouted. 'Punk band, you know.'

'That's the food ready!' announced Mrs Morrisson. Viv lifted the needle off the record and June clapped her hands. She ran to the table and climbed up into her seat and Mrs Morrisson put a plate of food down in front of her, which she began to eat immediately. Mrs Morrisson tied a tea towel around her neck and put another one over her dress.

'Now. There's sandwiches, all kinds, cheese and tomato and egg and salad and all sorts, and potato salad and coleslaw and pickles. Oh, and Mrs Gupta sent over samosas! There's plenty, help yourselves. Or there's beef casserole for those who want it.'

'I'll have that, please, Mrs.' Frank held his knife and fork, ready and waiting with napkin in his collar. She left the room and returned with a steaming bowl of chunky meat, carrots and potatoes in gravy and placed it in front of him.

'Father, would you like some, I can take the meat out?'

'No, no, thank you, I'm fine with sandwiches. This is lovely, Mrs Morrisson. Beautiful spread, very kind.'

'Very kind,' echoed Jean Paul as he looked for a seat. The only one left available was beside Jackie.

He nodded, smiled at her, then sat down. She returned his glance with a half smile, then looked at Viv who was looking down at her food and grinning.

'Would you like some casserole, young father... Jean Paul... son?' Mrs Morrisson asked Jean Paul.

'It's lovely,' said Frank, a forkful in his cheek, 'no offence.' He nodded towards Father Cleary who raised his eyebrows and shrugged.

'Ah, no, it's okay, Madame, Fronc,' said Jean Paul, 'I am good, I will try a samosa, thank you.' Jean Paul reached over just as Jackie was reaching for the coleslaw and they exchanged a smile.

'Oh, yes. Very exotic they are, samosas. I've never tasted one,' Mrs Morrisson agreed.

'Take a plate for yourself, Mrs Morrisson. Try a wee corner of the samosa.' Jackie passed a plate along from Jean Paul to Father Cleary to Frank to Mrs Morrisson. She put a samosa on the plate and cut it open and some filling tumbled out.

'Is that peas?' asked Frank. Mrs Morrisson tentatively put some on her fork and gently chewed a small mouthful.

'Quite foreign tasting.'

They sat around the table, eating. Frank scraped his plate loudly, keeping his head over the bowl so he didn't miss a corner.

'So,' asked Viv, 'how long have you been a vegetarian, Father?' Jackie looked wide-eyed at Viv and Viv returned the glance with a smirk.

'Not too long, Vivien, not too long. I must say this makes a nice change from ratatouille. It's all the shops sell – ratatouille. It's all I've been eating, that and toast, and Jean Paul has been trying to get me to eat a pizza. The baked potatoes are nice, from The Spud Spot. And of course there's chips.'

'Oh, chips, of course!' Mrs Morrisson frowned.

'What's ratatouille?' asked Viv.

'It's courgettes and aubergines in tomato sauce.'

'You said you like pizza!' exclaimed Jean Paul.

'I do, I do, it all takes a bit of getting used to, you know, trying new things from abroad and so on. Spaghetti – and not tinned spaghetti – boiled spaghetti, well, that's a challenge. You have to eat it with a fork and a spoon, in a twisting method.'

'You're talking another language to me, Father,' remarked Frank, mopping a white slice of bread around his plate without lifting his head. 'I only know carrots and peas,' he laughed. 'I couldn't do without my meat.'

'It's nice to have something plain now and again, Father. I do like a nice sandwich from time to time.' Mrs Morrisson pushed her samosa to the side of her plate and reached over to the sandwich tray.

'Pass me a sandwich as well, Mrs,' said Frank. 'Would anybody like another drink?'

'I'll get them, Dad. What would you all like?' Jackie took the drink orders and stood up from the table. Jean Paul stood up as she stood up.

'Something else they do in France, stand up when a woman stands up.' Father Cleary reached for the pickles.

Mrs Morrisson put her hand to her heart and sighed. 'So lovely, such manners,' she breathed.

'How long are you staying for, Jean Paul?' asked Viv.

'I am not sure yet, a while, I think.'

'You must be missing your mother?' Mrs Morrisson asked. 'Is there a special girl in Paris?'

Jackie clinked the tray of drinks loudly against her plate and Viv suppressed a giggle.

'Behave yourself, Viv,' said Frank.

'I do not have a girlfriend.' Jean Paul helped Jackie pass the drinks around. 'And I talk to my mother often.'

'No time for girlfriends, have you, Jean Paul?' scoffed Father Cleary. 'You've a future to think about.'

'Do you miss meat, Father?' Jackie stumbled over the question, desperate to change the subject.

'I wondered that as well. What else do you put on the space on the plate? Instead of the meat? Is it pizza right enough?' asked Frank.

'You know, I don't miss meat at all. I just went off it. All lined up in the supermarket, legs and thighs and bones and bits and bobs and necks and what have you, it just didn't seem right. I don't mind other people eating it, but I don't want to eat it anymore. But you know, let's not talk about it in front of the child. HOW IS NURSERY NOW, JUNE? ARE YOU KEEPING THEM ALL IN LINE?'

'I like the hula hooping!' replied June.

'AND ARE YOU GOING TO THE BIG SCHOOL THIS YEAR?'

June nodded shyly and looked at her mother.

'Yes, Father, she's off to the big school in September. We've got the uniform, just got to get the shoes, isn't that right, Junie?'

'Yes, Mummy, black shoes.'

'Aww, listen to her,' Mrs Morrisson tutted. 'She's great for the talking.'

'Don't they grow up so fast!' remarked Father Cleary. 'I bet she keeps you on your toes, Frank.'

'Oh, this one takes no prisoners!'

'If you'd excuse us, everyone, it's June's bedtime so I'm going to take her upstairs. Mrs Morrisson, don't clean up. I'll do it when I come back down.'

'I'll give you a hand upstairs, Jackie.' Viv stood up.

'Now say good night to everybody, Miss June.' June waved obediently and the table waved back. Viv followed Jackie out of the room and prodded her in the back, giggling all the way up the stairs.

SHIFTING CHAIRS

Daniel's mum took the stairs slowly and carefully with her forearms cradling a pile of ironing like she was carrying a full tray of scalding tea in bone china cups. Stopping at her son's room, she smiled and shook her head as she saw the usual unmade bed crumpled up at the corners, four pillows in one pile with a U-shaped dent where his head had been. She placed his clothes flat on the little blue chair that was too small for him to sit in anymore but she knew they'd never part with. She left the window blind down as it was getting dark. He'd be home soon and she wanted him to have a nice bed to fall into, although after all these years, she wondered if he'd flop into any old bed anyway, whether it was made or not. She separated the four pillows one by one and plumped each to its maximum and placed them down on the flat sheet on the mattress. She lifted the quilt and tucked it down neatly, folding it over at the top. She picked up a few rogue socks and put them into his wash basket. She reached for a pencil off the carpet and felt a twinge in her back and sat down for a second on his bed to recover. As she rested rubbing her lower back, she looked at the faces on the posters that covered the old *Doctor Who* wallpaper. She stared at the band members with the strange haircuts, then her eyes moved around the room to his little bits and bobs that lay on the table: his old watch that he intended to get a battery for, a lump of blue tack, a few rubber bands, his records in the wire rack, his alarm clock, some *Sounds* music newspapers and a worn out book by Bret Easton Ellis, *Less Than Zero*.

She noticed his side drawer was open and began to push it closed. The pad inside with writing and scribbles caught her eye, a page with a list, some things scored out. She could make out a few words, but didn't have her reading glasses on, which was just as well, as she didn't like to pry in her son's business. She continued to push the drawer into the cabinet until it was completely closed.

She placed both of her hands on her knees and sat there for a few seconds, until she heard her husband call up to her from downstairs.

'I'm just coming,' she called back.

She stood up and lifted the pile of ironing off the little blue chair and carefully placed it onto the different shelves of Daniel's wardrobe. Once finished, she surveyed the room again, picked up a glass with some milk left in it and a plate of crusts and went back downstairs.

Viv hugged Jackie goodbye at the front door, she insisted there was no need to say goodbye to the rest of them in the living room as the noise might wake June. Jackie had to laugh as a few minutes later, the phone rang loudly three times to signal that she had arrived home safely.

In the living room, the table had been cleared, wiped, tablecloth folded and Miss Piggy returned to the centre. Father Cleary was sitting on the couch with Jean Paul and Frank was deep into a story, gesticulating madly. Jackie could hear Mrs Morrisson sliding plates together in the kitchen and opening cupboards to put them away.

'I would have done that!' she said to her.

'Don't be silly now, you've a child to look after,' she waved away the idea.

'Okay but I'm taking the chairs back to your house, no arguments.' Mrs Morrisson tried to say no but Jackie put her hand up, led her into the living room and sat her down on the armchair with the others. She lifted one of the chairs and moved it into the kitchen. Jean Paul put his drink down on the carpet and jumped up.

'I will help Jackie with the chairs,' he said quietly. His voice wasn't noticed amidst the loud conversation between Father Cleary and Frank, who were now talking about a film they'd seen about a man from New York and a visiting mermaid with a high pitched shrill instead of a voice. Jean Paul lifted a chair and followed Jackie down the back street.

'Oh, thanks, it's just down here,' she said. She walked up Mrs Morrisson's garden path and opened her back door.

'No key?' asked Jean Paul.

'It's perfectly safe'. Jackie entered into the familiar clean Jif lemon smell of Mrs Morrisson's kitchen and into her living room and Jean Paul followed.

'Ah, yes, some places in Paris, it's the same. Old neighbours, trust each other.'

'Is it like that where you live, too?'

'Actually, I just helped my mother move house. She doesn't know the neighbours yet. My mother moved there after my father, how do you say, met another woman.'

'Oh! I'm so sorry. That's such a shame for her.' Jackie pushed the chair slowly under the dining room table so as not to disturb the fresh bowl of Mrs Morrisson's pot pourri.

'These things happen.' Jean Paul shrugged, copying her movements with the chair, but Jackie could tell he was covering his sadness.

'Had it been going on long? You know, your dad...'

'Some years, I think,' he replied. 'But for you... It is sadder, having no mother at all.'

'I'm okay,' she replied, adjusting his chair. 'It's still hard, I mean, don't get me wrong, I miss her every day. But you get used to it. Funny. Well, not funny, but I just found out that my mum had an affair, very early on, in her marriage.'

'Really? Oh no...'

'It was before I was born. My dad forgave her and took her back.'

'But that is very good of him, no?'

'Yes, but I'm sad he had to go through that, even though they went on to be happy, in their own way.'

'I am sorry.'

'Oh, don't be! It's okay. God, I don't know why I'm telling you all this! I'm really sorry about your mum and dad.'

'It's okay, I have known for a while that they were not happy. It will be better for them this way. And don't worry about telling me, I am good with the ears, remember?'

'Yes, I remember,' she smiled, feeling better.

'I'll go get the other chair.'

'No, I can go-'

'No, it's okay, wait here, I will get it.' He left the room and went out of the back door. Jackie thought of being alone with him and excitement rose within her. Viv's last words, 'Go for it!' were now ringing in her head. She walked swiftly to the mirror above the mantelpiece and checked her face and hair. She inspected her teeth to check there was nothing stuck between, then rubbed a finger over her lips to even out the lipstick. She realised that she was perfectly fresh and sober, having barely touched her wine at dinner, and she smiled and nodded confidently at her reflection. She heard the back door bump open and quickly lifted a framed picture of Mrs Morrisson's son.

Jean Paul entered the room with the chair. He placed it near the dining table. His hair had fallen forward into his eyes, and he pushed it back, like James Dean in a film Jackie had seen.

'*C'est tout*? No more?' he asked. Jackie placed the picture back down slowly. She noticed Jean Paul's face glow in the moonlight. She felt like she had no control over her mind, it was too late, she was lost to the idea of the moment. Her feet floated over so lightly she was standing right in front of him.

'That's it,' she said, 'No more.' The words barely leaving a sound. He reached up and placed a gentle hand on her face and his other arm pulled her in towards him. Her body folded as if she would faint, and she melted into his embrace.

'Hiya, Mum.' Daniel pecked his mum's cheek, as she sat in her chair, knitting with the television on.

'You're back late, son.'

'I went for a quick pint after work.'

'With Johnny?'

'Uh-huh. Is there any dinner, Mum?'

'On the side in there. Mince 'n tatties. Two minutes in the microwave.'

'Amazing.' Daniel's mum continued knitting as he put his trainers and jacket in the hall and came back into the room. 'Where's my dad?'

'He's away to his bed already. Do you know how to work the microwave or do you need me to do it?'

'I can do it, it's okay.' Daniel put the plate in the microwave and took his time to follow the instructions, pressing seven different buttons before it clicked on. He stood and watched the plate of food spin slowly. Three beeps later, he put it on a tray and took it to the living room to sit on his knee. The food was piping hot and he blew on a forkful.

'What are you watching?'

'*Panorama*. It's a repeat - some old rubbish about The Tories. It's just on, I'm not really watching it. Change it if you want.'

'No, it's okay.' Daniel and his mum sat quietly while he ate his dinner. She counted her stitches, then swapped the knitting needles around and began again. Daniel placed his knife and fork onto the empty plate. 'That was great! I could eat it again.'

'Did you like that, son? That's good.'

'I loved it, aye.' Daniel stood up and put his tray into the kitchen. He locked the back door, then the front door. He returned to the kitchen and washed his plate, knife and fork, then dried them and put them away. He wiped the tray and put it back into the cupboard. 'Night, Mum, love you.' He kissed her cheek.

'Night, son, love you too,' she replied. She continued knitting and looked back at the man on television. The reporter was talking but she wasn't listening.

CHEEKY COW

Jackie didn't remember arriving at work, being at work or leaving work, all she knew was that she'd had a wonderful day. All her patients had been lovely and she didn't mind washing or making cups of tea for anyone, she felt like she was skating from bed to bed like Jayne Torvill. Viv had made a phone call to Jackie's ward from the phone box outside the hospital and instructed her to come down to the hospital car park for five minutes at lunchtime. Jackie sneaked down and told her how the evening had unfolded after she left, in which Viv delighted and responded with appropriate gasps and squeals.

On the bus home, Jackie thought about the kiss, replaying it over and over in her mind, and blushing at her own daring. She hoped beyond hope that Jean Paul had no plans to become a priest. She wondered if he'd phone, and ran through scenarios in her head of how she would answer.

She toyed between the enthusiasm of 'Hi! Hello! *Bon apres-midi*!' and playing it cool.

As the bus rumbled along the back street towards Airdrie, she looked out the window at the empty swings in the park and thought of little June, who still didn't know who her father was, but, at the very least, had stopped asking questions about the man with the flowers. Perhaps, if they became closer, she imagined a scenario where she could ask Jean Paul for advice and his wise warm words of Frenchness would soothe her into a solution.

As soon as she arrived home, the phone rang in the hall. The kitchen radio was turned up loudly and she could hear her dad singing along to Roy Orbison's *In Dreams*. Her heart danced with possibility.

'I'll get it!' she shouted excitedly, and she threw her coat over the bannister. She cleared her throat and lifted the receiver.

'Hello?'

'Jackie... how are you?'

Jackie's back stiffened. It wasn't the voice she was hoping to hear. She pulled the living room door almost closed.

'What do you want?'

'Now, now... that's not a very nice greeting.'

'What do you want, Tommy?' she asked again, standing taller.

'You know what I want, Jackie. I told you before, remember?'

Jackie slid down onto the chair. 'I'm afraid, I think the answer is no,' she said, rubbing her head.

'You need more time? Of course, take it. I understand, of course I do,' replied Tommy, almost in a whisper. 'Take your time, but not too much time, eh? I feel I've lost enough time already, Jackie, not seeing her grow up.' Taken aback by his somewhat new feelings towards June, Jackie parted her lips, but no words arrived. 'Look, this is my number. Why don't you write it down, and you can phone me when you've had a chance to have a proper think.' Jackie took a small pen from the drawer and wrote his phone number on the pad. 'It would be nice if you could come and see the flat. Both of you. Next week? I could even pick you up in the car and bring you over.' Jackie leaned her head back onto the staircase, searching her mind for a reply. 'Just give me one chance, just one. You'll see.'

June ran into the hall and shouted 'MUMMY!' and wrapped her arms around her. 'Who's on the phone? Hello, hello?' She tried to take the phone from her mother and Jackie held a finger to her mouth.

'Ha ha! She sounds like a proper wee handful,' said Tommy.

'I've got to go. I'll call you.'

'Don't take long.'

'I won't. Bye.' Jackie hung up the receiver and buried her face into her daughter's soft jumper.

'Who was that, Mummy?' she asked, again. Jackie didn't know what to say.

'Is that you home, Jackie? Who was on the phone, hen?' called Frank. Jackie took a deep breath and stood up to walk into the living room, holding June in her arms.

'Wrong number,' she said casually.

Daniel's mum was washing the dishes when he came into the kitchen with his empty plate.

'Another triumph, Mum!' he said. She smiled and handed him a tea towel.

'No problem, son. How was work, today?' He picked up a plate from the sink and began drying.

'Usual. The crazy sister in Ward 14 made me do the corners again. She gets more mental every week.'

'Is that her off Jackie's ward?'

'Aye.' He slid the dry plate onto the clean ones and lifted another wet and foamy one.

'You off out with Johnny this weekend?'

'Maybe. No plans yet.' They fell silent as they continued washing and drying.

'You don't see much of Jackie these days.'

'I see Jackie at work all the time.'

She lifted out a pile of clean cutlery and it rattled across the sink.

'Still, Johnny seems... he seems like a nice boy.' She took the dirty pot from dinner and submerged it into the dishwater. She looked down into the suds as the water rolled over the sides and swirled into the centre.

'Johnny's a good laugh, aye.' Daniel dried a fork, first the prongs, then the handle. He repeated this until they were all dry and in a neat pile.

'You will be careful, won't you?' She turned to look at his face, and he noticed the stress behind her eyes, her furrowed brow, her kind smile. He dried the knives a little bit faster, unsure of where his mother was going with her conversation.

'Mum, I'm always careful. I never get into fights or anything.' She placed her wet marigold hand onto his as he reached for a spoon.

'You will be *careful*, won't you?' she repeated, looking directly at him. Her eyes had a piercing glow.

'Mum, you know I am!' She looked away and held the scrubbing brush above the pot.

'Daniel. Son. Please. Just promise me.'

He placed the spoon gently on top of another spoon in the cutlery drawer. 'Mum, for goodness sake! I haven't even made any plans yet.' The words left his mouth, both in truth and despair, confused and plain, as he danced around her questions in pointed ignorance. 'Stop worrying so much,' he smiled, in an effort to calm her, and himself.

She concentrated on scrubbing the pot and put it upside down onto the sink and he picked it up and dried it. She wiped around the formica surfaces and the top of the cooker. Daniel looked on, his mind frozen, his head spaced. He felt like a storm was coming towards him, but his feet were held in place. He put the dry pot in the cupboard and pushed the tea towel into the plastic star holder with his thumb.

'I'm going upstairs,' he said, leaving the kitchen. She stood still, arms outstretched, leaning on the counter, a cloth held in her hand that she couldn't feel.

'Is that the kettle on, Barbara?' she heard her husband ask from next door. His voice seemed so far away, like he was calling from a different time zone.

'That's me away, hen.' Frank buttoned his black coat up to the neck and pulled his bunnet onto his head.

'Oh, okay, have a good time.' Jackie brushed June's hair as June brushed her doll's hair. 'Tell Bobby and Maureen I'm asking for them.'

'I will do. You should come in one week and see me in action. I'll tell you, there's not an empty glass to be found on any of them tables.'

'I can believe that, Dad. Bobby's lucky to have you.'

'Right cheerio, my darlin'.' Frank kissed June on the head and Jackie on the cheek before he left. No sooner had the door closed than the phone started ringing. June jumped up and ran to the hall and Jackie ran after her.

'Mummy get it, good girl, now. Hello?'

'Jackie, can I come over for a wee while?'

'Daniel! Of course. What's wrong? Is everything okay?'

'Aye, it's fine. I just need to get out of this house.'

'No problem. Get here whenever. My dad's away out.'

Jackie hung up the receiver. She had never heard Daniel sound like that before. She took June upstairs to bed and read her the next chapter in her bedtime story. The little girl drifted into sleep, comforted by her thumb and the sweet soothing tones of her mother's voice.

Jackie was tidying up June's toys in the living room when the back door opened and closed. Daniel came in and flopped down onto the couch.

'Hiya. Cup of tea?' Daniel nodded. Jackie made the tea in silence and returned with two hot mugs and a plate of Bourbon biscuits.

'So... what's up? You sounded really panicky on the phone.' She handed him the cup. He took it and refused a Bourbon.

'No ta... I'm okay. It's just... my mum... She's doing my head in. I'll just stay here for a while if that's okay. I'll go home after she's in bed.'

'Stay as long as you like. *Your* mum though? I don't believe that! She's the loveliest woman *ever*.'

'Yeah, well, you're not with her all the time. She's not nipping at your head to do dishes and tidy your room. Talking to you like you're a big baby.' Jackie sipped her tea and glanced at the framed picture of her mum. 'Sorry, Jackie, I didn't think there...'

'It's okay.'

'I'm an idiot.'

'No, you're not. Don't worry about it.'

'I'm not getting anything right at the moment.'

'What do you mean?'

'My work, my pals, my mum... I just need to move out of that house. Fat chance of that with the job I do. I'd never make the rent.'

'I know what you mean. Same here. We could always move in with Viv!'

'Aye, right! As if she'd have us messing up her palace. By the way, did Thorn Birds phone?'

'No, not yet! I haven't heard a peep. I thought he might have phoned today but my dad said there were no calls.'

'I suppose it's only been one day. Are you staying in, just in case the phone goes?'

'I keep picking it up to check there's a dial tone. And then I double triple check it's hung up properly! Then I check it's plugged into the wall!' They laughed in unison. 'There was one phone call, but it was bloody - guess who? - Tommy. Asking to see June.'

'God, he's not letting it go, is he? You'll need to make a decision soon or he could get the social involved. They might say he's entitled to see her.'

'I know. He asked us to go over next week.'

'As much as I can't stand the guy, you should probably go, Jackie.'

'I'd have to tell June first... that he's her dad.'

'Oh, man, that's a nightmare. Do you believe him, when he says he's changed?' Daniel sipped his tea.

'I honestly don't know. I try not to think about it.'

'Will I stick the telly on?'

'Go on then.' Daniel jumped up and switched on the television. 'I've got *Wogan* taped. And this week's *Top Of The Pops*,' she said.

'Oh, cool, Who's on *Wogan*?'

'Larry Grayson. Do you like him?'

'*Shut that door!*' Daniel did Larry's catchphrase as best he could and Jackie laughed.

'*What a gay day!*' she replied. 'I love him. So does my dad. He loves Kenny Everett as well.'

'I know he does. And Freddie! Your dad loves all the poofs!'

'Daniel! Don't say that! And anyway, Dad doesn't know they're gay. He thinks Freddie is a man's man with his vest and tight jeans and all his get up.'

'Freddie is King Queer! He's actually Queen Queer! Your dad *must* know by now. His picture is in that paper every day, parties and boyfriends in his crown and cape.'

'I swear my dad doesn't know and if he does know, he definitely doesn't mention it.'

'Would it bother him?'

'What? If he knew Freddie was gay? Good question. I don't know. I don't think so. He's pretty open minded. Any time *I Want To Break Free* comes on the radio, he's out with the Hoover.'

Daniel laughed. 'I know. Remember he did that at June's christening? Mrs Morrisson's face was a picture.'

'You know what he's like. Any excuse and he's up.'

'It would bother my dad. Definitely. You want to hear him when he reads about it. He says the gay plague is *them getting what they deserve.'*

'Tell him it's not the fault of gay people. HIV started in Africa, anyone can get it. Straight people get it too. Even people like your dad. From blood transfusions and all sorts. It's actually very scary.'

'I know! It's terrifying! I've read the leaflet that came through the door! Bloody "AIDS KILLS"! My dad says that the gay community are to blame as they are the ones that keep on spreading it about.'

'Everybody would be okay if they use a condom. And they give them away for free at the clinic.'

'Or just don't do it in the first place! It's dicing with death! It used to be just about catching crabs or getting somebody up the duff.'

'All right, Daniel.' Jackie shook her head.

'Oh, sorry... I forgot you got pregnant.'

Jackie rolled her eyes and leaned over to press play on the video recorder. She sat down and folded her arms. The *Wogan* titles rolled up again and again as the picture jumped, then stabilised. They sat and listened as Larry told a story of how he and his friend used a tandem bike to ride up the hills of Torquay.

'His "friend",' said Daniel to Jackie. Daniel made a limp wrist. 'His special friend! I bet!' He continued to watch the television. Jackie felt that Daniel seemed a little agitated, not his usual gentle self. There was a hard edge to his words and she felt something much more than his mum was bothering him. She couldn't remember the last time he seemed happy. His head always hung low at work, he never mentioned girls, and he had very few friends. She thought of something her mum used to say, 'The best place to hide is in plain sight'. Her own thoughts poked round inside her head like tiny paper planes. Jackie felt she may have concluded incorrectly, but she needed to know.

'Is *Top Of The Pops* taped straight after this finishes?' Daniel asked.

'Yes, it comes on after a few minutes. Can I ask you something?'

'Mmm-hmm. Check him flicking his tie. Camp or what!'

'You won't take offence?'

'What do you mean, take offence?'

'Are you... are you, you know...' she pointed at Larry Grayson. 'Are you... have you got... anything in common with Larry?'

'Eh? You are *joking*. Is this cos of what we've just been talking about?'

'I don't mean, are you like him, you know, camp and all that, I mean, you know.'

'Are you asking me if I'm a poof?'

'I'm just asking, I don't mean any offence, and it's really fine, I'm really fine with it.'

'Are you kidding me, Jackie?' Daniel's face reddened and he crawled down onto the floor to hit the button labelled 'FFWD'. Jackie sat forward in her chair, her back straight. She was never more certain. Everything suddenly made sense. Daniel sat back on the couch. She turned and looked straight into his face.

'Are you gay?'

He stared back at her, catching his breath after hearing the word. This accusation, again, from someone else, except Jackie hadn't danced around it like Johnny or his mum, she had pointed it directly at him like a bow and arrow. He had nowhere to look and no answer ready. The boldness of her bubbled up inside him.

'That's none of your business!' he said, abruptly. 'How... how DARE you ask me that!' Daniel knocked his cup to the floor as he stood up to leave. Jackie stood up after him and grabbed his arm.

'Daniel, you don't have to pretend with me. All this 'poofs' business. I know it isn't you; you don't mean it. You're just doing it to try to fit in. You're just playing at being a bigoted old man. You're not Alf Garnett! It's not you.' He pulled away from her and headed to the kitchen door but she got there before him and stood in front of it.

'Move. Move, Jackie. I want to go.'

'Not until you've answered me.'

'Move!'

'I'll move after you answer me.'

'There's nothing to tell!'

'Well, if there's nothing to tell, say no then.'

'Okay, then. No.'

'Daniel, stop lying. We both know that you came over here to tell me something, so just tell me. Just say it. Stop carrying it around like a burden. It's okay to share it.' Jackie reached up to his shoulder and felt it stiffen.

'I need to go home, Jackie.'

'No, you don't. I'm not letting you run away. Let's go back in and sit down. You're safe here. It's... whatever it is... is safe with me, and I won't tell a soul.' She felt him soften and helped him turn around and move back into the living room and onto the couch, like she had so many times for her dad when he was tired after a walk or he couldn't find his slippers.

Daniel rubbed each side of his head. He melted into his words in a whisper, angrily, sheepishly, almost in surrender.

'I'm not like them.'

'I never said you were.'

'Larry Grayson, Kenny Everett, John Inman, Danny La Rue.' He pointed to the television. 'All figures of fun. *That's* how gay people are seen. I'm not like that. I'm not one of them.'

'You don't have to *be* one of them. They're people off the telly. It's not the same. You can just be like... you, like Daniel. You don't have to be camp to be gay.'

'So what am I? A guy that walks around with a big shameful secret?'

'Now you listen to me. It is not shameful! There's nothing to be ashamed of. Nothing!'

'Imagine if my dad knew, Jackie... he'd kill me! And my mum... it would be the end of her... of me... she'd be crushed.'

'You don't know that.'

'Yes, I do.'

'Your mum and dad don't have to know right now. There's no rush to tell *anybody*.'

'The worst thing is, I think she suspects. She keeps telling me to *be careful*.'

'She might just be saying that. Mums say things like that.'

'And I'm not like the men in the clubs either, dancing and feeling free... I just don't fit in anywhere!'

'You've been to one of those gay clubs? With the blacked out windows?' Daniel nodded. 'Did you go with... Johnny? Is he...?' Daniel nodded again. 'Oh, God! Of course he is,' Jackie said to herself. 'Why didn't I see it?' She shook her head. 'He is the spit of Jimmy Somerville.'

Daniel mumbled into his hands, 'Maybe you're more like your dad that you realise.' Jackie smirked. She could see Daniel half-smile through his fingers. He looked up. 'Jackie, what am I going to do?' His giant pupils were as wide as the black core of a sunflower. 'I can't be... I just can't.'

'Yes, you can.' Jackie moved closer to him and pushed his blond hair behind his ear. 'And you're going to do nothing. We're going to just sit here and be happy, together, Daniel. For a minute.' She held both of his hands. 'Happy that you are who you are, and that you were brave enough to finally, well, let's say finally let me figure it out. Now come here.' She pulled him into a cuddle.

'Well done, Daniel, honestly, well done.'

'Careful, you might catch something.'

'Right. A cold from a virgin.'.

'Cheeky cow,' he replied, wiping a small tear.

IN THE CLUB

'And how's Viv? Saw her the other night,' Frank shouted to Bessie Smith as the Working Men's Club house band Misty performed their rendition of Jive Bunny and The Master Mixers' *Swing The Mood* and couples jived and spun past their table.

'She's fine. She popped in to see us on her way out. She said she was staying in but she had half a ton of make-up on the face and the perfume was stinking out the kitchen.'

'At least the make-up isn't on our towels anymore!' shouted Tam Smith. 'She'd wipe her face and it was like a clown looking back at you!' He laughed and they laughed with him.

'Are we getting up to dance, Tam? We're the only couple sitting down.'

'We'll see how my leg goes.'

'This is a good one!'

'It's nearly finished.'

'Right, I'm off to get these back to the bar. See youse in a wee while!'

Frank carried his full tray of glasses back through the long tables. He pushed a few chairs in with his hips and kicked a handbag out of the way. He slipped past the bar queue and into the back sink where one of the barmaids was waiting to wash the glasses. Maureen was busy pulling a pint and Bobby was chatting by the door. His face didn't look its usual jovial self and he was gesticulating towards the street and then back inside towards the bar. Frank took a clean tray and ambled over towards the tables nearest to Bobby. He managed to make out the words 'He's barred' and could see that Bobby was wound up by the news he had received.

'Everything okay, Bobby?'

'Aye it's fine, Frank. That Tommy just tried to worm his way in here. As if we'd let him in after what he did the last time. I sent him on his way.' Bobby dusted his hands.

'No, you never!' the other man replied, 'it was Alec that got rid of him!'

'Under my instruction!' Bobby scowled at the man. He stood as tall as he could, folded his arms and looked towards Maureen. 'He's not getting back in here,' he mumbled.

Tommy stood in the street opposite The Working Men's Club with his hands in his pockets. He glared at the sign.

'It's all changed in there anyway', said Terry.

'That place never changes.'

'Look, I can do a quick pint somewhere else, then I've got to get off.' Terry twisted his watch.

'Off where?'

'I've got to go, it's my mum, she's not well.'

'What's the matter with her?'

'She's got a sore knee. Can't get about much.'

'So sit her in front of the telly with a cup of tea and a bun. No knee-d to use her knee then, is there?' Tommy sneered at his own comment. Terry looked at his watch.

'Like I said, I've got to go soon. Sorry, Tommy.'

'You'll go when I say you can go.' He paused and removed a cigarette from the packet. 'Now, let's find a pub. The Staging Post will do. They won't remember me in there. Or Penny's. What's it like in Penny's now?'

'It's okay but it's very quiet. Boring, really – not your scene. What about we go up to The Double A?' Terry began walking quickly, ushering Tommy up towards the other side of town.

'What is that aftershave? It's sticking in my throat.'

'Oh, it's just *Mesmerise*. My mum got me it for my birthday, do you not like it?'

'You want to go back to carbolic.'

Terry nodded. He rubbed his neck, worried he had over-sprayed for his special evening.

'Hold on! Why are we going all the way up to The Double A again, when there are pubs down here?

'The Staging Post is full of kids. There's no talent in there, Tommy! It's all in The Double A. Everybody goes there now.' Terry held two thumbs up as he said 'double'.

A taxi drove towards them with its amber light on. Tommy put his arm out and it swung around in a U-turn. The driver rolled the window down.

'Double A.' He opened the passenger side door and motioned for the driver to move his unopened bag of crisps and cigarettes off the seat. The driver put the cigarettes into his top pocket and shoved the crisps down the side of the door. Tommy swept into the seat as if the vehicle was his. Terry got into the back and shut the door. The driver asked Tommy to put his seat belt on but he waved him away. Instead Tommy pushed the buttons to change the channel on the radio. The driver shook his head. Tommy pushed five different buttons, until he found the intro to *Every 1's a Winner* by Hot Chocolate. The driver nodded along.

'Good one this. Classic,' he said. Tommy ignored him and pulled down the sun visor and slid open the vanity mirror.

Terry checked his watch again. If he could get Tommy chatting to a girl in The Double A within half an hour, he'd be able to slip away quietly, unnoticed and hopefully unwanted. Then he could grab a taxi and get to the other end of town, to Penny's, where hopefully, he'd arrive just before his date did. Terry smiled to himself.

'What are you smirking at?' demanded Tommy, his eyes framed in the rectangular mirror.

'Was I? Nothing! Nothing at all!'

They pulled up outside the club. Tommy flipped the visor up with a flick of his finger and opened the door. He put one leg out, then turned to Terry. 'Pay the man,' he said, exiting the cab. Terry mouthed 'Sorry about him' to the driver, as he had done, to so many people, over so many years.

'No bother. Be lucky, mate,' he replied.

Jackie couldn't get any answer from Viv's phone so thought she might have had an early night. She removed a cooked ham from the fridge and sat it beside the buttered bread. She cut a thick slice of the salty meat and placed it between two white slabs of bread. She cut the sandwich in two, then placed it onto a plate and covered it with a tea towel. She put a tea bag into a mug and boiled the kettle. She removed a pad and pen from the drawer and wrote, *DAD. EAT THIS.*

She drew a little heart, then signed 'Jackie' with a kiss. She put the note next to the sandwich and kettle, put the ham back in the fridge and headed up to bed with a mixture of thoughts of Daniel, Tommy, her mum and June, and a strong hope that Jean Paul would call tomorrow. She fell asleep thinking of the complete and utter love she had for little June and her dad, how strong he had been to take back her mum all those years ago.

As Misty hit their stride in the Working Men's Club with *Baby Jane,* every couple, including Betty and Tam, took to the floor. Frank sashayed around, enjoying the music and collecting his final round of glasses before finishing his shift. With a tray piled high, he approached the side door of the bar and heard Bobby and Maureen in a heated discussion. He paused by the door, unsure of whether to enter.

'Well, why, oh why, would he be trying to get in here? Of all places? There are plenty of other places he could go.'

'You know what he's like, Bobby! He likes to stir up trouble. That's his game. That's all he does!'

'I think it was more than that.'

'Bobby, stop! This petty jealousy has to stop! He is not in any way interested in me! Nor me him. Why can't you see it's only you I love?'

'I can, I just think... well, I just think he's after you, that's all.' Frank heard that as his cue to push the door.

'He's not after Maureen, nope,' he announced, placing the tray on the sink.

'Were you listening at the door?'

'I wasn't *listening* per se, I just *heard*.' The three stood staring at each other until Frank spoke, pointing to Maureen. 'She's right, and you're wrong. He's not after her. This I know for definite.' Maureen shrugged her shoulders at Bobby.

'What do you know, for definite, then?' asked Bobby.

'I bet he wants Jackie back, doesn't he?' asked Maureen. Frank nodded. 'I can't believe him.'

'Believe it.'

'Will Jackie take him back, then?'

'She's just thinking things through for now. He wants to see the wean. I doubt she'd make that mistake in taking him back, she's a damn sight smarter than she was.' Frank grabbed his jacket and bunnet off the hook. He put the bunnet on his head and buttoned his jacket right up to the neck.

'Pint before you go, Frank?'

'No thanks, Bobby, that's me done. You'll only have a few more rounds to do. There are no more glasses out there.'

Bobby reached into the till and took out £20. 'You're a gent, Frank, here you go. Thanks for your help.' As Frank said goodbye and left the club, Bobby pulled Maureen close. 'I'm sorry, my angel,' he said quietly. 'I just don't want anything coming between us.'

'It's okay, my stallion, nothing could ever do that.'

Tommy shook hands with the bouncers inside the club who seemed to recognise him. Terry scanned the room and vaguely recognised two girls from Cairnhill. One had long red hair and the other had long black hair. They giggled as the red head slid down a pillar and the black-haired girl helped her up again.

'Putty,' said Tommy over Terry's shoulder, 'Pure. Putty. Get the drinks in, Terry, you can watch the master at work.'

'I think they're quite nice girls,' Terry shouted into Tommy's ear as they waited for their drinks. 'I vaguely remember them from the other school, couple of years younger than us. They're sisters, I think. Not sure they live round here anymore.' Terry paid the barman as Tommy watched the girls and sipped his pint. They walked over to get a drink.

'Come here often?' called Tommy, as he moved towards them with his elbow on the bar.

'Depends whose asking.'

'What's your names?'

'Amanda.'

'Shamanada,' they giggled.

'But you can call me Mandy.'

'And you can call me Shandy.'

'Are those your real names?'

'Might be!' Shandy poked Tommy in the chest. 'Now, what are you buying us to drink?'

'Well, what are you drinking, little Miss Cheeky?'

'Let's get a cocktail!' She grabbed the cocktail list and perused it, her sister peeking over her shoulder.

'Have they got any Dirty Bananas?' asked Mandy.

'I don't think so.'

'I'll just have a Blue Lagoon then. I've seen that film so it must be nice. What's in it? It's a lovely colour...'

'Doesn't matter. You'll like it. Just get her a Blue Lagoon, and I'll have a Woo Woo please.'

Tommy waved the barman over.

'Woooooo! Woooooo!' Shandy spun in a circle. Mandy laughed and pulled a train horn. 'Woooooo! Woooooo!' They threw their heads back and laughed so hard that Mandy dropped her bag.

'Oh! Dropped my bag!' she shouted, crossing her legs and laughing. She bent down to pick it up and Tommy bent down with her.

'Let me get that for you,' he offered. Her red hair fell forward onto her face and he gently pushed it back.

'Thanks!' she said. The barman placed their drinks on the bar and Shandy asked for straws for both of them. As Tommy checked out the two girls, he decided that Shandy was a bit too stand-offish for his taste and that Terry could work on her. He was going to put all of his focus onto Mandy, then maybe reel Shandy in afterwards, if Terry wasn't interested.

'So, a cracker like you must have a boyfriend, somewhere.' He leaned into Mandy's face. 'You not with anybody tonight?'

'I'm keeping my options open.' Mandy nudged Shandy.

'Options open, legs closed, as your mother used to say!' They both erupted into shards of laughter.

Tommy gave a hesitant laugh.

'Very wise. I'm sure a couple of knockouts like you could have your pick of the place.' He waved his hands up and down at their outfits.

'Oh, please stop!'

'No, keep it coming!' laughed Mandy.

Shandy put a finger in her throat as if to be sick and Mandy told her to behave herself.

'Where are you from?' she slurred.

'Here and there. Up and down. Round and about. Down south, up north. All over. I have an apartment in Coatbridge at the moment.'

'Oh! An "apartment" in Coatbridge. Do you mean a flat, aye? I think he means a flat. Is it Council or private?' Mandy nudged Shandy to be quiet.

'It's private.'

'That's nice. You married? Leave the wife and kids at home, tonight, did you?' Mandy winked and gulped the blue drink through her straw. It made a loud bubbling noise as it rattled against the ice cubes. Her eyelashes fluttered as she looked coyly over the edge of the glass.

'I'm not married and I don't have a girlfriend, but I do have a wee girl. She has red hair, like you.'

'No way! Your wee girl has red hair? Oh, my God, so have I! I've got red hair as well! That's amazing! What age is she?' Mandy's eyes widened, and Tommy was confident he could reel her in. Women could never resist a man with a baby. The Athena poster had taught him that.

Shandy looked towards the dance floor. Terry excused himself to the toilet and Tommy waved him away to continue his chat with Mandy.

'I'm going to have lots of weans,' she continued, 'absolutely loads of babies. The more the merrier as far as I'm concerned.'

'Well, if you need practice...' Tommy winked. He gave as much charm as he could muster but noticed that she continued as if she didn't seem to hear him.

'And five poodles. I *love* their curly wurly curls! Actually I might have six poodles... six is my lucky number.'

'Six is actually my –'

'Captain Sensible!' Shandy dropped her drink on the bar and grabbed Mandy's arm.

'Come *on*!'

'I don't really like this...'

'You do!'

Mandy nodded towards Tommy to join them but he waited with his drink. He watched them take the centre of the floor. Two men tapped them on the shoulder to dance. Tommy stood taller, grinding his teeth. He felt annoyed that he had invested the time with them and now somebody else was going to swoop in. He lifted his pint, paused it to his lips then downed it in one.

Terry returned from the toilet to see Tommy walking towards the girls on the dance floor. His plan had worked flawlessly. He exited the club, down the stairs and flagged a taxi. It happened to be the same driver as he had before.

'All right, mate, no luck then?'

'Not yet, pal. Can you take me down to Penny's, please?'

'Aye, jump in.' Terry jumped in the back and ringed his hands, smiling.

'Do you mind if I say something?' asked the driver.

'No, go ahead?'

'See that guy that was in the taxi with you earlier … is he a good pal of yours?'

'Aye… well, kinda. We've known each other since school, you know?'

'Ah, fair play. I just thought he was a bit cheeky.'

'He speaks to everybody like that.'

'I'm just saying. No offence, like.'

'None taken. You're not the first to say it, mate. I'm Terry, by the way.'

'Good to meet you, Terry. Ronnie.' He reached one hand back to shake Terry's. They drove down through Airdrie while Janet Jackson sung quietly on the radio, asking what had been done for her lately. Terry considered, not for the first time, why Tommy treated everyone so badly, including his supposed best friend.

'That's eighty pence, please, pal.'

Terry gave him a pound note and waved goodbye. He stood up outside Penny's and straightened his jacket. Shoulders back, he walked in, ten minutes early for his late evening drink with Viv.

'She said Captain!
I said, Wot?
She said Captain?
I said Wot?'
She said Captain!
I said Wot?
She said Captain!
I said WOT YOU WANT?'

Mandy and Shandy were singing into each other's faces and flicking their hair. Tommy glared into the eyes of the two guys that were dancing with them and they walked away immediately. The girls turned toward Tommy as he stretched out his arms to motion them in closer. As they sang the song, their hair flicking got harder and harder and Tommy had to move back as he was getting whipped in the face or catching giant clumps of it in his mouth. A strand of Mandy's hair was stuck to her lip gloss and she pulled it away as she danced closer to Tommy.

'How about another drink?' he suggested.

'SHOTS!' the sisters shouted, in unison. Shandy grabbed Mandy's hand and ran her to the bar. Tommy scowled, hoping he wouldn't have to pay for *three* drinks. He looked around for Terry who was nowhere to be seen. By the time he pushed through the dancers and arrived at the bar, there were six shots lined up in a row. The girls also had six shots each but three of their glasses had been turned upside down already.

'What is it?'

'Flaming Sambuca. Get it down you.'

'What's the matter? You never had a shot before?'

'Behave yourself! Witness the master.' Tommy blew the flames out and rattled the six shots off one by one. The girls cheered and ordered the same again. Mandy winked at him.

'I'm very impressed with you, Don Corleone,' she said.

'Actually my name is –'

'Shh!' She placed a finger on his lips, squashing them slightly. 'We'll be calling you Don Corleone, for tonight.' He held her finger there and moved in to kiss her but her arm had been snatched away and her body tugged out of his grasp by her sister, who was dragging her back to the dance floor.

'£28, please,' said the barman.

'What?'

'Youse had thirty-six shots there. £28.'

'For Christ on a Bike! These WOMEN! Did they tell you I was paying?'

'They just nodded towards you.'

'Bloody hell, I'd better be getting something from this tonight.' He searched around for Terry. Reluctantly, he opened his wallet and handed the barman thirty pounds. Without thinking about asking for the change, he put his wallet back into his jacket, then walked unsteadily back towards the dance floor to look for the girls. He circled the club twice, getting confused by the gigantic mirrors and the different lights on the floor. He searched for Terry and couldn't find him. By the time he found Mandy and Shandy, they were back at the bar.

'Here we go, we got you a snakebite!' Tommy took the drink and sipped it.

'I hope you don't think I'm paying for this?' he complained.

'Be quiet, it's already paid for. DOWN IT! DOWN IT,' they chanted. He poured the cider and lager mixture down his throat and slammed the glass on the bar.

'WOO HOO! CHECK OUT THE DON!' shouted Mandy as she raised her glass. 'ANOTHER ROUND!' Some people at the bar cheered. Tommy leaned into both of them.

'Who fancies coming back to my place to keep the party going?' he slurred.

'Maybe later, we'll see how it goes,' said Mandy.

'I'm not going all the way down to Coatbridge!' shouted Shandy.

'On the edge, you, aren't you? You should be more like your sister and relax!' He reached out to touch Mandy's chin and Shandy pulled his hand away.

'Hands off her! Who told you we were sisters? We never told you we were sisters.'

'I guessed.'

'Oh, aye, been checking up on us, have you? Fancy yourself as a bit of a Poirot, do you?'

'I think he just fancies himself!' The two girls erupted in laughter. Tommy rubbed his head. He stared at Mandy's sequined belt as it reflected the disco ball and colours of the club.

'Oh! David Bowie! C'mon, Mandy! Let's dance!' Shandy ran off, knowing her sister would be right behind her.

'C'mon, The Don!'

Tommy felt one of his arms being yanked forward to the centre of the dance floor. He swayed from girl to girl as the lights spun around him.

'I'm going to the toilet,' he shouted towards them.

'What?'

'Toilet!'

'Over there,' Shandy pointed.

'I know where it is!' he shouted back at her. He walked through the club towards the Gents. A man walked towards him, out of the crowds. He was dressed in a suit like Tommy's and his arms moved in the same way. As he walked, the man got closer and closer. He even had hair like him. He felt for his knife in his trouser pocket, but it wasn't there. He immediately regretted not bringing it. He clenched his fists. Still he walked towards him! The gall! He wanted to ask him who the hell he thought he was staring at. This guy was going to get a good hiding. He was almost face-to-face with him when he leaned forward and slammed his forehead into his, as hard as he could. He felt immediate, searing pain and fell backwards to the floor, down onto his elbows. The other guy was gone. He had won. He heard people shouting and laughing.

'Oh, my God! That guy just took a header into the mirror!'

Frank finished off the last few bites of the sandwich that Jackie had made for him. He stood in the kitchen, chewing the crusts. Feeling too exhausted to make a cup of tea, he removed the teabag from the cup and filled it with cold tap water. He drank it all down and put the cup and plate in the sink, then locked the back door. He crept up the stairs and popped his head around Jackie's bedroom door.

'That's me in, hen, all locked up. Thanks for making me the piece, it was lovely and tasty.'

'No problem, Dad. Did you have a good night?' she asked, drowsily.

'All fine, hen. You go back to sleep. Night night.'

'Night night, Dad.'

Jackie was happy that he was home and safe. She struggled to get back to sleep, feeling freezing cold from her toes to her nose. She tucked her covers in as tightly as she could and waited for sleep to greet her. An hour later, she was still awake, listening to her dad's familiar snore from the next room. She kept her eyes closed, her body still and icy cold. Her shoulders shivered. Try as she might, she just couldn't heat up. She thought of getting up to find some bed socks and an extra blanket.

Slowly, she opened her eyes, expecting darkness, but strange lights danced above her. Stunning flashes of white light were suspended in the air above her body. They swooped and danced across each other, sometimes looking like lightning bolts and shooting stars crossing and diving and winding in a pattern like a kaleidoscope. She didn't feel afraid, she knew what it was, and she was happy to see it. It was one of the most beautiful sights she had ever seen. After the lights had conducted their dance, they swooped down upon her, and held a still focus above her feet. The tips of her toes began to warm up and the lights carefully and slowly moved up her body. Both her feet became warm, as if soft, warm wax was seeping onto her skin. The lights moved to her calves, then her legs, then her body, her shoulders, neck, face, up to the top of her head, right up to the crown, warming her through and through. She felt aglow, like a log fire was crackling above her. The heat travelled through her body and deep down into the mattress. She was warm again. Jackie smiled and closed her eyes. She drifted off, as the lights disappeared.

Terry was pleased to see that Penny's wasn't too crowded and there were a few free tables. After he said hello to Alyn and Jim at the bar, he took a seat down in the back.

He watched the door and he saw her walking in. She paused to say hello to a few people before she looked around and spotted Terry and waved. He stood up. She sashayed down towards him, her long coat open and flowing, and he breathed in her strong floral scent as she approached. He pulled out a chair for her and wiped it down with his hand.

'What a gentleman!' she smiled.

'Thanks, um, for meeting me, and that. Would you like a drink?'

'I'll have a white wine, please. We're in a wine bar, after all.' He nodded and went to the bar to get her drink.

Viv removed her coat and looked around as she patted her hair. She saw Alyn and Jim raise their eyebrows and give Terry a friendly punch. He blushed a little, then paid for her wine before returning to the table.

'Here you go. I got you a medium, is that okay?'

'It's lovely, thank you.'

They sat in silence for a few minutes, looking up at the TVs and sipping.

'I really love how you do your make-up.'

'Oh, thanks! I should be good at it by now.'

'I love all the colours.' Viv smiled and said thanks again. She struggled to find something to say. She begged herself not to talk about the number of people in the bar, but in the end, it was all she had.

'Quite quiet in here for a Saturday, isn't it?'

'It normally gets busy about now.'

'Oh.'

'Listen, thanks for meeting me. I wasn't sure if you would.'

'Why wouldn't I?'

'Oh, I don't know. Just, Tommy and Jackie, I suppose. She's your pal; he's mine. I had to go out with him earlier, that's why I arranged a later time.'

'Oh, that's okay. I had some stuff to do anyway,' Viv lied. Terry didn't need to know she had been ready since six thirty. 'I think I recognise your aftershave, is it an Avon one?'

'I don't know, to be honest with you. My mum got it for me. It's called *Mesmerise*.'

'Oh, that's definitely one of mine. You'll have to tell your mum I work for Avon. If she ever needs anything, I can get it for her.'

'Oh! Would you like to meet my mum one day?'

'Ha ha! Steady on!'

'God, she'd probably keel over if I brought a woman home.'

'Have you never brought somebody home before?'

'Well. I've had girlfriends but, I don't know. It's never worked out. She never met any of them.'

'Oh.' Viv took a large sip of her drink. She felt more nervous than she would normally and wasn't sure why. Luckily Terry seemed a bit more nervous than her.

'God. Ha ha! This is mad, isn't it?' He sat back in his chair and looked at her.

'Yeah, definitely.' She blushed.

'Ready for another?' Terry jumped up.

'Oh, no! Don't you dare! My round. Women's lib!' she pointed, awkwardly, unsure if it was funny.

Thankfully, Terry laughed and sat back down. He watched her as she walked up to the bar in her towering white heels. Alyn winked and Jim gave her a friendly nudge.

Terry giggled at the scene and looked at the floor. Viv returned to the table with the drinks.

'So how did it go with Tommy?' she asked, taking a sip.

'You know what he's like. I just left him in The Double A. There were these two girls he just honed in on. I vaguely remember them from years ago, from the other school, St Margaret's. Pretty sure they're sisters.'

'Oh, I went to St Margaret's. What did they look like? Were they my age?'

'Yeah. They were in their twenties. One had long, long, red hair and the other one had long black hair. I don't think they live round here anymore.'

'Oh, my God!' exclaimed Viv. She sat back in her chair and put a hand over her mouth. 'Was one of them quite flirty and the other one quite cheeky?'

'I don't know really, it was Tommy that was talking to them. I was just trying to get out of there to get down here.'

'HA!' screamed Viv. 'I think that's the Cassidy sisters! Oh, my God. They will eat. Him. Alive.'

'Oh! Ha ha! He might like that!'

'Oh, no no no no. I can assure you, he won't. I remember those girls from school. They are feral.'

'You all right, Tommy, pal? Here, let's get you up.' Tommy looked up. Two of the club bouncers loomed over him. He blinked - it could have been four.

'What happened?'

'You banged your nut on the mirror. Happens a lot in here.'

They helped him up.

'Don't worry, we'll look after him.' Mandy and Shandy marched over and looped their arms into Tommy's.

'Oh, I don't know... Have you seen Terry?' Tommy tried to protest.

'You sure, girls?' Maybe take it easy on the shots, eh?'

'You got it, Rocky. No more shots.' Shandy saluted. They marched Tommy back over to an empty table near the bar. 'You okay, Don Corleone? We were worried about you – couldn't see you after you went to the toilet, then suddenly there was this big circle all crowded round you.'

'I'm fine. Am I bleeding?'

'No. No blood. Just a wee bump. Hold this wet tissue on it.' Mandy dabbed his head with a piece of soaked toilet roll.

'You'll be fine. Drink some water.'

'Did you get me a water?' asked Shandy.

'Well, it's the same *colour* as water.' They both exploded with laughter again. Tommy looked on at the two girls, bewildered as to how they were still standing. They both looked as fresh as if they had just arrived. He sipped his water. His head spun like he was inside a tumble dryer.

'All better?' Mandy asked. He nodded. 'Right then. You wait here and we'll have a wee dance, then we'll be back to check on you.' They downed their drinks and headed to the dancefloor.

Tommy nodded. He looked around for Terry.

'He's not a nice guy, Terry. He's a liar, you know that. It was terrible how he treated Jackie. He left her with nothing. Not that she ever wanted anything from him, but that's not the point.'

'I know. I feel bad about that.'

'It's not your fault, but why do you still hang around with him?'

'I don't know. Just habit, I suppose.'

'Are you scared of him?'

'No. Well, not really, I mean, he can be pretty violent if he wants to, but never with me. I know his reputation... I know it's not good. I've seen him in action.'

'You know he's been trying to get back with Jackie? Taking her flowers, spinning her lies about how he's changed? He told her he's finished with women, his bad life. And now he's up in The Double A doing it all again? I mean, how can he think that he won't be seen or caught?'

'I thought he was just out on the razzle dazzle. I didn't know that he was trying to get back with Jackie. I had no idea. I suppose, as you say, he'll just lie and charm his way out of it.'

'You don't *have* to be friends with him, or work for him, Terry. You could go back to the market. It's an honest job. Besides, my dad is missing your apples. He says they really were the freshest. Dead crunchy and tasty. He liked your floury potatoes as well. My poor mum is on a permanent search for floury potatoes now.'

'Did he say that? Ha ha! I've always liked your dad. Your mum's nice too, she was up at my stall every week. I did enjoy the market. I've been thinking about it a lot, lately.'

'Last orders at the bar, please!' called the barmaid.

'Nothing for me, do you want another?' Viv reached for her bag.

'No, I'm good. I was wondering if it would be okay to walk you up the road?'

'That would be nice,' she said.

Alyn and Jim smiled and nodded goodbye.

The morning sunlight flickered across Tommy's face. He opened his eyes. His back hurt, and he realised that he was lying on the couch. He sat up quickly and looked around to check if he was alone. He felt a tightness around his stomach and looked down to see that he was wearing a sequined belt. He tore at the buckle to get it off and threw it across the room. The previous night's events flooded back through his brain like a burst dam.

'They lassies,' he seethed. He coughed and felt around the table for his cigarettes. He found them crumpled in his jacket pocket. He snapped off the end of a bent one and lit up and took a deep drag. He reached for his wallet and found it intact, with a few notes left in it. He tossed it back down on the coffee table and walked through to the kitchen and switched on the coffee machine. In the highly polished kettle, he saw his reflection. His hair was its usual messy morning style, but his expression looked different, a strange colour. He looked full of surprise. As the coffee filled the mug, he walked swiftly to the bathroom mirror to see his face was covered in eye shadow, blusher and lipstick. A large bump was sticking out of his forehead and a circle had been drawn around it. Two eyebrows had been drawn high on his forehead. He turned on the tap and scrubbed at the make-up. He looked back in the mirror. Most of it was gone, except the black arched eyebrows and the circle which remained just as black as before. He scrubbed again, but it didn't fade. He punched the sink and let out a howl.

PLUS ONE

Jackie and Frank were eating fried eggs on toast for breakfast when the phone rang in the hall and Jackie jumped up to answer it. She felt her heart sink to her knees when she heard the familiar jolly tones of Bobby.

She handed the receiver to her dad as he stood waiting in the hall with a napkin tucked into his shirt and a little bit of brown sauce on his cheek. She wiped the sauce off his face.

'It's Bobby,' she said. He shrugged as if to apologise. Jean Paul had not been in contact for weeks.

She half listened to her dad in the hall, laughing and seeming very happy about some news. After much excited chat, he said goodbye and waltzed his way back into the living room, as if dancing with an imaginary June.

'Well, you'll never guess what?'

'What?'

'You will *never* guess.'

'Bobby's won the pools?'

'Nope! Guess again!'

'Bobby and Maureen are also having fried eggs.'

'No! Much bigger than that! You need to think big, Jackie! Bobby and Maureen have got *engaged!*'

'Ah, no way! That's great!'

'And the best bit is... guess who Bobby has asked to be the best man?' Frank straightened an invisible tie at the collar of his pyjama shirt.

'Is it you? Aww, that's brilliant, Dad!' Jackie stood up and hugged him, still holding her plate.

'And you, little lady, you've to be a flower girl, if that's okay with you, Jackie. Maureen told Bobby to tell me to ask you... You have to be okay with that decision...'

Jackie smiled. 'Of course it's okay!' June bounced on the couch with excitement. Frank bounced his knees as much as he could with her, holding her hands, as his socks rubbed against the carpet.

'I love a good, big party!' he said, happily. 'Apparently, it's going to be in the next few months, too! Bobby's not getting any younger!'

'Maybe Maureen wants a baby?' Jackie considered.

'Is she not at the age of "the change"?' he whispered. He began singing *This is the age of the change* to music he had heard on a TV advert for British Rail.

'Dad! You're terrible.'

'How? She can't hear me.'

'Cooee!' shouted Mrs Morrisson from the back door. 'Hope it's not too early to call.'

'That woman's got an ear hidden down the back of our couch.'

'What's that, Frank?'

'Hello, Mrs! Come in, come in, sit down, now. Oh, there you are, sitting down already. Oh, June, I'm done in. C'mon sit on Granda's knee. You can tell Mrs Morrisson the big news, Jackie.' Frank sat down in his chair and June climbed up onto his lap. Mrs Morrisson clapped her hands together and looked at Jackie.

'Don't tell me! Has he phoned?' Jackie shook her head. Mrs Morrisson tilted her head to the side. 'Ah no,' she said. 'Still, there's plenty of time!' Jackie looked away from her sympathy, feeling her cheeks redden. 'And Father Cleary has said nothing to you, Frank?'

'To me? No. Not a dickie bird. None of my business.'

Mrs Morrisson rolled her eyes, 'It usually is!' she swiped.

'Go on, then, Jackie, tell Mrs the big news,' he added quietly, 'before she snorts it out of me.'

Jackie took a deep breath, and, ignoring her own feelings about the lack of a phone call, she smiled and broke the wedding news to her neighbour.

'Well, I never!' she gasped. Mrs Morrisson and Frank began speculating about where the wedding would be, what the meal would be like and what they would wear. She suggested to Jackie that she buy something new, and not off the market. Jackie said she'd go down to What Every Woman Wants in Coatbridge but Mrs Morrisson insisted she was not to do that, with a look of disgust. Frank shrugged.

'Why don't you just wear that thing you wore to the wean's christening?'

'She will not! It's a wedding! We all need something new for a wedding.'

'I don't. My grey suit will do. Unless Bobby wants top hat and tails,' Frank paused, 'but he can pay for that.'

Jackie brought Mrs Morrisson some tea.

'It could be Viv, next!' she said, accepting the tea. 'Is she still seeing the big Terry?'

'She is!'

'And is he a nice lad, now?'

Jackie nodded. 'He seems to be!'

'Ah, that's great for her. Don't you worry, Jackie, you'll be next! Your prince will phone, I know it.'

'Oh, I doubt that, but thanks!' Jackie smiled. 'I'm not really one for princes, anyway.'

'Quite right! Have you heard from Jack the Lad?' she asked, referring to Tommy.

'Oh! Him! Wait til you hear this...' Frank sat up.

Jackie interjected. 'I meant to tell you, Mrs Morrisson...'

'Oh, what's this now?' she smiled.

'Can I tell her, Jackie?' asked Frank. Jackie nodded. She couldn't find the enthusiasm that Frank and Mrs Morrisson had. Tommy was way down her list, but she felt forever tied to him, and exhausted with the drama of his life inside of hers. 'Apparently, he was out the other week and something happened at The Double A. Viv says Tommy told Terry he got into a fight. Terry told Viv that Tommy's been wearing a woolly hat to work and hasn't been out for ages.'

'A woolly hat? I mean, what's that about?' asked Mrs Morrisson. 'He was always one for the Bryclreem!'

'Well, here's the thing!' said Frank. 'Terry told Viv he thinks he's covering something on his head.'

'Oh. I wonder what it is! Have you seen it, Jackie?'

'No.'

'Has he stopped asking you to visit him, now?' she said, lowering her tone. 'In the fancy flat?'

'Oh, I don't know. I have no idea what he's playing at, to be honest.'

Jackie left them to their conversation and went to the kitchen to clear away the plates and mop the kitchen floor. She thought of the wedding, and how she had no one to go with. She considered Tommy, and wondered what would become of him, and if he had really been in a fight, or if he still wanted to act as June's dad, or have a relationship with her. She thought of Jean Paul, for whom she had allowed herself to fall, pinning her hopes and dreams onto him, and then he disappeared. Her brain whizzed for possibilities around every corner and down every avenue of her life and her eyes glazed into a stare.

She blinked as the hot water for the mop began to reach the top of the bucket. She twisted the tap very tightly to stop it squeaking and added a cap of bleach. She lifted it with two hands and placed it onto the floor. She dug the mop into the water, screwed it out and banged it into the corners of the checkered linoleum. She imagined everyone else coupled up at the wedding and June and her dad at the top table. She'd be sitting with Mrs Morrisson, Viv and Terry. Mrs Morrisson would be her plus one! She was going to a wedding with her elderly neighbour. She tried to console herself that it would be fine, and then felt guilty for feeling angry about it.

She wondered what her mum would think about the whole situation. If she was looking down at Jackie, tut-tutting and shaking her head, or would she see similarities with her daughter and be able to offer her advice.

She finished mopping the floor and rinsed and screwed the mop head into the top of the bucket.

She stood and stared out the window to the garden to calm her thoughts. Thoughts of her mother floated into her brain. She felt a sense that her mum was beside her, like she could turn around and see her in the kitchen, cutting bread or making tea. She wondered why this feeling was so strong.

The little robin landed. It darted around the grass, glanced into the window then flew away. As it landed on a nearby tree, she thought of her mother and Eddie O'Donnell together, and wondered again if her mum was really in love with him. She lifted the bucket and poured the water down the sink, wondering if this man was still alive.

Mrs Morrisson stood at the kitchen door with an empty cup, her shoes at the edge of the wet floor. 'Here, hen, take this. I'll go out the front door.' She turned and made her way towards June to give her a kiss. 'I'm just nipping home to get something,' she winked at Frank. 'I won't be long now!' Jackie heard the front door slam and the gate squeak shut.

Tommy removed his hat. He had bought some nail polish remover and pan stick from the chemist and managed to rub off the eyebrows some days ago but the bump had taken a while to go down. He dotted pan stick lightly over the fading bruise. He examined his face in the mirror and styled his hair, then spritzed his French cologne. In the living room, he pulled out a fake plug socket and put his hand in a hole in the wall. He removed a packet of £50 notes from the brown envelope, put the envelope back in the hole and replaced the plug socket.

He headed to Fine Fare and filled a trolley full of food, much of it frozen microwave meals. He put in crisps, sweets and a bottle of diluting orange juice. He put a small chicken in the trolley for roasting and some carrots and potatoes. He added gravy granules, Mother's Pride and a bottle of Lambrusco. In the deep freeze, he selected a Vienetta ice cream dessert. He paid with a £50 note and the young shop assistant looked puzzled.

'Oh, I don't know if I can take that?' he paused. 'Hold on a minute.' He took a deep breath and shouted, 'Ho, Veronica, can I take this?' He waved the large green £50 note in the air. Veronica approached the till, her eyes wide.

'Let me see, give us it here.' She held the note up in front of the strip light and inspected it as if she knew what she was looking for. 'Have you not got anything smaller?' she enquired, without looking at him.

'No,' Tommy replied, curtly.

The mother with two toddlers behind Tommy sighed deeply. 'Oh, for God's sake,' she said, exasperated.

The man behind her tapped his walking stick. 'Bloody ridiculous,' he uttered.

Tommy held his hands up to them as if to say, 'not my fault'. One of the toddlers loitered dangerously near Tommy's suit jacket with a sticky lollipop so he took a step away in precaution. The toddler moved a step closer, licking the lolly and staring at Tommy with the eyes of a kitten. Tommy recoiled in disgust that the boy's nose had not been wiped. Veronica called for the manager to take a look at the note. Again, he held it up to the light and gave Tommy a suspicious glare.

'Can we get on with this, please? My money is as good as anybody's,' he said. The manager nodded and told the shop assistant to take it and give him his change. He opened the till, handed Tommy a note and some coins.

'Have a nice day!' he called. 'Good to see you got the eyebrows off. Next, please!'

Tommy shook his head, puzzled, and carelessly threw the bags into the trolley as fast as he could then wheeled it out to the car park. He threw the bags into the car, pushed the trolley down between two cars and let it roll as far as it would go until it stopped. He lit a cigarette. Straightening his jacket, he felt a sticky patch along the seam. He cursed the toddler and marched down into the florists.

'I've ordered a bouquet. Fletcher.'

'Ah yes here it is. £20, please.'

He collected a bouquet and handed her the money.

'Bruising all gone, has it?' she asked. 'Sounded like a sore one.'

He walked out of the shop without a reply. With his head down, he went to John Menzies and bought a Tiny Tears doll that came with a bath. The shop assistant stared at him, and his head. She nudged the other shop assistant who was stacking batteries behind her. They both giggled.

'Something funny?' he asked.

'No, not at all!' they replied. He heard them laughing as he left the shop. One clutched her stomach as the other whispered, 'Do you think he needed any "double As"?'

He headed back up to the car and dropped the flowers and the doll in the back seat. He sat down in the driver's seat, removed his handkerchief and wiped the sweat off his brow, and some pan stick came off with it. He attempted to clean the sticky lollipop patch off his jacket. He started up the car and pulled out in the direction of Jackie's house.

'That's us away to the swings, hen. Won't be long!'

'Okay, Dad, thanks. I'll get this place hoovered while you're out.'

'Jackie, it's your day off. Sit down and relax, for goodness sake. Mrs Morrisson hoovered yesterday. We're going to have some fun, aren't we, Junie?'

'Yes, Granda!'

Jackie kissed June goodbye and smiled as she heard her dad telling June to keep her eyes peeled for fivers and tenners at the park. She enjoyed the comfort of her dad's never-changing phrases. She waited a few minutes to check that they had walked down the path, then went to get the phone book and flicked through for the number of the church.

Father Cleary answered on the second ring. His booming voice echoed down the phone.

'Hello, Father, this is Jackie McNeill. I was wondering if I could speak to Jean Paul?'

'Hello, Jackie! How are you? I'm afraid Jean Paul is not here at the moment.'

'Oh, okay. Do you know when he will be back?'

'I'm afraid I can't be sure if he's coming back at all, Jackie. He had to go back to France. Left in a bit of a rush. Wanted to see his mother.'

'Oh, I see.'

'Can I help you with anything, Jackie? What did you need him for?'

'I needed him,' Jackie's voice wobbled, 'I'm learning... I just wanted to brush up on my French.'

'Oh, I see,' Father Cleary laughed. 'Well, I'm a bit rusty with that! *Comme ci, comme ça* and so on!'

'Yeah.'

'Will I see you on Sunday? You've been working, I take it?'

'Yes. Yes, Father, see you on Sunday. I'd better go...'

'Jackie?'

'Yes?'

'You can drop in and see me you know, anytime, if you need to. If you need to talk.'

'I know. Thank you, Father. Bye.'

Jackie hung up and slid down into the phone chair. She placed her face into her hands. After a few minutes, she picked herself up and pulled the hoover out from under the stairs.

Mrs Morrisson turned the key in her back door, then pulled the handle twice to ensure it was locked. She put her keys in her handbag, checked the contents, then clipped it shut. She closed her back gate securely. She walked down towards Frank's house and opened the back door.

'Cooee!' she shouted. The hoover was on. She walked into the living room and pulled the plug out. Jackie turned abruptly to check the wire.

'Well, what are you standing there hoovering for? C'mon. Get your coat on.'

'What for?'

'I'm taking you into Glasgow.'

'Glasgow? I look a sight.'

'Oh, for goodness sake, Jackie, if only you could see yourself the way the world sees you,' Mrs Morrisson tilted her head. 'You're coming. No arguments. You need a break, hen. Let me treat you.'

'I couldn't do that, Mrs Morrisson, honestly, plus my dad will be back and what about June...'

'It's all sorted. I spoke to your dad already. Why do you think he took June to the swings? Now go and get your jacket and your bag. We're going wedding shopping for a new dress for you.'

Jackie smiled and leaned down to wind up the hoover wire. 'Okay, then, I suppose I could...'

'Leave that! I'll get it. Coat, please.' She wound up the hoover and put it back under the stairs.

'We'll go to Goldberg's. There will be a good selection there, good bargains.' Mrs Morrisson linked Jackie's arm and they walked up the street together towards Airdrie train station. 'I'm taking you away from all this!' she laughed.

'You're supposed to be tall, dark and handsome, Mrs Morrisson.'

'Well, short, fat and ugly will have to do you!'

'You stop that!'

Jackie nudged Mrs Morrisson and they both giggled.

Tommy's car pulled up to the front of Jackie's house. He got out and rang the bell but there was no answer. He retrieved the doll and flowers from the car and wrote a note with a betting pen.

Jackie, I would love it if you could just let me show you and our little June the flat, and for you to see how much I've changed. Come over for dinner. Call me please. Love, Tommy X. PTO: SEE BEHIND BIG FLOWER POT.

He placed the flowers and the doll behind the pot at the side of the house. Satisfied that they couldn't be seen and that it wasn't going to rain, he got back into the car and drove home.

STRAWBERRY TARTS

After finishing his most hated shift working through the night, Daniel had caught a few hours' sleep and was now wide awake. His open eyes must have sent a signal to his mother's hands as she was there at the door with a tray.

'Morning son,' she said quietly, 'just a wee bit of something for you to eat. How did you sleep, okay?'

Daniel rubbed his eyes and moved onto his elbows. 'Slept fine. What is it?'

'Toast and tea.'

'No, sorry, I meant what time is it?'

'It's just about half past one. Is that all right?'

'That's good, Mum, thanks.'

'You got any plans for today?'

'No, nothing.'

'Will you help me get a few things up the street?' Daniel smiled. 'Is that okay?'

'It's fine, Mum, I'll help you.'

Daniel's mum clasped her hands together. 'Is that a yes?' she asked, eyebrows higher than space, knees slightly bent. Daniel took a sip of tea and smiled.

'Go on, then, I'll come. But don't make me stand and wait at the knitting patterns in Woollies. Or the shoes. And definitely not bras!'

'Tsk! As if I would do that!' she smiled. She left the room and stood outside his door for a second, listening to him munching his toast and slurping his tea. She tugged at her apron strings and pulled her pinny over her head, folded it and put it atop the bannister. She had important work to do without it.

Tommy set about tidying the flat. The cleaner had been the day before so there wasn't much to do. He washed a cup and a plate and arranged all the food in the fridge for Jackie to cook, confident that the language he'd used in his note, 'our little June', was enough to entice her over.

In the living room, his flick knife was out on the coffee table beside his cigarettes. He lifted the knife and went to the kitchen. He tapped it on a drawer handle, thinking of where to put it; not in his pocket, it could fall out on the couch. A changed man doesn't carry a knife. He didn't want to put it behind the fake plug socket; if he needed it for any reason, she'd see where his cash was. He decided to hide the knife inside a Tupperware box that Terry had got him as a housewarming gift. He threw the

Tupperware into the low kitchen cupboard beside the fridge. Satisfied that the flat looked nice, he flopped down on the couch and lit a cigarette. He blew smoke at the ceiling fan, whist he waited for the phone to ring. The only clue left of the old Tommy was the smell of cigarettes, and he could get rid of that with a spray of air freshener.

Daniel and his mum had visited a few shops and her string bag bulged. Daniel offered to carry it to stop the plastic handles digging into her fingers. They decided to make a final call at Sharelle's café and got a booth just before it closed. The waitress came over and took an order for a burger, two strawberry tarts and two teas. The burger arrived quickly and Daniel blew on it and took a huge bite.

'You're going to get a sore stomach, eating like that.'

'I always eat like this!' he said, biting another bit of the burger, and pausing to examine his teeth marks on the bun. Daniel's mum took her strawberry tart out of the little foil tray and cut the strawberry down the middle.

'Look at the size of this strawberry! It's like the Eiffel Tower!'

'Was that the last two off the shelf?'

'Looks like it, son. We were lucky! They're usually all gone by now.' She took a small bite. Daniel watched and rushed to finish his burger to get to his strawberry tart.

'Hello there!' called Bobby and Maureen from a booth further down the back.

'Oh, hello, Bobby! Hello, Maureen!' said Daniel's mum, and he waved along with her.

'We're just in to see about our wedding cake!'

'That's right! We heard you were getting married!'

'Jackie told us,' Daniel smiled.

'Sharelle says we've to look at pictures and choose what we want!'

'Isn't that lovely!' Daniel's mum her fork down. She never liked to eat in front of people while they spoke to her, especially if they were not eating.

'Oh, well, better get back to it,' said Maureen, and she turned around. Bobby followed suit and they soon had their noses deep in plastic pages of colourful cake pictures.

Daniel's mum picked up her fork. 'That's nice, isn't it? They make a lovely couple.'

'Aye.' Daniel pushed his plate away and pulled the smaller plate with the strawberry tart towards him. The strawberry was nestled upside down on a pile of cream inside a shortcrust pastry with a runny jam glaze over the top. Daniel contemplated biting the entire strawberry off, then going in for the cream and shortcrust pastry in two further bites.

'What are you waiting for?' his mum laughed. 'For God's sake, bite it! Your eyes are doing cartwheels.' Daniel bit the top of the strawberry off.

'Mmm.'

'Lovely strawberries. Absolutely beautiful,' said his mum, as she finished hers off with her fork. 'Do you think you'll ever get married?' she asked Daniel. His chewing slowed, then continued.

'Doubt it. Maybe. One day. If it's the right person.'

Person, she thought. He said *person*.

'It's a shame the gays can't get married, isn't it?' Daniel sipped his tea too quickly and burnt his tongue.

'Suppose so.'

'Dangerous game now. Being gay.'

'Mum, do you have to keep saying that?'

She continued to eat her strawberry tart with the fork. 'I'm sure an old uncle of mine was gay. Poor man died alone. He was a happy man, but he had no wife. Never had a girlfriend or a boyfriend or anything.'

'Right.'

'You can get lady gays now. I saw it on the television.'

'Okay, Mum. Do we have to talk about this?'

'And they can *all* get the AIDS,' she whispered.

'Mum! Shh. We'll get kicked out.'

'Well, I can't mention it at home, can I? Not in front of your father.' Oblivious to their conversation, the well-manicured waitress placed a saucer with the bill onto their table and went off to wipe tables. 'What I'm saying is, Daniel, to you... is that I'm all right with it, as long as you're careful.' She placed pound notes onto the plate and stood up. 'Look at me.'

Daniel looked up at her crinkly watery eyes, sparkling in the low lights of the café. The last piece of pastry rested on his tongue, unchewed.

'Did you hear me? I'm okay with it,' she whispered. She turned around and began walking out of the café before he had time to respond. He picked up the string bag and followed her. As they walked home in the dark, she linked his arm into his.

'Mum. I'm not gay,' he said, lightly laughing awkwardly into the darkness.

'Daniel, let me tell you something. Just because you haven't done "it", doesn't mean you're not "it". There's a lot more to it than that.'

'How do you know I haven't done it?'

'So what you're saying is, you have done *something*?' She looked ahead, expectant of an honest answer.

'No, I'm not saying that.'

'Right then. That's what I thought. Are you prepared for when you do?'

'Mum, I'm not answering that. I told you I'm not gay.'

'I never said you were. But I went to the chemist and I left something in your drawer.'

'Oh, for God's sake!'

'Don't tell your dad.'

'Don't tell him what? That you left something in my drawer or that I'm gay?'

'And there it is. I knew it.'

'Mum!' He stopped. She stopped beside him and looked back up into his face. His face gleamed in the streetlight, still soft and barely stubbled. She reached up to touch his cheek.

'That's enough now.'

'I'm not...'

'No more now.'

Daniel felt sick and dizzy with a sour taste in his mouth. His whole body tingled. He knew she was right, that she knew him from the very inside. He couldn't deny it anymore. His words were useless and pointless; like flicking tiny toothpicks at a steel shield.

His head spun with the idea that she knew, and he knew that she knew. Just that fact was enough for him to disbelieve the situation, and he felt himself hang suspended in the moment, not knowing how to move forward, or backward or sideways. The thought nudged his brain that it was okay, she was *okay* with it, but he was unable to process anything more than his secret was out, acknowledged, by her, and now by him.

He thought back to what he might have done to show her, how she found out.

'How... how did you..?'

'Mums just know these things, darlin',' she said. 'I've suspected since you were very young. Very young. I've just been waiting for you to acknowledge it. And here we are.' She took the bag from his fingers and linked his arm and they began walking again. 'Oh, look. The Spud Spot has Macaroni Cheese. I'll make that tomorrow.'

Daniel looked in The Spud Spot window.

'I love you, son,' she said, words rarely spoken, saved for 'special' in their house, uttered less often than *Merry Christmas*. Silent tears washed his face. He couldn't reply. He had no words for the adoration that flooded his heart for his mother.

THIS TRAIN TERMINATES AT AIRDRIE

Jackie and Mrs Morrisson sat opposite each other on the Airdrie train. Mrs Morrisson laughed as her body bounced with the rhythm of the carriage. She placed her hand over different bits to stop them wobbling. Jackie laughed with her, then took an excited peek into the three bags with Goldberg's emblazed on the side.

'People say that shop is on its last legs but it was well worth it. They'll never close it down. It's been there years! And that dress – my Lord! Well, you'd never get that dress anywhere else, Jackie. I swear to God that dress is the nicest thing I've ever seen in my life. It's going to look stunning on you. Nobody else will have that. And with the bag and shoes, you can't go wrong. You'll get a lot of wear out of white high heels, you know.' Mrs Morrisson waved her hand in the air, and rested it on her knee, as if she'd made an important discovery about white shoes.

'Are you sure it's okay to wear white to somebody's wedding?'

'It's only an accessory to the outfit! The dress itself is pink. Cerise is a very pretty colour. Very rich. Very now. You're going look a million dollars.

And it all matches, with the white buttons and the white bag and shoes.'

'Thanks, Mrs Morrisson. For the dress, the shoes, the bag, everything. You're far too generous.'

'Not at all now. My pleasure. What else am I going to spend my money on, eh? You can't take it with you when you're gone.'

'We are so grateful to have you nearby. You've been a godsend to us. And June loves you.'

'It's my pleasure to help. Brings me a lot of joy. Now let's finish our day in style and get a taxi home after we get to Airdrie.'

'Okay, but I'm paying!' Jackie was feeling buoyant after her afternoon with her elderly neighbour. The dress fitted perfectly and the shoes and bag were beautiful. One white slide comb on the side of her hair and a pair of American Tan tights would complete the look.

'Oh, now, just wait until your dad sees you, all dolled up. He'll be proud as punch! You know you're the *image* of your mother at this age.'

'Am I?' Jackie's eyes widened.

'Oh, you must know that! Only the colour of the hair is different. Surely your dad tells you?'

'He doesn't say much.'

'Well, yes,' she shifted awkwardly. 'I saw that, with that... other business.'

'Mrs Morrisson, do you know where he is?' Jackie asked hopefully. 'That man?'

'Do you mean O'Donnell? Oh, he'll be long gone. Long, long gone. This is years ago now. All water under the bridge. Don't go digging up the past. It won't do you any good.'

'The thing is, I keep dreaming about my mum. Strange unusual dreams, upsetting dreams. I don't feel like she's, well, this will sound strange but, I suppose, "settled". I get the feeling she wants me to do something, find something, him, maybe, I don't know... though my dreams aren't making sense.'

'I doubt she wants you to find him, Jackie. To say what?'

'I don't know. I just feel, if I could ask him, you know, try to understand what it was they had. My dad won't tell me anything, and I don't want to ask him anymore.' She looked up. 'I found that picture for a reason. I need to know more. And these dreams. I can't explain them. They're all so... mad.'

'Well, I had so many nonsense dreams about our John after he died. Oh, my God! There was one when we were sailing on a raft. I tell you, our John had never been on a raft in his life! And another where we were running down a hill. Ah, for God's sake! With his hip? No way.' She laughed. 'You've just got to enjoy the little visit, whatever it is.'

Jackie looked out the window at the passing grey buildings of Shettleston. She was certain the dreams were more than that.

'Jackie, can I say something?' Mrs Morrisson looked around the train carriage. There was only one man across from their seats. He had white hair and a beard, asleep with his mouth open. An empty lager can rolled around the floor. Jackie nodded and Mrs Morrisson leaned in and touched Jackie's knees with both her hands. She could smell the Lenor on her clothes and her sweet tea breath. 'You never cry. I never saw you cry after your mum died.' Jackie looked down and her fringe fell forward. 'You carry so much. Sometimes I think you're going to burst open!' Mrs Morrisson pushed the hair from Jackie's eyes but it fell forward again. 'I know you're trying to be strong and you have the job and the little one and your dad and all the business with her father. But Jackie, it's so important to cry! You have to let it out or it will build up inside you like a big hard stone. Stress can make you very sick.'

'Don't worry about me! I'm fine.'

'See? That's what you always say! But it doesn't wash with me. I see you. I see the sadness behind your eyes. It's all in there, desperate to come out.'

'I do cry. I cry privately. I don't want my dad to see me upset. Or June. My mum was never one for big displays of tears. Anyway, she died nearly five years ago. I shouldn't be crying anywhere near as much.'

'Of course you should! I still cry for our John.'

'Do you?'

'All the time! There's no harm in it – why would there be? It's my loss, my personal loss, and my feelings.'

'I do think about my mum. Every day. I think about if I just had one more day with her, you know? The things I would ask. About growing up and my dad... and what she thinks of my little baby. And her advice with Tommy and Jean Paul and I'd ask her about this man, this O'Donnell man. If she... loved him.'

'We all want another day. I understand that. For you especially, you were robbed of your mum at such a young age.'

Jackie dabbed her eyes with her scarf. Mrs Morrisson unclipped her bag hurriedly and removed a tissue from a packet and gave it to her. She squeezed her hands.

'Losing somebody is so hard. It's like a long, slow, moan that never ends, a yearning or a hurt in your heart. Like that noise you make when you're giving birth. Remember that? Oh, it's painful. And it feels like it will never end. But, if you follow each moan, and you bear down for a very low, very sore day or two of tears, the next day you're okay. There is a little break for you to recover. That's why they call it a pattern. It's a pattern of hurt - over and over - again and again. And then survival. You live on, because you must, and you appreciate things, and others depend on you. And that person that died, they depend on you too, to carry on, do the things they can't. Once you realise this, you can allow your sad grief to turn to a different grief. And somehow, I don't know if it's to do with the mind or the human condition or whatever, but somehow, you're programmed to push through the whole thing. Just like the pain of labour, I suppose...' Jackie sniffed and wiped her eyes with the tissue. '... except we usually get a wee bouncy baby at the end...'

Jackie couldn't help herself and let out a little laugh at 'wee bouncy baby'.

'It is funny, isn't it? I suppose you have to laugh. That's what it's like. Crying one minute, laughing the next. There's just no rules.' Mrs Morrisson could see she was making Jackie feel better and felt encouraged to give her a second to blow her nose and wipe her tears. They settled into a few minutes of silence with their own thoughts. The train pulled into Coatbridge Sunnyside. 'Now I'm not your mum, and I'm not trying to be your mum or replace her. But here I am, two doors down, and you're there, two doors up, so it seems natural I should help. If you want to talk about Tommy or Jean Paul or clothes or June or *Coronation Street* or *Blockbusters*, or have a cry, I'll do my best to help. I might even join in.'

Jackie nodded. 'I know. I really appreciate that.' She paused and looked out at the train pulling away from the station. 'I want to find O'Donnell,' she said. 'I think I'm supposed to find him. I have a strong feeling... I don't know... I can't explain it. I think my mum wants me to find him.'

Mrs Morrisson sighed. 'Oh, Jackie, I don't know if it's a good idea. You've got enough on your plate with Tommy. And your dad...'

'You don't have to tell him. It's just for me. Please.'

'I don't like keeping secrets. Your dad is a good friend of mine. Please don't ask me to do that.'

'Please, Mrs Morrisson! *Please!*' Jackie implored. 'I just can't get past this...'

Mrs Morrisson sighed and looked down. The empty can rolled over to her feet and she picked it up and put it behind her seat. 'Okay then. If you think it will bring you peace, I'll help you.'

'Do you know where he is?'

'No. As I said, I don't know where he is.'

'So how do we find him?'

'Sadie Ward will know. She knows everything. I'll ask her.'

As the train pulled into Airdrie, Jackie helped Mrs Morrisson up out of the seat. She leaned over to the man who was sleeping and nudged him.

'End of the line now, Santa.'

'Where am I?' he woke up, baffled.

'The North Pole.'

'What?'

'You're at Airdrie.'

'Ah, for bucks sake!'

Viv and Terry sat in her flat on her two-seater red couch, his arm around her shoulders, his other hand eating a packet of plain crisps. Viv took one.

'I think you should do it. You should do it now.'

'I thought we weren't going to talk about it?'

'You're not happy at the bookies. You said so. And you know he's dodgy. Just tell him. Phone him and get it over with.'

'You don't know what he can be like, Viv.'

'Oh, I know fine what he can be like. Sure I nearly kicked his head in once.' Viv took another crisp from his bag. 'You're not frightened of him, are you?'

'Who? Me? No way!'

'So phone him. Tell him you're not working there anymore, and you're going back to the market.'

'I'll think about it. Maybe tomorrow.'

'Do you want me to phone him for you?' she teased.

He smiled and shook his head. 'You are something else.' She grabbed his packet and poured all the crisps into her mouth and munched them down. 'You had better have another packet in there, Miss Viv!' He leaned in and tickled her.

'There's... none... left...' she squealed. 'I'm putting you on a diet.' He tickled her harder and she laughed louder. 'You'll thank me when you're skinny!'

'Frank, would you put that kettle on, for God's sake? This daughter of yours has the hind legs walked off me.' Mrs Morrisson flopped down onto the couch as Jackie put the bags on the table.

'Granda found a dolly in a plant!' June jumped up and down and took Jackie's hand to pull her into the hall. Frank reached over to Jackie and handed her a note.

'This was put through the door.'

As Jackie read the note from Tommy, June pulled her towards the stairs to show her a dolly in a bath and a bouquet of flowers. June begged her mother to take the doll out of the plastic packaging.

'Granda says not to touch until Mummy got home.'

Jackie pulled out a Tiny Tears with its own bath and toys. June danced with delight and hugged the dolly.

'It's for me, Mummy, isn't it? Is it mine, Mummy?'

'Yes, darling, it's for you.' June ran into the living room to show Mrs Morrisson and Frank. Jackie sat on the stairs and took in the note. Exhausted, she felt overwhelmed by Tommy's generosity and seemingly genuine words. She came through to the living room with the toy bath and flowers.

'It seems he's not going to go away, until he gets what he wants,' said Frank. 'This is just his latest trick.'

'I think I need to get it out the way.'

Frank put his hand to his head and sat forward in his chair. 'No! Jackie, no! Don't!'

'Wait a minute, Jackie, are you sure this is the right thing?' Mrs Morrisson also leaned forward.

'I don't know. But as my dad said, he's not going to go away until I face him.'

'But I didn't mean that! I was only saying...'

She walked towards the phone in the hall and paused by the door. 'Dad, I promise you, now, he gets one last chance. I mean it. This is his last chance. Let's just see if he is what he says he is. He's never going to stop until I speak to him.'

'But what about the fight at The Double A? Jackie!' Frank stood up. He realised that his hands were trembling.

'Don't worry Dad. I know what I'm doing.' She closed the door behind her.

Frank looked over to Mrs Morrisson who was looking at the carpet. 'Well, that's it, now!' He pointed. 'If he gets his claws into her again...'

'He won't. As she said, she knows what she's doing.' Mrs Morrisson felt the sentence leave her mouth with the intention of consoling her friend, but her words were feeble.

'I don't know so much. He still has a hold over her. I can feel it.'

'Frank, calm down.' Mrs Morrisson reached over and took one of his hands into both of hers and rubbed it warm. 'The wean will hear you,' she whispered, and nodded towards June who sat with the doll on the floor. She had removed all the doll's clothes, put it into a seated position and was now feeding it with a plastic spoon.

'He's coming to pick us up in half an hour.'

'Jackie-'

'Dad.' She held up a hand. 'Don't say anything.

Let me just do this. Finish it or continue it, I don't know what. I need to get it out of the way and stop avoiding it. Who knows? There might be a future for the three of us.' She looked over at June.

'I can't believe you're even saying that!' Frank sat forward in his chair, shaking with fury.

'Well, he is her...' Jackie glanced over at June, then back to Frank. 'I'm not exactly swamped with offers, am I? The one I wanted doesn't want me. I have to think of the future. Of her future.' Jackie leaned down to help June dress the doll.

Frank rubbed his big toe into the pattern of the carpet. Jackie took a deep breath, holding her resolve. 'Mrs Morrisson, please explain to him that I have to do this.'

Mrs Morrisson smiled weakly and pushed her hand down on the armrest to stand up. Jackie stood up and to take her other arm and help her.

'I need to go.' She patted Jackie on the arm. She kissed her hand and placed a kiss onto June's head. 'Try not to worry, Frank.' She touched his shoulder, then hobbled out the back door.

NUMBERS

Frank watched from behind the curtain as Jackie and June walked down the path to the gate, both looking lovely in pretty patterns. Tommy got out of his car, walked around and opened the back door for June. He fastened her into the back seat and then opened the passenger side door for Jackie. He stood over her as she climbed in and shifted to adjust her skirt. He closed her door gently. He turned around and looked at the window. He gave a little wave with a smirk. He walked around to the other side of the car, saluted at Frank and then climbed in. They sped away, too fast for Frank's liking. He watched the car until it was out of sight. He dropped the curtain and smoothed it out. He turned and looked at the empty room. The Tiny Tears bath sat on the floor with little toys around it, and an expanse of patterned brown carpet around that. The brown and orange figures-of-eight swirled into each other. He had never noticed how huge the living room looked when there was nobody in it. He sat down in his seat and sighed. He took the remote control off the mantelpiece and squeezed the ON button. He flicked the four channels up and down, backwards and forwards, pictures flashing, faces staring out. He did this for a few minutes, then turned the television off. He rubbed his hand on the wooden arm of the chair and looked at the mantelpiece towards June's picture. He felt cold. Fear bubbled around inside him like a pot of porridge. He glanced at the clock to check the time. They had been gone ten minutes. He took the photo of June into his hands. He pulled his jumper sleeve down and wiped a small smear from the glass. He pulled his lips in between his teeth and bit them.

'She's going to go with him, isn't she? I know it. I'm going to lose the two of them again.' Frank began to sweat and little nervous pains tingled in his chest. 'She's going to move in with him again, I know it, I just know it.' Frank stood still, tapping the photo.

June smiled out from the picture, into the distance.

Tommy put the key in the door and opened it wide.

'Welcome to my little palace!' he announced. June smiled brightly and entered.

'Wow!' she shouted as she ran into the living room. She went over to a stainless steel ornament of ball bearings and began clicking it back and forth.

'You like that?' Tommy laughed. He bent down to show her how to make it go faster.

Jackie watched him, looking for clues that he was still the old Tommy, and not this new improved version. Conflicted, she kept her guard high. He always looked and smelled wonderful. As he clicked the ornament, she admired his checked shirt and navy crew neck jumper over the top. All well fitted, no doubt very expensive. She took in the beautiful immaculate room. It still had a new glue-like smell of fresh new furniture and air freshener. Everything seemed to gleam. She ran her hand across the back of the blue crushed velvet chesterfield.

'Shall I give you a tour?' asked Tommy. He walked over and cupped the small of Jackie's back. She brushed his hand away. He put both of his hands up. 'Guilty!' he said. 'Not my fault, can't blame me, coming round here looking like that. You don't know what you do to me.'

Jackie looked back at him puzzled, then looked down at her dress which seemed quite innocent.

'Did you try that on before you bought it?' he whispered into her ear. 'Sizewise, it looks a bit snug around there.'

Jackie swept her fingers down over her waist and hips, she had never been told her clothes were snug. June ran over to her and pulled her skirt.

'Mummy, I want to see all the rooms!'

'You heard the lady!' smiled Tommy, and he scooped her up into his arms.

'Uh, I don't think she wants to be carried...' Jackie began to protest.

'Don't be silly, Mummy! She likes me, don't you, darling? Come and see *this* room! It's the most *special* room in the flat. It was decorated by *fairies*!' He walked off with June in his arms and Jackie walked hurriedly behind. She followed him into a room of pink. He placed June down gently. She ran towards the doll's house underneath the window and began to play with the furniture and tiny family.

'Wow!' she said. Tommy reached for Jackie's hand but she declined. He looked over at June playing with the doll's house.

'That could be us, you know, if you wanted.'

Jackie smiled politely. 'We'll see,' she answered. He escorted her into the bathroom and showed her the his 'n' her sinks and towels. He pointed out the jacuzzi pumps in the bath and the expensive power showerhead. Jackie couldn't help but feel overwhelmed and impressed. She had only heard of power showers. At home, she washed her hair with a rubber pipe hose that fitted onto bath taps. She imagined June in the jacuzzi with her ducks and bubbles. She imagined her and Tommy and June living here, happily, as a family. The idea began to warm to her, but still there was something about Tommy that didn't feel right.

They walked down the hall to June's room and she was now at the vanity mirror, switching on the Hollywood lights.

'Look, Mummy!' she grinned. 'It has drawers!' She opened and closed the drawers of the dressing table.

Jackie laughed and replied, 'Yes, it does!'

They admired the wardrobe together as Tommy leaned in the doorway, watching them fall deeper and deeper into the idea of life in his flat. June sat down in front of the doll's house on the carpet and took the old man doll from the family. She placed him to sleep on the couch. 'And Granda can sleep here when we do sleepover.'

Tommy laughed. 'Oh, no, I don't think so. Granda will stay in his own house.' June's face was crestfallen. Jackie put her hand on her shoulder.

'Let's not talk about sleepovers just yet, Junie! Plenty of time for that.'

'Granda sleeps here for a sleepover!' She put a tiny blanket from a bunk bed over the figure and continued to play with the other dolls.

Jackie went into the kitchen with Tommy.

'All mod cons!' he said, opening the microwave door. 'Sparkling, grade A shiny stainless steel and marble worktops. Plus an island with stools. I can just imagine you sitting there, Jackie. After you've cooked us a lovely dinner. A little glass of wine in your hand. A reward for you, just relaxing and waiting for me to come in from work. And look, I didn't forget!' He reached up and took down the electric knife, still in the box. 'A buzzy knife, your favourite.' Jackie surveyed the beautiful, shiny kitchen, impressed. 'You wouldn't have to clean at first, I've got a cleaner,' he continued. 'Of course, that's not really practical long term. Long term, you'll want to be in charge of all that, won't you? Without another woman getting under your feet. You can give up the nursing if you like, it's not exactly high powered. You don't need to work. I've got us covered.'

'I want to keep working. I love what I do, it's my career,' she insisted. Tommy sniggered at the word 'career'.

'If you say so,' he shrugged. He opened the fridge and showed her the food. He ran a finger over her cheek. 'If you haven't eaten, there's no time like the present to test out the kitchen, if you like. I've got all your favourite things in and a Viennetta. Do you remember that time your dad came for lunch in the other flat? That was a lovely meal, that was. I often reminisce about that chicken, it was mouth-watering.'

'I remember that day. You left early. My dad built the cot.'

'Oh, I did, didn't I? I had work to do. I'll make sure I've got plenty of cans in for your dad, as usual. I take it he still likes a can? He certainly did back then.' Tommy laughed. 'He never brought his own, did he...?'

'I'm not sure he knew he had to-'

'Oh, come on! I'm only winding you up. Remember how we used to laugh? You need to laugh again, Jackie. It's good for the soul.' He pointed to a kitchen sign in calligraphy. *Laughter Is Good For The Soul!*

Jackie nodded, although she didn't remember much happiness. She sat on one of the bar stools as he talked and made a juice for June and a coffee with his new coffee machine. He mentioned how only he could touch it, as it was very expensive. She sipped her coffee and contemplated life with him. There was no doubt about it, the flat was beautiful. Jackie knew it would be security, maybe even marriage. She peeked around the corner at June still playing happily. She considered that she'd no longer be a single mum. She'd be with June's dad, her real dad, and not a boyfriend. June's blood. There was something so neat and tidy about the set up that appealed to Jackie, something that seemed right, a jigsaw puzzle finally fitting together. Maybe, with Tommy, she wouldn't be as happy as she could be but her happiness wasn't a top priority, June's was. No couple is ever truly always happy, no marriage or relationship is ever perfect. She placed down her coffee and followed him into his bedroom. A beautiful king-sized bed greeted her with white sheets. She slid the mirror doors open and closed as Tommy expressed his delight that they would be a proper family. He stood beside her by the mirrors and wiped her fingerprints off with his shirt cuff. He paused, fixed his sleeves, then turned towards her.

'You know it was my mum's dying wish that I find you again. You and June. To be together, as a family. It's what she wanted. It's what I want. I really want this to work, Jackie. I'm tired of running around. I'm ready to settle. All of that stupid stuff I was doing a few years ago – it's all out my system now.' He put both of his hands on her hips and she put her hands on top of his and slowly slid them away.

'You say you're tired of running around, but what about the girls at the Double A?' she asked.

'What girls? I barely remember any girls. That place is a hole, it should be condemned.'

'The Cassidy sisters. You were with them all night. I know, Tommy. And I know you got into a fight. How can I trust you? How do I know that you are really what you say you are? And not what you *were*.'

'Jackie, I *didn't* get into a fight. You'll never believe this, it's embarrassing. I'm sure somebody must have spiked my drink... I actually...' he looked down at her shoes. 'I never told you, because, well, it's mortifying... I actually banged my head on the mirror. I walked up to it, I could see the toilet sign, but it was behind me. It was an accident. I'm not proud of it. It was dead sore... I felt hazy and...'

'Oh, my God!' Jackie erupted into laughter. 'Oh, my God!' she repeated. 'That must have been agony!' Tommy shifted from foot to foot, angry at her reaction, then a smile cracked his lips, not reaching his eyes.

'You like that, eh?' He nodded. 'You find that funny? Okay, I see, fair enough. Whatever makes you laugh, I suppose.' He continued to feel slighted, wishing he hadn't told her. He felt his fists clench, then released them, keeping his soft approach. 'Anyway,' he waved an arm, 'I *have* changed. I don't mess around anymore. I have made all of this, for you, for us, for the three of us. I came back for you, Jackie.' He stared into her eyes and leaned in to kiss her. 'You smell so good. Look at all those tiny freckles. I do like your imperfections... quite unusual.' He kissed her neck and she tensed. 'Relax, Jackie! Relax! It's me.'

'I've got to check on June...'

'No, no, she's happy. One more minute.' Jackie could smell the coffee on his breath as his cold lips edged closer to hers. His hands held her tightly, and she tried to relax, to feel what it would be like to be with him again. She thought of this beautiful flat, him and June, all together. She let herself imagine the ideal family as he pushed a kiss onto her warm mouth. She persevered with the kiss, as her eyes darted around the room. This would be the type of life he could offer. Security, money. June would have a mum *and* a dad, and maybe she would feel less lonely. As the kiss progressed, Jackie tried, and failed, to get involved with it. Her mind and body seemed to be locked up from him, and she knew in that moment it was wrong. She began to push away, and he moved closer in towards her.

'MUMMY!' she heard June calling, followed by crying. 'MUMMY!'

Jackie pushed Tommy with such a force he fell backwards. She darted from the room into the pink bedroom but June wasn't there. She ran into the living room, then into the kitchen and found June sitting on the floor, a couple of tiny drops of blood visible on the white tiles and a flick knife in her hand.

'Oh, my God! Oh, my God!' Jackie grabbed the knife and threw it into the sink. She scooped the little girl into her arms and snatched a tea towel and wrapped it around her fingers. 'What happened? What happened? What did you do, sweetheart? Tell Mummy.'

'I was doing my numbers.'

June pointed to some scratches in the floor tiles. Several cupboard doors had been opened. Beside the scratches was an empty Tupperware box.

'What's all the drama?' asked Tommy, leaning out of the bedroom door. He walked forward and saw June's hand wrapped in a tea towel. 'What's happened to her hand?' Tommy quickly moved towards them in the kitchen. 'What the hell was she doing in here? We only left her for two minutes.'

'You... You! Again, you! Why the hell have you got a flick knife in your house? Actually, don't answer that. I should have known better. I'm an idiot.'

'Jackie, I can explain this-'

'I hate you. I HATE you, Tommy Fletcher. You could have done permanent damage to her hand.'

'Wow, wait a minute.' He held up his hands. 'She's the one that went looking in my private property.'

'What? Your *private property*? She's *three* years old, for God's sake! Oh, my God! You care about nobody but yourself and you know nothing about children.' Jackie looked under the tea towel and the bleeding had stopped.

'Well, by the sounds of things, neither do you. Leaving her to wander about like that!' Tommy took a step forward.

'You stay back! You stay away from us. Don't you ever contact me again.' Jackie grabbed her bag. 'Don't come near me, or my house, or my dad, or my baby ever again. Do you understand? I HATE YOU! And I hate myself for EVER thinking this could work. Go to hell!' Jackie ran through the front door of the flat. Her daughter felt light in her arms as she took the four flights of stairs with ease. She ran outside into the warm evening air and flagged a taxi. She slammed the door shut and it sped away.

Upstairs, Tommy looked at the kitchen floor. Three of the floor tiles had the numbers *one, two* and *three* scratched into them. He tutted and swore. He picked up his flick knife and ran it under the tap, dried it, closed it and put it into his pocket. He took a kitchen cloth from a new packet and wiped up the tiny droplets of blood. He threw the cloth into the sink, all the while cursing June's name. In the hall, the phone rang. It was Terry.

'Just to let you know, I've got my job back on the market. I'm not coming back to the bookies.'

'What? Do whatever the hell you want! You're useless, anyway.' Tommy slammed the phone down and noticed a giant scratch all the way around the bottom panel of the kitchen door. It was in the shape of a six.

THE WORST MUM, THE BEST MUM

'Jackie, stop torturing yourself. You have to stop this!' Viv had her arms around Jackie's shoulders as she went through events again. Frank sat in his chair and Mrs Morrisson stood in the kitchen, waiting for the kettle to boil.

'I-I-took my eyes of her, for a second, she was playing with the dolls' house and I went to look at the other bedroom... How could I ever? How could I ever have put her in danger like that?' Frank tapped his fingers on the edge of the chair. 'Don't!' shouted Jackie. 'Don't say a word.'

'I never said anything!'

'You don't need to,' she sniffed. 'Your mouth was hanging open. I know you warned me. All of you warned me. You, Viv, Mrs Morrisson, Daniel, everybody. My God, everybody told me! And I still put her in danger like that.'

'Now, shh... Jackie' Mrs Morrisson entered with tea and a plate of Jammie Dodgers. Frank reached for two but received a glare and took one. 'She's fine! It was just a tiny little cut. Not even a quarter of an inch. You won't see it in a couple of days. She must have just trailed it lightly across her hand.

You know how she loves to colour and draw. It's no worse than a paper cut.'

'But it could have been much worse! I can't bear to think about it. I'm a terrible mum. The worst mum. I was just thinking of a future for her...' Jackie sniffed.

'Listen, Jackie.' Viv took her friend by both shoulders. 'I know you. You wouldn't have rested until you found out for yourself. And now you have. You may have prevented something worse from happening later on. What if you *had* moved in with him? Maybe it would have been fine for a few weeks then... well, God knows. Fighting, arguing, maybe worse. You've done yourself a favour, knowing all this now. You've done June a favour. There's no harm done to her.'

'That's it, Jackie. Listen to your friend. You're out of it now.' Mrs Morrisson handed her a cup. 'For good, this time.' She looked hopefully towards Frank, who was still tapping his fingers.

'But... but he's her dad...' Jackie tried to breathe through her tears, 'And it would have been nice... it would have been nice to marry her dad. In a church. How it's meant to be. The three of us. If he wasn't such a ...'

'Jackie, that is not how it's meant to be!' Frank raised his voice. 'You don't stay with a person like that, just for a child! Nobody does that and nor should they! Times have changed, for the better. And, listen, I don't say that lightly.' Frank looked at his biscuit, sighed and placed it on his knee. He sipped his tea. None of this was giving him any comfort. He did want Jackie to find happiness but not with Tommy; with anybody but Tommy.

'You and June are much better off here,' Viv added.

'Destined to be a single mum forever? Living with my dad? Nobody wants me.'

'That's not true, there was Jean Paul-'

'And he ran for the hills!' Jackie was suddenly aware of how loud her voice was and lowered it. 'I come with too much baggage,' she said, sinking into her shoulders. 'I'm done with men.'

Viv hugged her. 'Don't say that. It's just how you're feeling right now.'

'I'm going up to check on June.'

'You just checked on her, she's fine.'

'I know, but I like to watch her sleeping.'

'Do you want me to come up with you?'

'No, it's okay. You stay here. Thanks, though.' Jackie left the room and took the stairs two by two.

'Poor mite. She's been through so much,' Mrs Morrisson observed. 'There's more behind those tears than we know.'

'I still say we should phone the police. He shouldn't be allowed to have that knife.'

'That knife will be well gone! He'll have hidden that somewhere by now, Frank, and then it will be her word against his, and he can afford big lawyers. Police wouldn't be able to do a thing about it. Let Jackie have a chance to think.'

Frank nodded. He thought of calling the police, relishing the thought of them finding the knife and arresting Tommy. But he knew Viv was right. The knife would be gone. In any event, Frank knew calling the police would be the worst thing he could do, for his family's safety. He contemplated Tommy's next move. 'We need to make sure he doesn't come after the wean,' he mumbled.

'No chance,' replied Viv. 'Too many stories about him. Plus, the whole town knows what he's like, and those that don't, I'll make sure they do.'

Jackie lay upstairs next to June. She tucked her knees in behind the tiny bend in June's and listened to the soft sound of her breath. She wrapped her arm around her, over the top of the quilt. Both lay silently on their sides, as Jackie's silent tears fell softly into June's red curls.

'I'm sorry, my baby,' she whispered, 'Mummy's not very good at this. I'll never leave you alone again, ever.'

Jackie stiffened as she heard the sound of the letterbox from downstairs, wondering if it might be Tommy.

Frank saw a shadow at the window and got up to investigate. Relieved, he watched as Bobby ran down the path and into his car. Frank went immediately to the door and picked up two envelopes off the carpet.

'I've got it!' he called up, in a stage whisper. 'It's okay.' He knew what she might be thinking, because he was thinking the same thing.

One envelope had Jackie's name on it, and one his own, written in old-fashioned handwriting. He nodded and went about opening his as he walked back into the living room. He placed Jackie's envelope on the table.

'The wedding invitations are here,' he said, trying to muster enthusiasm.

'Ah! Some good news for a change.' Mrs Morrisson clasped her hands together.

'Let's see!' Viv stood up and leaned over Frank's shoulder.

'Me plus one, it reads. Well, that looks a bit... strange, doesn't it?' He looked over to June's picture, then back down to the words.

'Two o'clock up at St Margaret's and then after at The Working Men's Club. That'll be a nice day.'

'You'd better get to work on that speech! Best man duties and all that. Who are you going to take as your plus one?' asked Viv. Mrs Morrisson folded a handkerchief on her lap, in and out of diagonal folds and triangles, then into a square again. Frank shook his head.

'I'd best be making a move,' said Mrs Morrisson. 'I've a pile of ironing up to the clouds!' She pushed herself up. 'Say goodbye to Jackie for me.' She walked towards the back door, saying 'cheerio' quietly.

'Ask her!' whispered Viv. '*Ask her.*'

The back door closed.

'I will not be asking her.'

'Why not?'

'I don't want anybody thinking we're up to any funny business.'

'People won't think that. They know you're only pals.'

'Well, people think a lot of things that they shouldn't.'

'She might not get an invitation and then she won't be able to go. I'll probably only get invited to the evening do, if I'm lucky. But Jackie might bring *me* as her plus one! But then me and Terry might get invited to the night time, I suppose he could meet me there later, couldn't he? I'll go up to the church, anyway, to see Maureen's dress and all that.' Viv paused.

'Sorry, I thought we were talking about me there, for a minute,' muttered Frank.

'Oh, God, look at the time. It's nine o'clock already. Ill need to be heading off. Some of us have got work in the morning!' Viv playfully nudged Frank on her way past. 'I don't think she's coming back down the stairs. Tell her I'll phone her tomorrow.'

'Will do. Thanks Viv. You're a good friend to our Jackie.'

Frank smiled and Viv nodded. He collected the cups and put them in the kitchen sink. He locked the doors. He took the steps upstairs and peeked into Jackie's room. She was fast asleep, cuddled into June. Jackie's own bed lay empty. He took a blanket off the top of her bed and placed it over her. He looked down and watched them both in perfect stillness.

Two cut hands in a number of months. One broken heart. One little girl without a daddy. I've got a lot to fix.

THE BIG DAY

'Well, I just can't believe it's finally here.' Mrs Morrisson walked into the church with Jackie and Viv. 'When did you get the invitation? Was it May?'

'Three months ago.'

'Did your dad ever send that RSVP out?'

'I don't know if he posted it or gave it to Bobby. I told Bobby we were all coming, anyway, and he said Maureen was happy about that. So you can stop worrying, you're invited!' Jackie smiled. She reached over and adjusted Mrs Morrisson's flower on her dress.

'You look beautiful, Jackie.'

'So do you. And so do you!' Jackie squeezed June's little hot hand and they took the steps into the church. Viv rushed to catch up behind them.

'Did you get a parking space?'

'I did, in the end. I had to drive down to the other car park.'

'Oh, Viv, sorry about that, I hope it wasn't a lot of trouble.'

'Don't be silly, Mrs Morrisson!' said Viv. 'We needed to drop you off at the gate. Can't have you walking too far in your new heels.' Mrs Morrisson looked down at her low-heeled sparkly shoes that Jackie and Viv had helped her choose from the catalogue. They squeezed into a row and then one of the bridesmaids came and collected June.

'Aren't you adorable?' she said, as she smiled and led her out of the row. She placed the handle of a basket of petals in her hand and June closed her little fingers around it. Jackie recognised the bridesmaid as one of Maureen's sisters.

'Just remember to do what you did at the rehearsal, Junie. I'll be watching. I love you and I'm so proud of you!' June smiled at her mother.

'Her wee lemon dress looks beautiful against that blue satin,' said Viv in admiration.

The bridesmaid took June to the vestibule and they waited for Maureen. The church was busy and Jackie strained to see her dad in the front row. She finally caught a glimpse of him, shaking hands with people with a great big smile of pride across his face. Her heart bloomed. She shook her head as she saw him pass Bobby a hip flask and he took a swig. He put it away hurriedly as he heard the first bossy note of the booming church organ. The bride had arrived.

Jackie turned around along with the rest of the congregation to see little June walk down the aisle scattering petals. The two bridesmaids walked carefully behind her, wearing beautiful flared blue satin dresses in a pleated detail and blue comb clasps with artificial flowers on each side of their hair.

Maureen entered with an old man that looked like her dad, although Jackie had never met him. Her hair was pinned up and decorated with artificial flowers and a white veil covered her face. Her dress was an elegant off the shoulder style, also in satin, and it floated freely to the floor. As she walked towards the altar, Jackie could see she had the expression of a woman who had waited a long time for this day. Sunlight streamed in through the stained-glass windows and bounced off the white shine of her dress, making her every bit the beautiful bride she felt she was and deserved to be. As she passed Jackie, she felt a look of history and kindness pass between them. It was impossible to feel anything other than joy on this day, as the smiles and awes were plentiful and people cooed over the happy couple.

Jackie watched as Bobby gently turned his head around to catch a glimpse of Maureen as she walked towards him. His face blushed red and she saw him gasp as his lips parted to tell Maureen something, but the words never came. Frank's face beamed from just behind Bobby, caught up in the euphoria of his friend's big moment. Jackie's heart lifted at the sight of Bobby and Maureen brushing fingers, then dropping hands in front of the priest. She watched Bobby looking at Maureen like there was no one else in the room, and she laughed as the priest had to repeat his name twice. Jackie knew what she was witnessing was something different, unbreakable, untouchable, remarkable love, love that would never crack. Her thoughts were with Maureen and Bobby and their love that blossomed from the spot where they stood.

Church was always a great place for Jackie to gather her thoughts. 'The great brain tidier, always makes you feel better.' Her mum's words echoed around in her head. She felt her presence. Jackie thought her mum would have loved this part of the day. She thought of how shamefully she had behaved, drinking her mother's vodka to find out if she had inherited her alcoholism, or maybe even drinking it to get closer to understanding her mother's state of mind. She felt bad for her dad, picking up the pieces, but things had returned to normal between them since that fateful visit with Tommy.

Jackie glanced over at Daniel, sitting with his mum on the other side of the church. She grinned and he grinned back, and his mum gave her a little wave. She had visited their house quite a lot since Daniel had confided in her, and Jackie had grown to love Daniel's mum even more than she did before. His dad and many other people still didn't know, and maybe wouldn't ever know, but at least he had his mum and his friend, behind him and beside him, whatever his future might bring. Johnny had introduced him to a few more friends in the gay community but none yet that could turn Daniel's head. For now, he was happy to stay in the cocoon of Airdrie, just near enough to Glasgow, and just far enough away.

Viv squeezed Jackie's arm and pointed to Frank who was handing over the rings. He turned around as he moved backwards to the pew, as if to ask, 'Did I do okay?' Jackie, Viv and Mrs Morrisson all let out a little sigh of laughter, as if he had been talking to each of them.

Jackie considered that the abundance of love and fortune that she had around her was enough - a loyal and loving friend in Viv, a soft and doting dad, a warm home, a perfect little girl, a selfless and generous neighbour, and a job she loved. She wondered why she had been searching for a man to make it all better, when she was perfectly fine without one, and her life was actually full of fun, everyday, normal stuff, the stuff that other people wished they had. She realised that a great part of this low feeling was to do with losing her mum, and pieced a puzzle together that maybe she had never allowed herself to explore her grief, that instead she had avoided it, not permitted herself to 'indulge' in it. She had been searching for another thing or person to replace it as a distraction to her constant pain and longing.

Between her dad's grief and running a house and keeping a job, and all the other dramas in between, Jackie had never really focused on herself, and when she did, her thoughts overwhelmed her. Mrs Morrisson had taught Jackie that it was natural to want to avoid the pain, but eventually she had to face the hard truth. The person you love is gone and they're never coming back.

'Make sure you always carry a tissue,' she'd advised.

As the service continued and the couple finished exchanging vows, hymns were sung and communion given. June came back to sit with her mother. She leaned her head into her mother's hip and Jackie reached for her hand. She held it between both of hers and rubbed to get her own hands warm. She looked down at June's little palm and felt relief again that there was not a trace of a scar. At last, one thing she was finally certain of was to never welcome Tommy into their lives again, and never be stupid enough to think he was anything other than a manipulator and someone who didn't truly love her.

He hadn't been in touch about access to June, but Viv had got her ready with a case against it. She knew she would bump into him from time to time, but at least he had stayed away from their door. She wondered if him staying away had anything to do with Terry, who had recently started a new fitness regime with Viv, called Step Class. He had also invested in some weights that he kept in his mum's garage. The weights had made quite a difference to Terry, and, at any given opportunity, Viv's new party trick was to proudly ask Terry to display his new biceps for all to admire.

She looked up to her mother's star and was immediately reminded of the time she'd met Jean Paul in the church, and his soft touch. She dismissed the feelings as silly dreams of romance and felt a fool for how quickly she had fallen. She felt stronger now, more in control, more able to feel her own confidence as a single mother.

She stroked June's hair, her little yellow flowers looked so delicate and pretty against the glorious red fire colour. Jackie still had to face the fact that she had to tell June who her father was but wanted to leave it a few more years until she was old enough to understand. Thankfully, June seemed to be more focused on being four, starting school and making friends.

The one strong feeling that Jackie couldn't let go of was the undiscovered truth about her mum and Eddie O'Donnell. She felt the nagging wind of her mother behind her to search for this man. The strange dreams had lessened but the signs remained, and something in Jackie's skin told her that this wasn't going away. She wasn't going to give up until she found him.

Alone upstairs, he watched. How cute the little girl in lemon looked as she climbed back over the kneeler and onto her mother's lap. He carried a plastic box with a small corsage of red roses inside. He hoped that Jackie would like it. He could only see the back of her in her fitted pink dress, and how shiny her brown hair gleamed and bounced as she turned her head from side to side to shake hands with others. He willed for her to turn around and look up at the sole figure on the balcony and wondered how she would feel when she saw him. He took a deep breath and hoped she could forgive him.

MY FRANK

'What's your teacher's name?'

'Mrs McGuigan.'

'And what was she saying today?'

'We did plasticine and painting and singing.'

'Oh, now that sounds like it was a great first day. C'mon up and sit on Granda's knee and tell me all about it. I've been waiting all day to hear!' June climbed upon Frank's knee and leaned her chin onto his shoulder. Jackie kissed them both on the head, then went to the kitchen to peel potatoes. The back door opened, and Mrs Morrisson entered, quietly. She motioned for Jackie to close the door between the kitchen and the living room.

'What is it?' Jackie asked. 'You okay?'

'I'm fine,' Mrs Morrisson nodded. 'She's found him.' Jackie gasped. 'They thought he was actually dead, but then new information came through from one of Sadie's contacts at the Pilgrim Church that there was a brand new tenant up in that place at the bottom of Arthur Avenue – the old folks home – and she's positive it's him.'

'How did she find him? How does she know it's him?'

'This is Sadie Ward we're talking about!' Mrs Morrisson squeezed Jackie's hand. 'Got to dash, see you soon!' She took the steps backwards, looking around her as if she was on a spy mission, then closed the door.

'Was that somebody at the door?' called Frank.

'Just the radio,' said Jackie, and she turned the volume up.

Jackie boiled the potatoes and cooked the crispy pancakes and carrots as fast as she could before announcing she had to nip out to see Viv about an eyeshadow and she'd be back to put June to bed. Both June and Frank rolled their eyes at each other.

'Important stuff, eh, Junie?' motioned Frank. June nodded very expressively.

Jackie grabbed her coat and said goodbye, leaving the dishes in the sink. Ideas flew around her head with what to say as she raced towards Cairnhill. It might not even be him. Should she be going in the first place? She saw a small estate with little white cottages and knew it was the place. She passed a sign, 'No Ball Games', and up a hill to the main building. White paint on the tarmac parking area read 'RESVERED'. She guessed it should have spelled 'RESERVED' but wasn't sure if it was an old person's term for something else. A small windmill spun around in the centre of a pleasant lawn. She walked around the garden that was in the shape of a semi-circle surrounded by a knee-high white picket fence. There was a pond with some fat goldfish swimming around inside it and a little fountain splashed up through the middle.

She pushed one large, heavy, glass door, then another, and was met by a very smart official-looking woman in a fitted pencil skirt, soft blouse and heels. Jackie explained who she was here to visit and the woman informed her that the man was in the common room, up the stairs. Jackie took the fire stairs up to the first floor. She entered the room through a crowd of empty beige Parker Knoll chairs and saw an old man, sitting alone, playing Solitaire with a pack of cards. She stood staring at him for a minute, trying to decide if he looked like the big bulky guy in the picture in her bag. If it was him, he had definitely shrunk.

She walked over to his table. 'Excuse me?' Her voice wobbled.

'No thanks, I don't want any tea,' he replied, without raising his head.

'No, sorry, I'm here to... visit you...'

'You don't sound very sure.' He moved a card from one position and placed it underneath another. 'Who are you looking for?'

'Mr O'Donnell? Is your name Eddie O'Donnell?'

He looked up. 'What did you say your name was?' He adjusted his hearing aid. 'You look familiar.'

'Are you Big Jock?

'Well, that's what they used to call me... forty odd years ago... but I've not been called that for a long time.' He leaned back in his chair. 'Why do I know your face? Are you John Sheldon's lassie? I told him to forget about what he owes me.'

'No.'

'I know you. Your eyes...' He tapped the chair arm. 'I know those eyes... don't tell me now...'

'I think you knew my mum. Years ago.' Jackie edged closer.

'Well, go on, then.' He motioned for her to sit down, so she sank into a high-backed squashy chair adjacent to his table.

'My mum's name was June. June Ann McNeill.'

'Well, I never!' He swallowed hard.

Just then the lady in the pencil skirt entered and came over to the table. 'Is everything all right, Mr O'Donnell?'

'Yes, yes, everything is fine, thank you. Just got a visitor.'

'Pull the cord if you need me.'

'I will do, yes.' The lady wandered over into the kitchen.

'Say the name again.'

'June Ann McNeill.'

'June. Ann. McNeill. Well, I haven't heard that name for years and years and years,' he smiled fondly. 'And you're her daughter, you say?' Jackie nodded. 'Of course you are. You're her spitting image. The hair is different but... God, you're like her. Tell me now, how is she? Is she all right? She's not in here, is she? Is she in here?'

'No.'

'Is she still with, what's his name...?'

'Frank. Yes, but-'

'That's it! Frank! The lucky bugger. I wanted to marry her, you know, I had plans for her and me.'

'You wanted to marry her?' Jackie began to dread what she came to find out.

'Oh, I did. I wanted her to leave him and marry me. Is Frank your dad? I suppose he must be.'

'He is.' Jackie felt a strange sickly feeling come over her - *don't go digging if you don't like what you'll find* – she straightened up, she had come this far, and would carry on.

'Ah, it was a long time ago. Your mum did the right thing. I wasn't any good for her. And I've been no good for any woman, ever since.'

'What do you mean? *She did the right thing?*'

'Well, sorry to say this, because I wasn't used to rejection, you see. But I begged and begged her to stay with the singing and go out with me. "No," she said, "my heart belongs to my Frank." I'll never forget those words. She said she was done with me and singing, said she wanted to settle into her marriage and have a family.'

'Hold on,' said Jackie, 'are you saying that *she* finished with *you*?'

'Well, it never really started. She finished the whole thing and went back to Frank.'

Jackie found it hard to understand why, if this was true, that her mother never said anything to her father. 'But my dad, well, everybody was led to believe that you ended it...'

'Well, usually I did end it with the clingy ones. But not her. Not June. If I had my way, she'd be beside me now. But, as I said, she did the right thing. Your dad is a better man than I am, or than I was, anyway.'

O'Donnell looked down at his cards. Jackie tried to put the pieces together in her head. She reached into her bag and removed the photograph and stared down at her mum. She hadn't noticed the disconnect between them before. He stood slightly behind her, not beside her, and she was looking elsewhere, away from the club.

She looked up to the solitary old man in front of her. One who had clearly adored her mother, thought he could have her, but had been rejected in favour of her dad. The once great O'Donnell slouched in the large chair, a shrunken frame of regret.

'Here.' She pushed the photo over on the table, next to the cards. 'Have this.' He picked it up and his eyebrows lifted his eyes and cheeks and smile into happiness.

'Well, there's a memory! My, oh my!' He sat back, away from the cards. 'Look at her!' He tutted. 'She was only *just* married, you know. It never used to make a difference to me if they were married or not. I was a bit reckless. Not proud of that. You know she never even let me kiss her?' He paused. 'I never found a singer as good as her again.' He looked up. 'But I left her alone, as she asked, after she said she was finished.'

'You never even got to kiss her? You never had an affair?'

'Oh, God, no. She wouldn't have any of that. She was a touch of class, your mother. Far too good for the likes of me.'

'So, all these years...'

'What do you mean, *all these years*?'

Jackie felt heat rise inside her. Every window was closed and heavy curtains and thick carpet made the room overly snug. The clock ticked loudly. 'I've got to go.' She stood up.

'Wait! What was your name! You never told me how your mum was! Is she looking for me?' Without speaking, Jackie shook her head. She looked down at the carpet. 'Oh,' he nodded, 'that's a great shame. How long ago?'

'Five years.' Jackie had said as much as she could, her body now filling with sadness at another reminder of losing her mum.

He held up the picture for her to take. 'Here, I'm sorry. Take your picture.'

'You can keep it,' she said, 'it's a copy. I've got another one.'

'Oh, thank you,' he said weakly. He turned away from her and looked out the window to the small garden. Jackie decided to go. Before she left, she took one last look back at him, and he was staring down at the photo as the lady in the pencil skirt rested her arm on his chair. He was pointing to himself as a young, successful man with a woman he had once loved.

Jackie walked back down the stairs and pushed the heavy outside door. She enjoyed the freshness of the light Airdrie drizzle on her forehead and cheeks. She marched down the hill with her hands in her pockets and didn't bother to put her hood up.

The anticipation of telling her dad welled up inside her, and she hurried down the muddy path shortcut, and leaped over the last mucky puddle.

THE VISITOR

Frank had to open the back door and go outside to take in the news. The drizzle had stopped and the sun was threatening a visit as it began to prise the clouds apart. He stood on the back step, staring out at the perfectly shorn green hairs of his velvet lawn. His first thought, if this was true, was why hadn't June told him the truth? She'd had forty years to tell him the rumours were lies. But then, maybe she didn't *know* there were rumours. After all, they never talked about it, ever. One minute he felt proud of her - she didn't even let O'Donnell touch her - but the next, he felt angry at himself for believing the gossipy undercurrent that ripped through the small town. No woman turned O'Donnell down. Why should they believe June would be any different?

He wished he had asked her, instead of living with it, silently for all these years. He was wrong to think she drank her vodka because she missed him. She drank because she drank, and in crept the slow realisation that there was no reason other than she was an alcoholic.

He felt Jackie touch his shoulder, ask him if he was all right. He responded he was fine. She talked softly behind him, about how happy he should feel, that her mum loved him beyond everything else.

'It was you she wanted, Dad. It was always you,' Jackie whispered, as she patted his jumper and walked back into the house.

He gathered himself together and went back inside to his chair. Jackie was upstairs putting June to bed. He picked up the picture of the mantelpiece and shook his head. *Why didn't you tell me?* He wondered, *Why didn't I ask you?* Too much was silent in the marriage. Too much was unsaid, to avoid argument. He whispered the words he wished he had said back then, *I'm sorry*.

She smiled back out into the distance. He felt a knot slowly untie somewhere deep in his stomach, the release of a great big misunderstanding.

A few days later, Mrs Morrisson called round in the evening to explain that she had spoken to Sadie Ward, and the town would be 'put right'.

'People need to know the truth, Frank,' she claimed. 'A woman's name can't be tarnished like that. God forgive us all.' She blessed herself. 'Of course, I never really believed in the first place, you know, but still...' she faded off.

'What do you want to watch?' he asked. She took that as his signal he didn't want to talk about it anymore.

'Anything. I'll watch anything. Just stick it on for ten minutes, then I'm off.' Frank rolled his eyes, knowing she'd still be sitting there when the news came on. He turned on the television and it was *Top Of The Pops*. Mrs Morrisson tapped her knee along to the song to try and lighten the mood. 'That's a nice name, isn't it? "The Happy Mondays". We should all be happy on a Monday. Look at that one, dancing away there, having a nice time with his maracas. What did he sing? Did he sing about chocolate?'

'I'll get the biscuits.' Frank returned with a plate of Club Orange.

'Oh, what a lovely treat! Those are the ones with very thick chocolate, Frank. We should only have the one.' Frank offered the plate to Mrs Morrisson and sat down and unwrapped his.

'This music is damnable,' he said, biting a chunk of chocolate off the end of the biscuit. Jackie entered the room with her keys in one hand and her bag in the other. She had changed out of her work clothes and blow-dried her hair. Frank thought she smelled nice and noticed that she had put a little bit of make-up on.

'That's her out for the count. She loved the swings today, Dad, thanks.'

'No bother, hen.'

'Are you two all right? I don't have to go out, you know.'

'Go out, Jackie!' Mrs Morrisson protested.

'Go out, for God sake!' Frank added.

'I'm excited for you!' Mrs Morrisson laughed.

'Oh... I don't know... I don't feel so sure.' Jackie put her keys in her bag. Frank screwed up the biscuit wrapper.

'Everybody deserves a second chance,' he said, nodding at the television. Mrs Morrisson gave Jackie a knowing glance. The doorbell rang.

'Oh, God, I told him to knock, I hope June doesn't wake up.'

'She won't,' they echoed. 'Go and enjoy yourself.'

'Okay.' Jackie smiled nervously. She opened the front door.

'*Bonsoir,*' smiled Jean Paul. 'You are quite... beautiful.'

Jackie blushed and pulled the door behind her. She followed him to the waiting taxi, inhaling his fragrance that she had sorely missed. As the taxi drove away, he touched her hand.

'I am so happy that you agreed to meet with me.' Jackie could see how genuine he was, so earnest in his approach. She relaxed her hand and allowed his to rest on top of hers. 'I thought, after talking to you at the church, you may not want to see me again.'

'Everybody deserves a second chance,' she said, echoing her dad's words.

'I am sorry I went away.'

'It's okay. It's fine, really,' she lied.

'I had to see my mother. To talk things through, you know? It took some time to tell her that I do not want to be a priest, but she understands now.'

'Does your uncle?'

'He knows. He is fine with it, he said I can stay with him for as long as I like, and it doesn't matter, as long as I am happy.'

'Are you doing this because of what happened between us?'

'Well, I'd be lying if I said you didn't help with my decision.'

'I feel bad about that.'

'You don't have to. You helped. I didn't ever want to do it. I was trying to please my mother, but she is happy now. She even has a new friend who is a man!'

'Oh, that's nice for her,' Jackie smiled. 'Why did you decide to come back to Airdrie?'

'I was coming back in a few weeks. But then Fronc called my uncle, and they talked of Bobby's wedding. Fronc told my uncle you would be there alone and asked if I was returning. So I came sooner, as weddings make people happy and in good mood.'

Jackie smiled and shook her head. Her dad worked in mysterious ways.

'Are you going to be staying for long?' She looked across with such hopeful and honest eyes he wanted to hold her again. He inched across the seat and his hair fell forward. A wayward curl dangled at the side of his forehead.

'If you would like me to.'

She beamed a smile at him and nodded lightly. The taxi pulled up outside the restaurant. He jumped out his side of the car and opened her door for her. He offered his hand and she took it. An urgent thought darted into her mind.

Oh, Jean Paul, please don't hurt me!

Somewhere else deep inside her head, a familiar voice answered,

`He won't.`

ABOUT THE AUTHOR

Julie Hamill is a London-based Scottish author and radio broadcaster. She is the creator of the Life and Soul trilogy of novels, *Frank (2017), Jackie (2019)* and *June (2023),* about the love and loss of a family in 1980s Airdrie, Scotland.

Her non-fiction book, *15 Minutes With You* was first published in 2015.

She features regularly on radio and television in podcasts, documentaries, shows and panels surrounding her work in music and literature. Prior to her writing and broadcasting career, she worked in advertising in both London and New York.

She lives in London with her husband, two children and Dolly.

Printed in Great Britain
by Amazon